DOWN THE BROKEN ROAD

ALSO AVAILABLE BY J. R. BACKLUND

Among the Dead

DOWN THE BROKEN ROAD

A Rachel Carver Novel

J. R. Backlund

CROOKED
LANE

NEW YORK

Published in the United States by Crooked Lane Books, an imprint of The Quick Brown Fox & Company LLC.

Crooked Lane Books and its logo are trademarks of The Quick Brown Fox & Company LLC.

Library of Congress Catalog-in-Publication data available upon request.

ISBN (hardcover): 978-1-68331-740-1
ISBN (ePub): 978-1-68331-741-8
ISBN (ePDF): 978-1-68331-742-5

Cover design by Melanie Sun
Book design by Jennifer Canzone

Printed in the United States.

www.crookedlanebooks.com

Crooked Lane Books
34 West 27th St., 10th Floor
New York, NY 10001

First Edition: October 2018

10 9 8 7 6 5 4 3 2 1

For my mother, my hero, the strongest person
I've ever known.

ONE

The pink light of daybreak. The rattling of an ancient air conditioner, struggling against the summer heat. The smell of freshly cut grass and fertilizer and pesticides.

And urine.

Officer Ashley Ramirez wrinkled her nose as she approached the body. It lay faceup on the slope of a drainage ditch, just west of the chain-link fence that bordered the old man's property.

Right where he said it would be.

"I seen the commotion just before dawn," the old man had said. Standing on the front porch of his farmhouse, pointing a shaky finger in the distance, pausing every few words to lick at toothless gums. "Out yonder. There was a big fella. Looked like he was draggin' somethin' heavy. Too dark for me to see just what it was. But I figured he couldn't have been up to no good. So I waited till he left. Then I got my flashlight and my twenty-two and went out to see for myself. That man, whoever he was, went and dumped a body over there."

Ramirez had asked him to wait inside while she went to have a look. It didn't take her long to find it.

There was a street lamp attached to the top of a telephone pole by the road. It gave her just enough light to see the form but no details. She clicked on her flashlight.

White male.

Early thirties.

Unresponsive.

She slid on a pair of blue gloves as she looked him over. He was thin and clean-cut, wore a purple polo half-tucked into his soiled jeans. There was a brown leather shoe on his right foot. Only a sock on the other.

"Not from around here, are you?" she muttered, glancing around for the missing shoe. It had probably fallen off while he was being dragged across the grass. Not that it mattered. It wasn't her job to figure out what had happened here.

He had blue lips and cool gray skin, but his shoulder gave a little when she pushed on it. Rigor mortis had yet to set in. She checked his wrist for a pulse, just to be sure, then called it in and knelt down beside him to start CPR. Whoever he was, he hadn't been dead for long. There was always a chance the EMTs could revive him, if she could only keep oxygen moving to his brain while she waited for them to arrive. A *slim* chance, but it was worth a try.

She put her hands together on his chest and started compressions. "Stayin' Alive" played in her head, which helped her keep a steady rhythm. An instructor had once told her it was the perfect song for CPR; it had just the right tempo for circulating the blood until someone with advanced medical training and equipment could take over. He had also said compressions needed to be two inches deep to be effective. The slope of the ditch made that difficult. Made it hard for her to get her weight behind the effort.

She moved to his other side to try for a better angle. Got her hands in position and rose up on her knees to start again. Then she heard something that made her freeze.

The air conditioner had stopped. There was the Doppler effect of a car passing by on the highway—the change in pitch as it shot across the landscape to the east. Then it was quiet again. She leaned forward, put her ear just above his mouth, and heard it clearly.

Gurgling.

Faint wet breaths that told her he was still alive.

"Shit!" She rubbed her knuckles on his sternum. "Sir? Sir, can you hear me?"

The air conditioner came back on. Another car passed on the highway. It masked the sound of his breathing, which made her question if she had heard it at all. She reached for his wrist again to check for a pulse, wondering how she had missed it the first time. As she lifted it, the man's sleeve fell slack, and she spotted something wrapped loosely around his upper arm. A closer look and she knew exactly what it was.

A tourniquet.

Ramirez jumped up and started running, yelling at the radio mic on her shoulder to update the dispatcher. Her voice shook with each stride over the uneven terrain. When she got to her patrol car, she popped the trunk, grabbed the orange kit, and ran back. She hit the ditch without slowing down, slipped on the wet grass, and fell to her back. Cursing, she rose to her knees and shuffled the last few feet to the man as she tore the kit open and shook out the contents.

There was a syringe, three capsules filled with naloxone, and an atomizer that was supposed to turn the lifesaving liquid into a mist.

"Hang on, sir. Stay with me."

She fumbled with the capsule and the syringe, trying to remember exactly how they went together. Then she remembered that the rubber cap on the capsule had to be removed first.

"Dammit!"

She slid it into place, put the atomizer on the other end, and stuck it into the man's nostril.

"Here goes nothing." She squeezed until half the capsule was drained, then put it in the other nostril and delivered the rest. "Come on. Wake up for me."

She waited a few seconds, wiping sweat from her brow as she watched for any sign that he might be coming around.

Nothing.

She grabbed a second capsule and tried again.

"Sir? Can you hear me?"

She gave his sternum another rub with her knuckles and felt movement in his chest. Then his breathing grew louder. He moaned, and his head slowly turned toward her.

"It's okay, sir," she said. "I've got EMS coming. They should be here any minute. Just stay with me, all right?"

The flashing lights of the approaching ambulance caught Ramirez's attention as she updated the dispatcher. It turned off the highway and came to a stop next to her patrol car. The EMTs jumped out and ran toward the house. She grabbed the flashlight from her belt, clicked it on, and waved it at them, but they didn't seem to notice her.

"Damn." She patted the man on the shoulder. "Hang tight, sir. EMS is here. I'm gonna go get them for you. I'll be right back."

She started to stand, but he reached up and seized her hand.

"Jesus," she said with a start.

His grip was impossibly strong. His eyes were still closed, but his mouth was moving. Raspy breaths tried to form words with each exhalation. She leaned in to listen.

"Ra . . . Rachel . . ."

"Rachel? Who's Rachel? Is she someone you want me to call?"

A mumbled response and a weak nod.

"Sir?"

"Rachel," he yelled suddenly. He opened his eyes, fixed his gaze on Ramirez's face, and said, "Please, call her . . . Rachel Carver."

TWO

Rachel Carver was being dissected. Sitting in a conference room in the twelfth-floor offices of the Robertson Burke & Porter law firm in downtown Raleigh, she watched the attorney pull her life apart, page by page. The file was thicker than it should have been, Rachel thought. Far more than just her résumé, the copy of her private investigator license, and the letters of recommendation she had provided.

There were newspaper clippings and printouts of stories from Internet news sites. Excerpts from case files that could only have been obtained through public-records requests. Other documents that Rachel didn't recognize. The attorney appeared to be moving backward in time, quietly absorbing her career in reverse.

"I apologize for the delay," he said, keeping his eyes down. "But we, of course, like to do our research."

"Of course," Rachel said. "It looks pretty thorough."

He looked at her, pushed his wire-framed glasses further up onto the bridge of his nose, and smiled. "I'll just be a few more moments." Then he went back to reading as if she were no longer in the room.

Rachel had already forgotten his name. She stole a look at the business card he had handed her while introducing himself. *Calvin Grant*. She judged him to be in his midthirties. He wore a navy suit with a silver tie that had one of those perfect dimples just below the knot. He sat straight and rested his forearms on the edge of the table, taking care to keep the band of his Rolex from scratching its shiny surface as he flipped through the pages.

"UNC," he said with an approving nod. His eyes ran quickly through her college transcripts, tracing her coursework in vertical columns.

"Fellow Tar Heel?" she asked.

"Cornell," he said, looking up. He sat back in his chair, took his glasses off, and laid them on the table. "So, help me understand something. Why would a special agent with the SBI, with a stellar reputation and nowhere to go but up, quit after only seven years to become a legal investigator?"

His eyes were small without the lenses in front of them. Almost piercing.

"Several reasons, I guess . . ." Rachel had anticipated the question. She had prepared a response, but her answer suddenly seemed inadequate. The accusation in Grant's words, the way he peered at her from across the table, told her he wouldn't accept anything less than the unvarnished truth. "Better hours. More free time. I liked the idea of—"

"Miss Carver, you have an impressive résumé," he said, glancing at his watch, "but we have no shortage of ex-cops turned PI applying for this job. If you want to be considered, you're going to have to be straight with me."

Rachel flushed with irritation. "I didn't ask for this interview, Mr. Grant. Your office called me."

"And here you are. Was it a mistake to assume you might want a position with this firm?"

It was no mistake. After abandoning her career with the

North Carolina State Bureau of Investigation, Rachel had decided she was done with law enforcement. But, at thirty-nine, she was too young for retirement, so she had settled on her next best option—working as a private investigator for criminal defense attorneys.

At first, she had wanted the independence of being a freelancer. Working by contract, choosing only the cases that interested her. Unfortunately, those typically went to firms that could afford full-time investigators. The smaller firms, as it turned out, didn't have enough good cases to keep her busy. For Rachel to make a living, she would have to take any work that came her way. That made a permanent position with Robertson Burke & Porter much more enticing. Better work with steady pay, a retirement plan, health benefits . . .

So Rachel put on a smile and said, "It's true. Working here would certainly be a step up."

"Well then," Grant said, "let's try this a different way. Why don't you tell me about Lauren Bailey?"

The name hit Rachel like a gunshot to the chest, leaving a familiar black hole that swallowed her heart. "What would you like to know?"

"How about we start with what happened?"

"It isn't written up somewhere in that giant file?"

"It's a lot to read. I'd rather hear it from you, if that's all right?"

She cleared her throat. "Miss Bailey was a suspect in a homicide investigation."

"Your last case with the SBI?"

"Yes." She straightened in her seat and tugged on the lapels of her blazer to flatten a wrinkle on her back. "That's correct. Her boyfriend, Tyler Larson, was found dead in her car with a single gunshot wound to the head. The car was found about two miles from where she was living at the time."

"And where was that?"

"Her mother's house, just outside Wendell. Before that, she was living with Larson in Fayetteville."

"He was a soldier, right?" Grant asked. "Stationed at Fort Bragg?"

She nodded. "A platoon sergeant assigned to the five hundred eighth infantry regiment."

"I see. And why did Miss Bailey decide to move back in with her mother?"

"Bailey and Larson had a volatile relationship. One night, about three months before Larson was killed, Bailey found out he was cheating on her. They had a nasty fight. Lots of yelling and screaming. Things breaking in the house. The neighbors called the police. The responding officers didn't see any signs of domestic abuse, so they just calmed things down and issued them a warning for the noise complaint. Bailey took her son and left that same night."

"But that didn't end their relationship?"

"No. They seemed to patch things up pretty quickly. They were even talking about moving back in together."

Grant leaned his head against the seat back and looked up at the ceiling, thought for a second, and said, "So Sergeant Larson turns up dead in Miss Bailey's car. The Wake County Sheriff's Office works the case for four months before getting frustrated and calling the SBI for help. The SBI sends you in to save the day."

"Something like that," Rachel said.

"And I take it you had a breakthrough?"

She nodded. "I discovered that Larson was still cheating on Miss Bailey. With a different woman this time. One the sheriff's office didn't know about. That gave Bailey motive, which was the missing piece of the puzzle."

"So where did it all go wrong?"

She hesitated, unsure of how to answer.

"Forgive me for being blunt," he said, "but you shot and killed Miss Bailey while attempting to arrest her—"

"She had a gun," Rachel said quickly. "She was pointing it at a deputy."

"Of course." He gave her a conciliatory wave of his hand. "By all accounts, your actions were entirely justifiable. Even worthy of praise, according to your superiors. I didn't mean to insinuate otherwise. But now there's this." He dug through the file and withdrew a newspaper clipping, laid it on the table, and pushed it a few inches in her direction. "I assume you recognize this article?"

She needed only a glance. "I do."

"It says you think Lauren Bailey was innocent."

"Yes, it does."

He stared at her quietly for a moment. Then he said, "That's a stunning admission, Miss Carver. Especially considering that you're—"

"The one who killed her?"

"I was going to say, named in a wrongful-death lawsuit."

"Right. I don't suppose you'd be willing to help me out with that?"

"One thing at a time," he said. "Tell me about Ross Penter."

Another name that made Rachel feel like her heart had seized. She fought to keep her composure as she said, "He was the special agent in charge of the Capital District. After I left, he was promoted to assistant director for field operations."

"He was your superior?"

"Yes."

"And he disagrees with you about Bailey? He believes she was guilty?"

"You could say that."

Grant put his glasses back on, reached into the file, and pulled out another clipping. "In this interview, he questions your motivation for speaking out. He intimates that you were riddled with guilt after the shooting."

"Intimates?" She couldn't help but laugh. "He seemed pretty clear about it to me."

"He goes on to say that, in addition to feeling guilty, you tend to be obsessive about your work. That once you get started on something you can never let it go."

"Are you asking me if I think he's right?"

"No, Miss Carver." He gathered the articles and slid them back into place. "Everything in here tells me he's right."

Rachel tugged at her blazer again.

Grant said, "My question is, if that's the case, why aren't you out there right now trying to solve Tyler Larson's murder?"

"You mean, aside from the fact that I'm no longer an agent?"

He nodded at the file. "You weren't an agent when you solved the Lowry County murders a few months ago."

"That's different," she said.

"How so?"

"I was working as a consultant for the sheriff's office."

"So, since you have no *official* involvement with the case that ended your career, you're willing to just let it go?"

She took a deep breath and said, "I guess so."

"I don't believe you."

Rachel felt herself tensing, her body preparing to spring out of her chair. She didn't know whether she wanted to stand up and yell at Grant or walk straight out of the room without saying a word. In that moment of indecision, he pressed on.

"I think you're conflicted," he said. "I think you want to be out there searching for the real killer, but you're afraid of what might happen if you actually solved the case. What harm it might do to the SBI's new assistant director. The man who actually made the decision to arrest Lauren Bailey. He was, after all, your mentor, wasn't he? Taught you every-thing you knew about being an agent?"

"He was." A little sadness crept into her voice. "Where are you going with this?"

He leaned forward, put his forearms on the table, and laced his fingers together. "Miss Carver, this firm defends a number of clients who've been investigated by the SBI. If we decided to bring you on board, we would need to know that your past loyalty to AD Penter wouldn't interfere with your ability to perform your duties."

"That won't be a problem for me," she said. "I can promise you."

"You're certain of that?"

"I am. The truth is, you're right. I *did* feel a sense of loy-alty to him. But that's over now." She looked at the file, felt anger and resentment rising within her. "I'm done caring about Ross Penter. You won't have to worry about him getting in my way."

Grant seemed to recognize the resolve in her voice. He gave her a nod and said, "Very well then. I appreciate your time, Miss Carver."

"That's it?"

He smiled. "We'll be in touch."

THREE

Rachel left the interview feeling spent, and the three-block trek back to her car didn't help. The sidewalk on Salisbury offered no shade, and the late-morning sun was relentless. The only respite came from a cloud of concrete dust that billowed from a construction site across the street, but the gray mass made the humid air all the more stifling.

When she hit the public parking lot, the freshly coated asphalt seemed to soak up the little bit of life she had left in her. Her feet dragged across its black surface as Grant's questions played in her mind.

So where did it all go wrong?

He had cut right through Rachel's pitiful defenses, forcing her to relive the worst day of her life.

The screaming child. The nervous deputy. Lauren Bailey waving her dead boyfriend's pistol.

It had been one of several from Larson's collection. A .40-caliber semiauto, similar to the one deputies had found in the car next to his body. It was too large for Bailey's tiny hand. It likely would have launched free from her grip had she pulled the trigger, but that didn't make it any less dangerous.

Rachel begged her to lower it, to put it on the floor. But she was defiant, intoxicated, and proclaiming her innocence.

The deputy had heard enough. He stepped forward and yelled at her to drop her weapon. She pointed it at him instead.

So Rachel shot her. Eight rounds to the center mass, and Bailey went down, dying in the living room of her mother's house. Rachel scooped up the child and carried him outside as the deputy secured the gun and called for backup and an ambulance. It was all over in less than a minute.

Nine months had passed, but it took only an instant to put Rachel back in that moment.

She dropped into the driver seat of her Camry and started the engine, turned up the air conditioner but left it in park. She stared blankly at the world outside the windshield. After a few minutes, she realized she was sitting there with nothing to do and nowhere to go. Nowhere but an empty apartment on the north end of town.

The days had been passing quickly, as Rachel had moved from one freelance job to the next. The Lowry County murders, as the media had called them, had been her biggest case. She had solved it on her own, receiving a lot of news coverage in the aftermath. Free advertising, as it turned out, which had provided her numerous opportunities. But the buzz was dying down, and so was the workload.

It bothered Rachel to admit how much she wanted the job with Robertson Burke & Porter. In some ways, it made her feel like a failure. Of course, she was always welcome to rejoin the SBI. Penter had said as much during their last encounter. But she hated the thought of going back, tail tucked between her legs, and she couldn't see herself ever working for Penter again.

She opened her briefcase and took out her phone. It was almost a reflex, or an instinct. As if the little device would hold some answer for her.

She thought about calling her best friend, Danny Braddock.

Is that what he is?

They had been partners in the Raleigh Police Department's homicide unit before she left to join the SBI. Soon after, Braddock had moved away to the mountains, where he'd become the chief deputy of a tiny sheriff's office. It was at his insistence that Rachel had been asked to consult on the Lowry County case. That job . . . that *crisis* had brought them closer together. Perhaps too close.

She wanted to be near him now. Wanted to hear his voice, though she didn't know just what she hoped to hear him say. She stared at the phone for a moment, then turned the ringer on, and checked the screen for any notifications. There was a missed call and a voicemail.

She played the message: "Uh . . . hi . . . I'm trying to reach a Ms. Rachel Carver? My name is Chad Hughes. I'm a detective with the Siler City Police Department. If you could give me a call back at your earliest convenience, I'd greatly appreciate it."

He had left a number and a time; the message was less than ten minutes old.

It wasn't unusual for Rachel to get calls from detectives, especially ones she had worked with in the past. Sometimes they needed help remembering details from old cases. Sometimes they wanted advice on solving a new one.

And she had worked in Siler City, just one county to the west, on several occasions. But it had been a while. Perhaps a few years. She didn't know Chad Hughes, and he sounded like he didn't know who she was either. He had even called her "Ms." instead of "Agent."

She hit redial, and he answered immediately.

"I'm sorry to bother you, ma'am," he said, "but, by any chance, do you happen to know a Bryce Parker?"

"Yes, I do," she said, a little alarmed. "Is he okay?"

"Mind if I ask how you two know each other? Are you family or . . . ?"

Rachel adopted an official-sounding tone as she said, "Up until January, I was a special agent with the SBI. In that capacity, he interviewed me on several occasions."

"Interviewed?"

"Bryce is a reporter."

"Is that so?"

"Yes," she said, growing annoyed. "He works for the *Raleigh Herald.*"

"Huh. I wouldn't have guessed—"

"Can you please tell me what's going on? Is he okay?"

"Actually, no," he said. "I'm afraid not. Mr. Parker was brought in to the ER a few hours ago. It appears he overdosed on heroin."

★ ★ ★

Rachel took off for Siler City right away. An hour later, she was standing by a nurse's station in the emergency department of Chatham Hospital, waiting for Hughes to finish a call.

"Right . . . mm-hmm . . ." he said, rocking from his heels to the balls of his feet. The rubber soles of his slip-on dress shoes squeaked against the vinyl floor. He glanced at Rachel and mouthed an exaggerated *sorry*, which bunched the chins beneath his puffy face.

She offered him a smile and tamped down the urge to snatch the phone from his hand and drop it into the nearest biohazard receptacle. One of the red ones with the safety lid meant for disposing of hypodermic needles.

"Mm-hmm . . . okay . . ."

She thought about how much fun it would be to watch him try to dig it out.

"Well, listen, I'd better run," he said, as if he'd read her mind. "I got someone here waiting on me." He ended the call and put his phone away. "I'm sorry about that, Ms. Carver. What was it you were saying?"

She smiled again. "I was just explaining that I haven't seen Bryce in a few months. If I remember correctly, it was around the end of March."

"Right." He thought for a second. "And he hasn't been in contact with you at all in that time?"

"No," she said.

"No emails? No text messages?"

"Nothing."

"That's kinda strange, don't you think? That he would ask us to call you before anyone else?"

"A little."

"Yet you rushed straight over here to see him," he said, eyeing her suspiciously.

"We may not have seen each other in a while, but I consider Bryce a friend. And he's helped me out in the past. I owe him."

"Helped you out with what, if you don't mind me asking?"

"A case I was consulting on for the Lowry County Sheriff's Office."

Hughes rocked back on his heels, scratched his chin, and said, "Hmph."

Rachel didn't like being on the defensive. She asked, "Is this normal for you, Detective? Do you always get called in when someone ODs?"

"Me? Oh no, of course not. No, I'm just here 'cause the old man who reported it said he saw your friend being dragged into a ditch, like someone was dumping a body. Given how he was dressed, the responding officer didn't think he looked like an addict. She thought she might have stumbled onto some kind of a kidnapping or something. Like someone had drugged him against his will."

"And what do you think?"

"Hard to tell when he won't talk to me. But if I had to guess? I've seen addicts that look plenty enough like normal folks. At least in the beginning. I think Mr. Parker just had one hit too many and it turned out to be more than he could handle. Whoever he did it with probably thought he was dying, so they panicked and took him for a ride."

"I guess that's one theory," she said, glancing over his shoulder toward the room at the end of the hall. "Are you planning to charge him?"

He shook his head. "He didn't have anything on him. Not really worth our time. Besides, he's got a tough enough road ahead of him."

"You mind if I go in to see him?"

"Knock yourself out."

As she started down the hall, he said, "You will, of course, let me know if he wakes up and says anything interesting?"

"Of course," she said without looking back.

When she reached the room, she knocked on the door, then cracked it to peer inside. It was dark and quiet. She didn't want the light and noise from the hall to intrude, so she opened it just enough to slide in. As she stepped through the doorway, she glanced back and saw Hughes watching her. He was on his phone again.

Inside, Parker lay on his back, inclined in the tilted bed, sweat-soaked and shaky. He had an IV taped to his arm. An oxygen tube was slung over his ears and hooked beneath his nose. His lips quivered, and there was a line of drool descending his cheek. The bed rails were up, as if the hospital staff was afraid he might roll over the side and crash to the floor.

"Damn, Bryce," she whispered. "What the hell have you done to yourself?"

"Rachel?" His voice was weak and hoarse. "That you?"

She stepped around the foot of the bed and stood at his side. "It's me."

He lifted his head and opened his eyes, gazed at her for a moment before dropping back to the pillow. "They took me."

"*Took* you? Someone kidnapped you?"

He didn't answer. He seemed to be drifting off to sleep. "Bryce? Should I go?"

His eyes opened again. "No . . . don't."

"Okay." She tried to sound reassuring. "I'm here."

"I found—" He cleared his throat, looked like he was struggling for the right words. "—something."

"Okay. What did you find?"

"You were right. I knew all along . . . you were right." His strength was fading.

"Right about what?" she asked.

"Bailey and Larson."

"What . . . ?" The word stuck in her throat. She swallowed hard and said, "What are you talking about?"

He didn't answer. Rachel shook his arm and said, "Bryce?"

His only response was a soft snore.

★ ★ ★

Rachel had been sitting in the dark, waiting, for nearly thirty minutes when a nurse came in and told her that Parker would likely sleep for several more hours.

"Even if he does wake up while you're here," she said, "I doubt you'll be able to get much out of him. He probably won't be making any sense for a while."

Rachel thanked her and decided to leave.

Out in the hall, there was no sign of Hughes. He wasn't in the lobby either. He had apparently made up his mind about Parker. Another addict working his way toward an early grave. It was an epidemic. Even in this tiny town, fifty miles outside Raleigh.

Rachel wondered what Parker had been doing here. She hadn't spoken to him since their last interview when she had come clean about the Larson murder case. When she had told Parker she'd had her doubts about Lauren Bailey's guilt from the beginning—inadvertently blaming the special agent in charge, Ross Penter, for ordering an arrest that led to a standoff.

A standoff that ended with Rachel shooting Bailey dead.

Parker had been fascinated by the story, by the tragedy and the injustice of it all.

"If she wasn't the one who killed Larson, who did?"

Rachel hadn't been able to answer him. The SBI, at Penter's insistence, had closed the case for good. As far as he was concerned, justice had been served. When the time had come for Rachel to make her official statement about the shooting and the decisions that had led to it, Penter had pressured her into agreeing with his version. Soon after, the SBI's internal review found that Rachel had acted appropriately, and she and Penter both received praise for their handling of the case.

"I found . . . something."

Had Parker really discovered a new lead?

Rachel feared she could drive herself insane with a question like that. It would turn in her mind, forcing endless speculation. And Parker wouldn't be answering it anytime soon. There was also the matter of how he had overdosed on heroin in the first place. Had he really been kidnapped and drugged?

While waiting for him to wake, Rachel had inspected his arms. There were no tracks, the little sores common to habitual heroin users, though it was possible he had been injecting himself in a more discreet location. Intravenous drug abusers could be quite adept at hiding the signs of addiction.

Rachel had known Parker for a few years. She was a

good source for him, and she'd given him at least half a dozen interviews in that time. He didn't strike her as an addict, but she'd been surprised by people on more than one occasion. It was, in fact, an occupational hazard in her line of work.

As she stepped into the midday heat and crossed the parking lot, she wished she could force the questions away. That she could bury them, at least until Parker was well enough to talk to her again. But the investigator in her couldn't let them go.

She hopped in her car and headed for the highway, resolving to try the one place she might find some answers.

FOUR

The *Raleigh Herald* was on Salisbury, two blocks south of where Rachel had parked for her morning interview. She turned into the same public lot, got a new ticket from the attendant, and lucked out with a better spot under a shade tree. She took out a steno pad and a pen, then stuffed her briefcase behind the passenger seat to keep it out of sight.

The buildings were casting longer shadows across the pavement, and there was a light breeze that made the walk almost pleasant. Rachel quickened her pace as she approached the two-story office complex and checked the time on her phone as she reached the entrance. It was getting close to three. Hopefully, whoever she needed to talk to hadn't decided to leave early for the day.

At the reception desk, she spoke to a young man who suggested she try the newsroom director. Or maybe the senior editor for investigations, if she wasn't in a meeting. Then he hit a speed-dial button and waited several seconds as it rang on speaker. It went to voicemail, so he ended the call and said, "Let's see if Cara's around."

He hit another button and a woman answered. He picked up the handset to keep Rachel from hearing too much and spoke in a hushed voice. Then he hung up and said, "Cara will see you. Just take the elevators to the second floor. She'll be there to meet you."

When Rachel got off the elevator, there was no one there to meet her. She followed the hall to a large bullpen filled with cubicles. Surrounding it were offices, a pair of conference rooms, a break room, and what looked like a tiny library. Rachel walked the perimeter and read the names inscribed on the glass walls.

"Can I help you?" asked a man's voice from the bullpen.

She turned to see him watching her from his desk. His hands were on his keyboard, and he looked annoyed by the distraction. She suddenly felt like she had made a mistake walking around unescorted.

"Who are you looking for?" he asked impatiently.

"Cara," she said. "She was supposed to meet me by—"

The man threw a thumb over his shoulder and went back to work. Rachel followed his direction until she found the office. The name next to the door read CARA MARSH, SENIOR EDITOR. She stuck her head inside and said, "Ms. Marsh?"

"What . . . ?" Marsh looked startled. She pulled her glasses off and stood, pushing her chair into a bookcase behind her. "Shit. I'm sorry. Are you the one they called up about?"

"Yes. Am I catching you at a bad time?"

Marsh rubbed her eyes, which turned her pale lids pink. She squinted at Rachel and said, "No, no. Just got a little sidetracked." She had wild strawberry hair and freckled skin. She waved Rachel toward an empty chair with a bony hand. "What can I do for you?"

"I think we've spoken on the phone before," Rachel said. "Back in March. You called me to fact-check one of your reporter's stories. Bryce Parker? My name's Rachel Carver."

"Oh . . ." Marsh dropped into her chair and scooted it back to her desk. "Right. It's nice to finally meet you in person. What brings you here? Is it about that article?"

"I'm not sure. Have you heard from Bryce lately?"

"Not today." She glanced at the ceiling. "Come to think of it, he didn't check in yesterday either."

"When was the last time you saw him?"

She closed her eyes and said, "What's today? Thursday . . . ? Let me think." Then she looked back at Rachel. "Not since before Tuesday morning's budget meeting, actually."

"Is that normal?"

"For Bryce? It can be. It all depends on what he's working on."

"Would you happen to know what that is? I mean, did it have anything to do with the story he wrote about me?"

Marsh smiled, then gave Rachel a wary look as she tapped a pen on her desk. "It must be a habit for you."

"I'm sorry?"

"Walking into someone's office and thinking it's okay to interrogate them. But you're not an agent anymore, if I'm not mistaken."

"Maybe I'm trying to see if I have what it takes to be a reporter."

Marsh chuckled. "That's right. You were a journalism major, weren't you?"

"Once upon a time."

"Well, since you've been out of school for a while, let

me give you a bit of advice. Being a reporter doesn't carry the same weight as being a cop. We don't get much out of people just because we work for a paper. It's always a good idea to let the source know what kind of story you're working on before you hit them with a bunch of questions."

"I see." In many ways, Rachel was used to doing the opposite. As a homicide investigator, it was a good tactic to get as much from an interview as she could before she provided information that might make the subject clam up. Tell some people that a friend or a coworker had died and they might become distraught, overcome by grief. Or guarded with their answers, fearful that they might be suspects. But Marsh was right. Rachel had lost a crucial part of what made that work. She was no longer an agent. "I got a call this morning from a detective with the Siler City Police Department."

Marsh sat forward, concern on her face. "What happened? Is it about Bryce? Is he all right?"

Rachel relayed everything she knew about Parker's overdose, which wasn't much.

"Oh my God." Marsh looked dumbstruck. She was quiet for nearly a minute, then said, "I can't believe it. I mean, I really can't . . . Bryce Parker? *Heroin*?"

"I'm guessing he didn't strike you as an addict."

"Never."

"Me either." She gave Marsh a little more time to process the news before she asked, "So, by any chance, do you know what he was working on?"

"Uh . . . yeah. He pitched me a story idea about the State Employees Association. He has a source who says the director's been misusing funds. Maybe even stealing."

"That's it? Nothing about the Larson murder case or Lauren Bailey?"

Marsh shook her head quickly. "No. He hasn't mentioned anything about that in a while."

"How long is a while?"

"I'm not sure." Her eyes drifted away as she searched her memory. "It's been a month or more, at least."

"Do you remember what he said to you about it?"

"He was asking for some time to go out of town, if I remember. Something had happened to one of his sources, and he wanted to look into it."

"Did anything come of it?"

"Not that I know of. I had another assignment for him, so I couldn't let him go. I don't know if he did it on his own time, but he never brought it up to me again."

"Do you think that might be why he's in Siler City?"

"Could be. He didn't even tell me he was going. Maybe he was afraid I'd tell him not to . . . Wait, why did the police call *you*?"

Rachel shrugged. "Apparently, Bryce asked them to."

"Why would he do that?"

"That's what I'm trying to figure out. I only spoke to him for a minute or two before he passed out. He said he'd found something, but he didn't say what. He also said he knew I was right about Bailey and Larson."

"Wow." Marsh's eyes went wide. "Does that make any sense to you, or do you think it was the drugs talking?"

"I wish I knew." It suddenly occurred to Rachel that she might have put Parker's job in jeopardy. "Listen, I know this doesn't look good, but before anyone jumps to any conclusions, I think you should know something."

"Okay?"

"There's a chance that Bryce didn't do this to himself. The investigator said there was a report that he had been dragged into the ditch where they found him. And when I talked to him, he said someone had taken him. It's possible he was drugged against his will."

"Oh my *God*."

"Yeah. I thought you should know that before anyone starts talking about firing him."

"I don't think they'd do that," Marsh said. "Not without giving him a chance to get clean first. But, like you said, it doesn't look good. Are the police treating this as a kidnapping?"

"They're looking into it." Rachel decided not to mention that Hughes had probably discounted that possibility already. "But a lot will depend on what Bryce tells them. And how much he remembers."

"What about you? I mean, can you help him?"

Rachel wanted to say yes, but there was too much she didn't know.

"I'm going to try."

FIVE

The meeting with Marsh had not been very enlightening. Frustrated, Rachel walked back to her car repeating one thought to herself: Parker was working on a story about corruption.

A powerful government official, fearful that he might be caught stealing state funds, would have a lot of incentive to get rid of a nosy reporter. Abducting him and dosing him with heroin would've been one way to solve that problem. If that was the case, Parker had been lucky to survive. Or perhaps his survival had been part of the plan. A way to discredit him and ruin his reputation. After all, who would trust the word of an addict?

As convenient as that scenario was, it didn't explain why Parker had asked the police to call her. Nor did it explain his words to her at the hospital.

You were right.

His ashen face, sunken and flecked with droplets of sweat, hovered in her vision.

I knew all along . . . you were right.

There was a part of her that didn't want to be. As Grant had pointed out during their interview, Rachel could be obsessive. It was a trait that made her relentless as an investigator, but it also took a toll.

During her time with the SBI, Rachel had developed a tendency of letting her work take over to the exclusion of everything else in her life. Her family, her friends, her personal finances, her health . . . all pushed aside in favor of whatever case she'd been desperate to solve. Her supervisor, Ross Penter, had warned her about it after she'd resigned. Warned her about her habit of diving in too deeply.

"Sooner or later," he had said, "you're going to disappear down a dark hole again. And if you're not careful, no one will be there to pull you out. Not even me."

Rachel caught her reflection in the black window of her car door. It held her there for a moment, key in hand, eyes fixed, as she realized what had been holding her back. Why she wasn't, as Grant had put it, out there right now trying to solve Tyler Larson's murder. It was that fear of losing herself. If Parker had found a new lead in the Larson investigation, it was sure to happen again.

Rachel left downtown and headed home. The drive took fifteen minutes, which gave her too much time to think. When she got to her apartment, she heated up a microwave dinner and tried to lose herself in a sitcom as she ate on the sofa.

Chicken parmesan over spaghetti. Reruns of *Modern Family*. But the questions kept barging in.

She needed a better distraction. Two options came to mind: she could leave an hour and a half early for her Brazilian jiu-jitsu class, or she could start drinking.

There was a bottle of pinot grigio in the fridge, along with a six-pack of raspberry-flavored wheat beer from some microbrewery in Colorado. A third of a bottle of Maker's Mark sat in the cabinet beneath the sink. If she started now, she could work her way through all of it before bedtime.

Rachel went to her room, hung her blazer up in the closet, and changed into a pair of shorts and a T-shirt. Then she grabbed her gi, the uniform she used in jiu-jitsu training, and her brown belt and stuffed them into her gym bag. Getting drunk would have to wait.

* * *

Jiu-jitsu class turned out to be the perfect diversion. The instructor taught lapel chokes, which included numerous ways to use an opponent's own collar against him and make him lose consciousness if he wasn't willing to admit defeat. The right grip from a good position, the right motion of the arms, and Rachel's partners had to choose between tapping out or going to sleep.

Tap or nap, as the saying went, and it was no fun waking up disoriented and drooling on the mats.

After the lesson, there was a half hour of free sparring. By the time it was over, Rachel was exhausted. She had a sore neck and aching fingers but felt elated as she changed out of her gi.

She said bye to her classmates and walked back to her car, admiring the distant view of downtown along the way. The evening sun cast an orange glow on the cityscape, a mass of stark geometry jutting above the rolling hills of the Carolina Piedmont. The soft landscape in the forefront faded to black as the buildings above it held on to the last bit of daylight.

Rachel put the view in her mirrors as she made a U-turn

and headed home. Along the way, she realized there was no more food in her apartment. She felt like stopping for a cheeseburger and a large order of fries, but that would negate too much of her workout. She settled on a healthier option—a chicken sandwich, grilled, with a small order of fries and a diet soda. She was sitting in line at the drive-through when her phone rang.

"Good evening, Miss Carver." It was Calvin Grant. "I'm sorry to bother you so late, but I thought you'd like to know I have a job for you, if you're interested."

"I am," she said, though it didn't sound like he was offering her a full-time position.

"Excellent. There's a lot to discuss. How soon can we meet?"

"I can be at your office first thing in the morning."

"How about tonight at my house?"

"Um . . . well . . ."

"I know it's a little unusual for me to ask that of you," he said, "but this case is somewhat sensitive."

The driver behind Rachel honked his horn. The line had moved, leaving a gap between her car and the menu board. She let off the brake and lowered her window, heard a distorted voice offering to take her order.

"Okay," she said quickly. "Text me your address, and I'll be there as soon as I can."

SIX

Grant's house was in an affluent suburb in the northeast section of town. Rachel pulled up in front and looked it over as she ate her sandwich. A two-story colonial, clad in red brick and adorned with stucco accents. It was on the lower end of the spectrum for this neighborhood. An entry-level home for a young professional with high aspirations, no doubt hoping to trade up one day for a grander model. Like one of the petite mansions further up the street.

Rachel finished eating and left the Camry parked at the curb. She got out, climbed the steps to the front door, and rang the bell. Grant answered a minute later.

"I appreciate you agreeing to meet me here," he said, beckoning her inside. He had loosened his tie and rolled up his sleeves, but he still looked like he could slip into a jacket and walk straight into a courtroom, ready to deliver some flawless opening argument. It was a talent, appearing that pristine after so many hours in the same suit. Long days usually turned Rachel into a disheveled wreck.

"You have a nice home," she said.

"Thank you. I'm sorry I can't introduce you to my wife. She's upstairs getting our son ready for bed. She doesn't really like being around for this sort of thing anyway."

He led her to a dining room and a long oval table with ornately carved legs. He pointed to a spot and said, "Please, have a seat."

As she drew the chair out and lowered herself into it, she saw a thin three-ringed binder sitting on the place mat in front of her.

Grant took the next chair over and sat facing her, one arm bolstered by the top of the seat back. "I hope you can forgive me, Miss Carver, but I'm afraid I've lured you here under false pretenses. I don't actually have a job for you. Not exactly."

"Okay." She gave him a look that showed a little irritation and a lot of confusion.

"It *could* be an opportunity for you, though, should you decide to take it."

"What kind of opportunity?"

"The kind that would get you off the bench, so to speak."

Realization hit her, and she felt a sting of disappointment. "The interview this morning . . . that was just an excuse to question me about the Larson case?"

"To gauge how you felt about it, actually. To see if there was any chance of persuading you to take it up again."

"Why not just ask?"

Grant shifted in his seat, cleared his throat, and said, "The person we represent wishes to protect the information he's given us. Especially where it came from. If it was clear to me that you had no desire to continue the investigation, we wouldn't be offering it to you."

"And I suppose you're not allowed to tell me who this person is?"

"I'm afraid not."

She studied him for a moment. "Does this have anything to do with what happened to Bryce Parker?"

The name appeared to surprise him. "The reporter who wrote the story about you? What's happened to him?"

"Never mind. It's not important." She turned to look at the binder. "So what sort of information does this client of yours have for me?"

"During your original investigation," Grant said, "do you remember speaking to a man named Adam Hubbard?"

"Yeah." A face popped into Rachel's mind. A young face, filled with anxiety and sadness. "Once by phone and twice in person."

"What was your interest in him?"

"Hubbard was a member of Larson's squad for about a year. Right up until he was medically discharged. Phone records showed several calls between them in the days leading up to the murder."

"And what were those about?"

"Hubbard supposedly hurt his back in a training exercise, so his doctors put him on prescription painkillers. After he got out of the Army, he became addicted to them. He said Larson was trying to help him get clean."

"So he wasn't a suspect?"

"He had an alibi." Though that didn't tell the whole story. Rachel remembered the feeling she'd had when questioning Hubbard face-to-face. The suspicion he'd been holding something back, reluctant to tell her the whole truth. Unfortunately, she'd never had the opportunity to find out what he might be hiding. Once she discovered Larson's affair, the focus shifted entirely to Lauren Bailey.

Grant reached over and opened the binder. The pages

within were divided by tabs. The first was labeled INITIAL REPORT. He turned it over, exposing a document from the Union County Sheriff's Office.

"Mr. Hubbard was killed a little more than a month ago."

Rachel recalled what Marsh had told her earlier. About Parker wanting permission to go out of town. *Something had happened to one of his sources, and he wanted to look into it.* She pulled the binder closer and started reading.

Grant said, "You'll find witness statements, some crime scene photos, and the medical examiner's report in there. Along with an arrest report."

"Arrest report," Rachel said. "Who did they get?"

"It's in the back."

Rachel turned to the last tab. The page behind it was a printout of a mug shot. A young man, probably in his late twenties, though his face looked weatherworn. He had leathery skin and purple bags beneath his eyes. A few days' worth of stubble surrounded his razor-thin lips.

"Meet Kyle Strickland," Grant said. "The sheriff's office believes he and Hubbard got into a fight over drugs. In the heat of it, Strickland allegedly picked up a brick and used it to bludgeon Hubbard to death. I should warn you, it's not a pretty picture."

"It's okay, Mr. Grant. I've developed a strong stomach over the years." She turned to the medical examiner's report and found the autopsy photos. "I'd say bludgeon is a bit of an understatement."

The left side of Hubbard's face was a disfigured mass of tissue. The cheek and brow were crushed. The eye was either hidden beneath the swollen flesh or destroyed altogether. There was a massive tear to the scalp near the hairline that revealed a strip of white skull. The other side of the face, still intact, was mottled in shades of brown and purple.

"They really think this was over drugs?"

"Oxycodone, to be exact. They found a few varieties stashed away in his house. OxyContin, Percocet, Percodan . . . Apparently, his doctors refused to renew his prescriptions, so he had to start buying them illegally."

"And Strickland?" she asked. "He's an addict too?"

"Allegedly."

She went back to the arrest report and read through it for a minute. "So far, I'm not seeing how this has anything to do with Tyler Larson's murder."

"Our client," Grant said slowly, as if choosing his words carefully, "has a compelling reason to believe that the sheriff's office has the wrong man. And that the cases are, in fact, directly linked to one another."

"A compelling reason," she said. "Any chance you can tell me what that is?"

He offered an apologetic smile. "Sorry."

"Okay." She flipped through the other tabs, scanning the pages within them. "That doesn't give me a lot to go on."

"No, but it's more than you had before you walked in here."

"I guess that's true." She turned to face Grant. "Is that everything?"

"That's everything."

"Well then," she said, standing, "I guess I'd better get to work."

"So you're back on the case, then?"

Rachel didn't like the feeling of being manipulated by

Grant and his mystery client, but she couldn't ignore a new development in the most important case of her career. Add that to Parker's abduction and the pull was too much to resist. She closed the binder, cradled it in her forearm, and started for the door. "Was there ever any doubt?"

SEVEN

Rachel went home and spent the rest of the night studying the material in the binder. By the time she went to bed, it was after 2 AM, but she woke as soon as the first slivers of morning light cut through the blinds of her bedroom window. She made coffee and spread the crime scene photos across her kitchen table. Then she brought up Google Maps on her laptop and zoomed in to get a look at the location from overhead.

Hubbard had been found lying in the yard of an abandoned textile mill, a massive, three-story structure with a collapsed section near its southeast corner. That broken portion of wall had provided the implement used to rob him of his life. There were photos of the bloody brick in the binder. A weapon of opportunity, seized in the fury of a desperate fight.

Rachel wanted to see the location for herself. It was on the outskirts of Monroe, a small city to the southwest, just twenty-five miles from Charlotte. Her phone said it would take two hours and forty-five minutes to get there.

She took a quick shower and slid into a pair of jeans and a white T-shirt. She decided to bring along one of her black blazers, just in case she needed to talk to anyone about the case. It always helped to look a little more professional. As she slipped on her shoes, her eyes moved to the tiny gun safe on the floor of her closet. It housed her Glock 19, a compact 9mm she hadn't touched in several months.

It wasn't the gun she had used to shoot Lauren Bailey. That had been her service weapon, issued by the SBI. Nevertheless, there was something disconcerting about the thought of handling it again, of carrying it around as if she were still an agent. She left it in the safe.

She went to the kitchen and gathered the photos and put them back in the binder. Stuffed her laptop into her briefcase and double-checked that her license, credit cards, and a bit of cash were tucked into her phone case. Then she loaded everything in the Camry and headed out.

Her mind was on Hubbard's murder as she maneuvered through the parking lot toward the road. She didn't notice the black F-150 pickup sitting in a spot near the entrance. Nor did she see the man inside it, who was watching her as she passed by.

★ ★ ★

It was an easy drive, once Rachel cleared the rush-hour traffic on I-440. The route took her to an industrial zone on the north end of Monroe. When she reached the intersection near the mill, she spotted a convenience store on the corner, one that had figured prominently in the police investigation.

The sign by the entrance said SHARKIE's. Rachel guessed the store was as old as she was, though it hadn't aged as well. A dilapidated canopy stood over an uninhabited concrete curb, the gas pumps having been removed long ago. There were stickers and painted ads covering the dirty windows, which made them nearly impossible to see through. One of the doors had a paper sign with an arrow drawn on it, a handwritten note that said THAT ONE'S BROKE. USE THIS'N INSTEAD.

Rachel parked and went inside.

The cashier was a teenager in a ball cap. He had a bad complexion and thin lines of facial hair that looked like they had been drawn with a black marker. He sat on a stool by the window and kept his eyes on his smartphone as Rachel walked by, went to the coolers, and picked out two cans of Monster Energy drink.

When she stepped up to the counter, he sighed and put the phone down, rang up the total and mumbled it to her. She gave him cash and took the opportunity to look around while he dug her change out of the register drawer. There was an old monitor showing a security-camera feed overlooking the counter, another watching the aisles behind her, but nothing that showed the view outside.

He dropped the change in her hand and then climbed back onto the stool to continue staring at his phone. Rachel considered asking him if he knew anything about the murder but decided it would be best to wait. She wanted to walk the scene first, to get a look at where it had happened before she started asking questions. And she knew he hadn't been the one minding the store at the time anyway. The police report said the clerk working that shift was a thirty-one-year-old Hispanic male.

She went outside and cracked open one of the cans, drank half of it as she walked over to the intersection and looked around, taking in her surroundings. There were a few old houses directly across the street, most of which looked dilapidated. To the left, a rundown strip mall had a single store selling electrical supplies, though it didn't appear to be open. Red-lettered placards taped to the other windows begged for new tenants. A warehouse complex to the right showed the only signs of life in the vicinity. A pair of forklifts loaded tractor trailers with cellophane-wrapped boxes on pallets.

Deputies had canvassed the area immediately after discovering the body, looking for cameras and witnesses. Aside from what they'd found inside Sharkie's, they'd come up empty on both counts.

Rachel turned around to look back at the parking lot and the store. Beyond it, the red facade of the mill lay dead, like the fossilized remains of some prehistoric giant. Green vines climbed its walls. The branches of a withered maple pressed against its side, piercing one of the windows.

Things come here to die, she thought.

According to the affidavit detectives had prepared for the arrest warrant, everything had started here in this parking lot. Hubbard and Strickland had come to the store together, in Strickland's car. He had pulled up in front, then gone inside to buy a pack of cigarettes. Hubbard had stayed outside, where he met with his dealer to buy a bottle of Percocet. After the deal was done, Hubbard and Strickland had gone behind the store, sneaked through a hole in the chainlink fence surrounding the mill yard, and found a quiet place to divide the pills between them.

But something had gone horribly wrong.

Rachel went to her car, set the unopened can in the cup holder, and grabbed the crime scene sketch and the photos from the binder. She walked around to the back of the store and found the tear in the fence. She pushed against the rusty mesh to make the hole bigger and squeezed through. Then she used the sketch to orient herself as she slowly approached the mill.

There was no sign of the violence that had taken place here. Nearly six weeks had passed, erasing all traces of it. Rachel had to rely on the photos to take her back in time. With each step, she shuffled to a new one, moving in a circle around the spot where Hubbard had died.

A pair of teenagers had stumbled upon him. They had been passing through the mill yard, using it as a shortcut to get to and from the store, as they did almost every day. Occasionally they would explore the building, looking for a place to kill time, or maybe get high amid the rubble of red brick and rotting timbers. This time they had found a man, lying on his back with half his face battered to a pulp.

Strickland and Hubbard had argued over the Percocet, according to the affidavit. Most likely because Strickland had thought he wasn't getting his money's worth. The detectives had speculated that the dealer had raised the price he was charging for each pill. Desperate for a fix, Hubbard had agreed to pay it. But that meant walking away with less than he'd originally planned. Strickland still wanted the amount he had agreed to pay for, which would've left Hubbard with even fewer for himself.

That disagreement had turned into a fight. A fight Hubbard lost.

Rachel stared at the photo of his face. Blood and bone with bits of grass and gravel and brick . . . it would have taken several blows to do that kind of damage. Relentless pummeling fueled by wild rage. It didn't seem right that someone could do this over a few pills, although Rachel had seen crazier things in her career.

A prior history of violence would help to explain it. She wondered if the detectives had discovered anything like that in Strickland's background. If he had been known for dishing out severe beatings, it would certainly help their case. She didn't see anything about it in the binder, but that didn't mean they hadn't found something. Unfortunately, she didn't know anyone in the Union County Sheriff's Office. If she was going to learn more about the man accused of killing Hubbard, the best place to start would be his court-appointed lawyer.

EIGHT

The office of Charles Dunn, Attorney at Law, was on the second floor of a rehabilitated foursquare house, just west of downtown Monroe. Rachel found him sitting at his desk, eating what looked like an egg-salad sandwich and a bag of potato chips. He was in slacks and an undershirt with a paper napkin tucked into the neckband. A jacket, tie, and pin-striped dress shirt were draped over the only other chair in the room.

Rachel tapped on the doorjamb to get his attention. He looked up and stared for a second until he seemed to realize the state of his appearance. "Shoot . . . I'm sorry." He jumped out of his chair and jogged around to clear her a seat. He tossed the jacket and tie onto a cluttered credenza, then faced away from her as he slipped his shirt on. "The AC up here ain't worth a damn, but I guess I can't complain too much. That accountant downstairs pays almost twice what I do."

Rachel thanked him and sat down.

Dunn settled in behind his desk and pushed his sandwich aside. "I have to say, you're not exactly what I was expecting when you called."

"I get that a lot," she said, trying not to sound resentful. She was a brunette with deep green eyes, a square jaw, and an athletic figure. Most of the men she met found her reasonably attractive, but in the insular world of criminal justice professionals, she was all but a perfect ten. Occasionally, that could be an asset. More often than not it proved to be a hurdle.

"So you're here about Kyle Strickland," he said. "You have some information for me?"

She told him about her background as an SBI agent and her experience with the Larson investigation. How she had questioned Adam Hubbard, though nothing had come of it at the time. Then she told him how the case had ended.

Dunn's expression became a mixture of sympathy and awe. "That's quite a story. How do you think Hubbard's death fits into it?"

"I'm not sure, but I have reason to believe that the murders are linked, and that your client may be innocent."

"Mind telling me what that reason is?"

"I guess you could say I've received an anonymous tip."

"Uh-huh. And did this tipster give you anything I can use to keep my client out of prison?"

"Afraid not. But I believe there's something to it, and I'm committed to finding the truth."

He dropped against the seat back. "Well, I certainly wish you the best of luck with that."

"It might help if I knew Mr. Strickland's side of the story."

He laughed. "I'm sure it would. But you know I can't tell you that. Not without his permission. Hell, the only thing I've got going for me in this case is the fact that Kyle was smart enough to keep his mouth shut when he was arrested."

"You could tell me if I was working for you."

"I'm sorry?"

The suggestion had seemed to spring from Rachel instinctively, though it made sense when she thought about it. "If I was your investigator," she said, "you could tell me everything."

Dunn sat dumbstruck for a moment. "That's true, I suppose. Are you serious?"

"Absolutely. You want to prove your client is innocent, and I want to figure out who really killed Hubbard and Larson. Seems like a good fit."

"An alignment of interests, so to speak?"

"You could say that."

"And if there comes a time when those interests no longer align?"

She shrugged. "I guess we'll have to cross that bridge when we get to it."

He drummed his fingers on the arms of his chair. "I take it you're licensed?"

"I am."

He took a minute to consider the idea. "I should be jumping at the chance to have an ex–SBI agent on the case."

He pushed his chair over to the credenza, opened a drawer, and dug through it. When he rolled back, he had a one-page form in his hand. He laid it in front of her like it was a challenge. "If you're really sure about this, all you have to do is fill that out."

Rachel grabbed one of the dozen or so pens standing in a black coffee mug and started writing.

"I'll be damned." Dunn sat back, looking pleasantly surprised. "You know how this works, right? As far as the money goes? I can only pay you forty dollars an hour. That's all the Office of Indigent Services will reimburse me. And I'll have to get their approval before you start."

"They'll reimburse you up to fifty." She signed the bottom of the form and slid it toward him. "But let's not worry about that now. I'd rather get started right away."

"Suit yourself." He held the paper up and looked it over. Satisfied, he set it down on the corner of his desk, cleared his throat, and said, "Kyle claims he had nothing to do with Adam Hubbard's death. He says they were friends and that he never would have hurt him.

"On the day of the murder, he gave Hubbard a ride to Sharkie's convenience store and left him there. Supposedly, Hubbard was expecting to meet someone, but he wouldn't tell Kyle who it was. He says Hubbard told him he would order an Uber to get home. Kyle went in to buy a pack of cigarettes, and when he came back out to leave, he saw Hubbard standing by himself near the corner of the building, watching the road. That's the last time he saw him."

Rachel thought for a moment, comparing that story with the narrative from the sheriff's office and her own tour of the crime scene. "Do you believe him?"

"Isn't it my job to?"

"It's your job to tell everybody else that you do. You and I have to be honest with each other."

The corners of Dunn's mouth hinted a smile. "Well, to answer your question, I do believe him. For the most part. I assume you'll want to talk to him yourself?"

"Eventually. I want to get as much background as I can

first. You said, 'For the most part.' Do you think he's hiding something?"

"Maybe. The sheriff's office thinks Kyle killed Hubbard during a fight over some pills, like he was desperate for a fix. There's no doubt, Kyle's an addict, but he says he was working on getting clean. He swears he was completely off oxy for more than a week before the murder. The problem is, it's going to be hard to prove that. We're waiting for enough time to pass so we can test one of his hairs. The test can detect opioids for up to ninety days, so we gotta get the timing just right. We need to make sure it's been more than ninety days since he quit but less than ninety days since Hubbard was killed."

"Even then," she said, "that doesn't prove he wasn't itching to get back on them."

"That's true." He spun his chair and gazed out the window. "It also doesn't stop the DA from attacking the accuracy of the test. But what really worries me is what'll happen if the test comes back positive. You ever tried defending an addict before?" He didn't give her a chance to answer. "I think it's highly unlikely that Kyle's as clean as he says he is. On top of that, the sheriff's detectives are out there right now looking for a witness to shore up their narrative. One way or another, they'll find someone who remembers seeing him using when he says he wasn't, even if he is telling the truth."

Rachel was immediately offended by the implication, a knee-jerk reaction, though she couldn't deny that it was possible. "Is there any other way to demonstrate that Kyle was trying to get clean?"

"Oh yeah. He was a regular over at the local drug clinic.

The Monroe Outpatient Treatment Center. As a matter of fact, that's where he met Hubbard."

"Hubbard was a patient too?"

"Yep."

She took her steno pad and pen from the pocket inside her blazer and made a note. "I have to admit, it's not the strongest defense I've ever heard."

"It gets worse," he said. "Just wait till you hear what they found in Kyle's house."

Rachel recalled the inventory from the binder, the detailed list of what detectives had seized when they'd executed the search warrant on Strickland's house. There were six items altogether, the most interesting of which had been discovered in a trash can in the corner of his garage. "The shirt?"

Dunn turned to face her. "I guess you've been down to the courthouse."

She didn't respond, deciding it was best not to tell him who had given her the binder.

"That damn shirt," he said, "has Adam Hubbard's blood all over it."

"How do you know it's Hubbard's?"

"Kyle told me it was. He says Hubbard was helping him replace some shingles on his roof and cut his forearm. Kyle handed him an old T-shirt to stop the bleeding and just threw it away after Hubbard left. Didn't think anything of it when it happened. Completely forgot it was even there. At least, that's what he tells me."

"That's unfortunate," she said.

"That's one way to put it." Dunn leaned forward, put his elbows on his desk, and laced his fingers together. "What was the other guy's name again? The one who died last year in Wendell?"

"Tyler Larson."

"Larson," he said, like he was trying to commit it to memory. "Well, Miss Carver, let me put it like this. My goal right now is to keep Kyle off death row. The DA's gonna treat this like a capital case. I'm sure of it. Even if it *was* just a fight that got out of hand. They'll try to say Kyle planned to kill him all along so he could have all the pills to himself. They'll wave the needle around to scare us into a deal. And unless something changes, I'll probably do everything I can to convince Kyle to take it. In other words, I really hope you're right about the connection between Hubbard and this Larson fella. 'Cause it's about the only chance Kyle has of seeing another day of freedom in his life."

NINE

Rachel had spent the last few minutes of her meeting with Dunn staring at his sandwich. She didn't mind being hungry, but the caffeine was wearing off, and that was unacceptable. She pulled away from the foursquare and found herself cruising through downtown a minute later.

Once the center of commerce for the county, Monroe had suffered years of decline, much of it due to a steady drain of economic resources to nearby Charlotte. But now the money was starting to come back. Suburbanites were fleeing the congestion of the largest city in the state, searching for a smaller community to call home. And the City Council appeared to be doing its best to attract them.

The downtown area was in the midst of a revitalization campaign. The signs on the streetlamps said so, as did the new blacktop and the facelifts given to the facades lining Main Street. Buildings from a bygone era repurposed to accommodate new tenants.

Rachel's eyes caught one as she passed it looking for food. A large hardware store that was being split down the middle. The signs out front promised that a boutique clothing outlet and an Italian restaurant would be opening in less than a month. A poster on a window offered second-floor luxury condos for sale or for rent. A block away, Rachel found a pizza parlor situated on the corner and parked in the shadow of a bulbous oak.

In the passenger seat, there was a manila folder containing a case file Dunn had thrown together for her. In addition to his own notes, he'd made copies of all the discovery materials the DA's office had handed over to date. She collected it, made her way into the restaurant, and settled in at one of the larger tables near the back. When the server came by, she ordered a lunch special—two slices with pepperoni and sausage and a large Mountain Dew. Then she read through the documents while she waited.

The T-shirt, blotched and smeared with blood, was a damning piece of evidence. The detectives suspected that Strickland had used it to clean his hands after the murder. Presently, it was at the State Crime Lab in Raleigh awaiting DNA testing. Eventually those tests would confirm what Dunn and Rachel already knew. That the blood belonged to Hubbard.

A woman in a red-stained apron appeared with a tray of food. She spotted Rachel and shuffled over, set the tray on the edge of her table, and went back to the kitchen.

Rachel covered her pizza in crushed red pepper, then flipped through the file until she found a sheet labeled INTERVIEW. The pages that followed were scans of handwritten notes, a detailed account of the detectives questioning Strickland at his home. She read while the cheese cooled off, sipping on her soda and growing discouraged.

The interrogation had lasted for more than half an hour and had been a mess from the start. Strickland had been terrified. It seemed his nerves had gotten the best of him, and, like a lot of murder suspects, he'd made the mistake of trying to talk himself out of trouble. The pair of detectives had taken him apart with ease. Rachel could hear the conversation in her mind.

I just dropped him off at the store. I don't know who he was waiting on. He didn't tell me. I mean it, I just dropped him off and left. Hell, I didn't even get out of the damn car.

You sure about that? one of the detectives asks.

Yeah, I'm sure. How many times do I gotta tell ya? I just dropped him off and hauled ass.

So, if we talk to the clerk at the store, he'll tell us you didn't go inside?

Yeah. I mean, no, he won't. He shouldn't. Unless he's telling you a bunch of bullshit.

You didn't go in to buy a pack of cigarettes? asks the other detective.

No. Well . . . I mean, yeah. Just a pack of cigarettes. But that's it, man, I swear.

Lies and inconsistencies. Confusion and backpedaling. By the time Strickland announced he was done talking, the damage had already been done. They arrested him three days later.

Rachel took her phone out and called Dunn.

"Didn't take long," he said.

"You were right," she said. "There's not much here."

"That sounds suspiciously like regret."

"Not yet." She tested a slice of pizza with the tip of her finger, then dug a piece of sausage out and dropped it into her mouth. "I'm calling to ask for a favor."

"All right. How can I help?"

"Would you mind calling the drug treatment center for me? Let them know I'm coming by to ask a few questions. I'd like to talk to some of the counselors, if I can."

She heard him chuckle.

"What is it?" she asked.

"Oh, nothing," he said. "You'll see when you get there."

Rachel ended the call and ate her lunch. She got a refill of Mountain Dew and lingered at the table so she could comb through the file, looking for every reference to the treatment center and its staff. She wanted to be prepared when she got there. Interviewing doctors could be difficult. Sometimes fruitless. They were always touchy when it came to talking about their patients. Even the dead ones.

TEN

Parker stood in the ditch, dizzy and nauseous. His body was confused, enduring a cold sweat in the afternoon heat with no clouds to shield him from the sun. His bones and muscles ached, and he felt nearly incapacitated by fatigue. He couldn't concentrate, which made him agitated. Or maybe that, too, was just another symptom.

It was the worst he'd ever felt. Like having the flu with food poisoning and a hangover. But worse than any hangover he'd ever experienced. Even worse than the day after he'd spent fourteen hours power-drinking tequila and Irish whiskey with three of his awful friends in Orlando.

And the doctor had said he could expect another week of this. At least.

The nurse had all but begged him not to check himself out. He would have agreed to stay had the diarrhea not subsided. For practical reasons.

"You shouldn't be here."

She was probably right, whoever she was. A female voice, vaguely familiar. But Parker had gone there for a reason. He was looking for something. Standing there, sweating and shaking and fighting the urge to lie down in the grass, trying to find it, though he couldn't remember exactly what it was.

"My phone," he said weakly.

It was just a guess, but it turned out to be right. His hand moved to his front right pocket, and it was empty. He reached around and felt for his wallet, found it in the wrong back pocket, then felt the front again and found nothing.

No phone. No keys.

He turned around to look behind him. The yellow van was gone. There was a police cruiser there instead. And a woman in uniform, slowly walking toward him.

"Do you remember me?" she asked.

"What?"

"I'm Officer Ramirez. I'm the one who found you here yesterday morning."

None of that made any sense to him, so he went back to searching. "I gotta find my phone."

"Okay," she said. "Maybe I can help you."

She walked around with her head down, trying to look helpful. Parker stumbled in a circle, covering the same ground again and again until the dizziness became too much. He stopped and lowered himself onto the rise, dropped to his side, and vomited.

Ramirez approached and stood by his feet. "Sir, don't you think it would be a good idea to go back to the hospital? They can help make you feel better."

"Don't want no more drugs," he said, spitting into the grass. "Stupid drugs."

"Stupid drugs," she said sympathetically.

"I need my phone."

"Yeah." She looked around again quickly. "I don't think we're going to find it here, hon. Maybe you left it somewhere else. Before you came here. Can you remember where you were before?"

"Yes," he said, but then he thought about it. "No."

He pushed himself up, rested his elbows on his knees, and put his head in his hands. The frustration was overwhelming. He wanted to scream and cry. He wanted to rage against . . . someone. Whoever had done this to him. If only he could figure it out. He needed to be able to focus, but the only clear thought he could muster was how much his hair hurt when he touched it.

"I can't think straight."

"It's like that," Ramirez said. "It'll come and go."

Which made sense. He had been so lucid when he'd walked out of the hospital earlier. When he'd gotten to the parking lot and realized he had no way to leave.

"I don't have my car."

"I noticed that. Did you call a taxi to get you here?"

"Yeah," he said, closing his eyes and rubbing his temples to fight another wave of nausea.

"Why don't you come with me? I can give you a ride. Maybe we can figure this out together."

He nodded and stood up. Took a second to steady himself, then followed her to her car and got in. He sat still and enjoyed the air conditioning while Ramirez spent a few minutes talking to the dispatcher. She gave him a bottle of water, which helped a lot. The chill had passed, for the moment, and so had the queasiness. He used his shirt to wipe his face, then leaned against the headrest and stared out the window.

When Ramirez got off the radio, she looked over at him. "Feeling better?"

"A little," he said.

She turned the car around and started heading toward the highway. "How did you know to come back here?"

"The nurse told me. Said she knew the old man who called 911." He looked at her out of the corner of his eye. "Did she tell you I was here?"

"No. The old man called us again."

"Figures." He closed his eyes. His mind was getting clearer. He tried to recall everything that had led to him lying in the ditch, dying of an overdose. "Thank you, by the way."

"For what?"

"For saving me. The nurse said you saved my life with the Narcan or whatever it was."

"Well, you should be thanking that farmer. If he hadn't called us, you'd probably be in the morgue right now. It's lucky for you he was awake at that time of the morning."

"Wait." Parker opened his eyes and looked around. "Where are we going?"

"I thought I'd take you back to the hospital."

He was about to protest when an image appeared in his mind. A ranch house sitting behind a horse fence. It sprung into view with near-perfect clarity, followed by a memory. Then a string of memories, piecing together a story that managed to shine through the confusion.

"I know where I was." He sat up and turned to face her wearing a look of excitement. "I remember where I was."

She glanced at him with doubt in her eyes.

"Seriously. I was going to meet someone. My car should still be there. I can tell you exactly where it is."

"And the hospital?" she asked.

"I don't need a doctor. I need to figure out what happened to me. And I need to get ahold of someone."

"Rachel Carver?"

"Yeah. How did you know that?"

"You were begging me to call her for you."

"Did you?"

"Detective Hughes did. He said she came to see you at the hospital."

"Really?" He dropped back in his seat. "I thought I imagined that."

Ramirez paused at the intersection, waited for a car to pass, and then turned onto the highway.

"Listen," Parker said, "I know what you're thinking. And I don't blame you, but I promise, I'm not a heroin addict. I've never done anything like that in my life. I may drink more than I should, but I've never, ever been into drugs. I mean, I may have hit a bong once or twice in college . . . maybe rolled a couple of times . . ."

"You're not doing yourself any favors right now."

"The point is, I didn't shoot up, okay?" He leaned forward to catch her eye. "I swear to you, someone did this to me."

"Why?" she asked, though her tone wasn't as skeptical as he'd expected it to be. "Why would anyone want to drug you?"

"It's because of something I found. Some*one*, actually. Someone who witnessed a murder."

Her eyebrows went up. "You're serious?"

"I am."

"What were you doing trying to find a witness to a murder?"

"It's what I do. I'm a reporter for the *Raleigh Herald*. A few months ago, I wrote a story about an SBI agent. Rachel. She was working a homicide, and she shot a suspect. Her supervisor closed the case, but she thinks the real killer is still out there."

"I think I heard about that," she said.

Parker put his eyes on the road. He was feeling nauseous again. The excitement had held it at bay, but it was returning now with a vengeance.

Ramirez was quiet for a minute. She seemed to be considering whether to help. "You know, that old man's property is just barely inside the city limit. A hundred feet to the west and you would've been the sheriff's problem. Just my good fortune, I suppose." She sighed, dug her phone out of her pocket, and checked the screen. "And I'm off now. You were my last call. Lucky for you, it's my ex's day to pick up my daughter. Where are we going?"

"I'll tell you in a minute," he said, feeling the sweat build on the back of his neck. "But right now I need you to pull over. I'm gonna be sick."

ELEVEN

The Monroe Outpatient Treatment Center was housed in a new single-story building with a flat roof and accents of gray stone and stainless steel. Rachel parked in the visitor lot and walked the meandering path to the entrance. Along the way, she passed a koi pond and what looked like a meditation garden surrounding a giant vase that burbled water over its rim.

Inside, the setting was clinical. White and sterile. A potted ficus sat in the corner by a window, alone in its attempt to add a little color to the tiny lobby.

Rachel stepped up to the counter and identified herself to the receptionist seated behind the glass. It took a few iterations of explaining why she was there before the young woman finally seemed to understand. She left her desk and disappeared through a doorway, then came back a couple of minutes later and said, "Ma'am, if you'd like to have a seat, someone will be out to see you shortly."

Twenty minutes later, a door opened and a tall woman in a gray suit emerged. She said, "Miss Carver," and motioned for Rachel to follow her. They walked silently into a hallway, turned a corner, and entered an office. The woman waved Rachel toward a chair, then closed the door and walked around to stand behind her desk.

"I'm Dr. LeMay," she said. "I'm the medical director of this facility."

Pamela LeMay, Rachel recalled from the file. A psychiatrist specializing in the treatment of drug addiction. She was responsible for overseeing the staff, supervising the treatment of each patient, and writing all the prescriptions.

She also owned one third of the clinic.

LeMay lowered herself into her chair, leaned back, and folded her arms. "I apologize for the wait, but we didn't get much notice that you would be coming. I'm sure you understand."

"I do," Rachel said.

"Good. Before we get started, I should say something right up front. I know your firm represents Kyle Strickland and that we have his permission to talk to you, but that only covers him. I can't discuss any of my other patients. And I really don't know what more I can offer you about Kyle that I haven't already told Mr. Dunn."

"Can you tell me anything about the relationship between Kyle and the victim, Adam Hubbard?"

The lines at the corners of LeMay's mouth curled into parentheses. Something resembling a smile but devoid of any real emotion.

Rachel studied her for a moment. She appeared to be in her early fifties, though she could have passed for younger had she adopted a warmer expression. She was beautiful but harsh, a long face with a sharp chin and penetrating gaze.

"Nothing at all?" Rachel asked. "Not even about their relationship outside the clinic?"

LeMay shook her head. "You have to understand, Miss Carver, our patients' personal relationships are often addressed in the course of their treatment. It would be a betrayal of their trust for me to discuss what I know about them in any way."

"In the course of their treatment . . ." she said, trying to think of a different way to get the information she wanted. "You're referring to their counseling sessions?"

"I am," LeMay said with a nod.

"And Kyle attended those?"

"He did."

"One-on-one? Group?"

"Both. And a couple of family sessions as well, while his parents were still involved."

"Why did they stop coming?"

"I'm not sure exactly, but I know it was hard just getting them in here at all. Especially his father."

"Who paid for his treatment?"

"A good portion of our funding comes from the state," LeMay said. "It's meant to help with patients like Kyle, who have limited means. On top of that, he was still on his mother's insurance at the time. It wasn't the best policy, but it helped."

"I see." Rachel made a couple of notes in her steno pad. "When you say that a patient's personal relationships are addressed, I'm assuming that's because those relationships can cause stress? The kind of stress that might trigger a relapse?"

"That's right."

"Was Kyle's relationship with his father like that?"

"Yes."

"Were there any others?"

"I'm sure there were."

Rachel waited, hoping for more, but LeMay just stared at her. "Okay . . ." She made a note and decided to change the subject. "How about anger management issues? Did Kyle have any of those while he was here?"

"I'm sure he did."

"I haven't read anything about it in his file. Mind telling me a little more?"

"I'm not sure what there is to tell. It's pretty common for our patients to experience anger. Recovery is exceedingly difficult. Aside from dealing with the physical symptoms, the withdrawal, the cravings, patients also have to face the thing that led them down the path to addiction in the first place. The underlying issues that made them turn to drug dependency. It's a battle on two fronts, and they fight it every waking moment of every day. Frustration, depression, anxiety, anger . . . they're all very common."

Rachel couldn't help but think about Parker, lying in the hospital bed. About the struggle he had before him. She shook it off and asked, "In Kyle's case, did that anger ever cause him to lash out? Violently?"

"Not that I'm aware of."

"Doesn't that seem strange to you, Doctor? Given the way Adam Hubbard was killed?"

LeMay's brow tensed. "The way he was killed?"

"Yeah," Rachel said. "I'm no psychiatrist, but beating someone to death with a brick . . . hitting him over and over again until half his face collapses . . . seems a little like uncontrollable rage to me."

LeMay cleared her throat. "I'm afraid that's not my area of expertise."

"No, I guess it isn't." Rachel was starting to feel like she was wasting her time. She flipped to a page of notes she had made at the pizza parlor and found a name she had written—the name of Strickland's counselor. "Would it be possible for me to speak with Mr. Gulani?"

LeMay appeared to mull that over for a few seconds. She said, "I don't see why not. He should be finishing up a session shortly. If you'd like to wait in the lobby, I can send him out to see you."

"I'd appreciate that." She stood and slid the steno pad back into her jacket. "Just one more question though, before I go?"

"Sure," LeMay said with another forced smile.

"Obviously, I'm here to investigate the possibility that Kyle may be innocent. Given everything you know about him, do you believe he's capable of killing someone?"

"Capable?" LeMay's expression softened. She stared at Rachel for a moment. A despondent haze settled in her eyes, and she looked away. "Under the right circumstances, Miss Carver . . . anyone is capable of killing."

★ ★ ★

Manish Gulani had a slight build and a disarming smile. He introduced himself with a sweet voice and a weak handshake.

"Perhaps if we could step outside," he said, motioning toward the door.

Rachel followed him out of the lobby. They walked the

flagstone path from the entrance back to the koi pond and sat on a bench at the edge of the grass.

"It really breaks my heart, what happened between those two," Gulani said. "It has been such a shock to all of us here."

"Because they were friends?" she asked.

"Yes. But also because Kyle . . ." He took a moment to find the right words. "It just doesn't seem like something he would do."

"So it was a surprise to you, when they arrested him?"

"Oh yes," he said with a nod. "Definitely. The whole thing didn't make sense to any of us." He shrugged and put his hands up. "But what do we know? It just goes to show how difficult it can be for some people."

Rachel sensed that he felt responsible, as if he thought he could have done something to prevent the murder. "Were you teaching Kyle how to manage his anger as part of his therapy?"

"Anger? No, no." He shook his head, looking confused at the question. "Not any more than any other patient. That isn't what I was referring to."

"I'm sorry," she said. "What exactly *were* you referring to?"

"The fact that he was using so soon after rejoining the program. He had only been back for a week. That's usually the time when it's easiest for a patient to be sober. When they're getting the most help and they seem the most determined. Once they've been at it for a while, when the pressures of their lives start to weigh on them again . . . that's the biggest test for a recovering addict. Usually."

Rachel considered that for a moment, then asked, "Did

it surprise you to find out that he was hanging around Adam Hubbard?"

Gulani looked warily over his shoulder at the entrance.

"Manish," she said, leaning toward him, "it's okay. We know Adam was still using. The police found a bottle of pills on him when they discovered his body. I don't need you to tell me anything about that. I'm just trying to find out everything I can about Kyle. If you thought he was doing his best to get clean, then it should have surprised you to find out he was hanging around with Adam, right?"

He shook his head quickly.

"Why not?"

He glanced at the door again and said, "Kyle told me he had become friends with Adam. He wanted to help him clean up his life. He said he felt sorry for him. He was trying to get him back in the program too."

"You're sure about that?"

"I was," he said glumly. "At least until I saw them on the news."

Rachel thanked him for his help and walked back to her car, trying to make sense of what she had just learned. Either Strickland had fooled Gulani into believing he was dedicated to getting off the pills or the narrative of the murder was dead wrong. She would have to do more digging to find out which was true.

But first, it was time to learn more about Adam Hubbard.

TWELVE

"They didn't give you anything to help with this?" Ramirez asked.

It was their second stop. Parker was on one knee, coughing and spitting into a bank of tall grass on the side of the road. He shook off the foul taste and said, "Just the names of a couple of places in Raleigh."

"Methadone clinics?"

"Yeah." He wiped sweat away with his forearm and braced his other hand against the ground to keep his balance.

"I'm surprised they wouldn't give you something to hold you over."

"I know, right?"

She handed him the bottle of water. He took some in, swirled it around, and spit it out. Repeated the process twice, then tried to swallow a sip.

"I think I'm good," he said.

"You sure? We can take a minute if you need to."

"I'm good." He stood and walked back to the car, took a deep breath, and climbed in.

Ramirez, back in her seat, shifted into drive and said, "Okay, where to now?"

He pointed at the next intersection. "Take a right into that neighborhood. Should be on the left, a little way up. Arcadia Lane."

She eased forward and into the turn, sped up a little until she spotted the street sign, then made a left and slowed to a crawl. "Recognize any of this?"

"I do," he said, pointing ahead. "That's the house. Right there on the left. I don't see my car, though."

A bulky Panasonic laptop sat on a stand mounted to the side of the center console. Ramirez parked and flipped it open, typed in the address, and studied the information that came back. "John and Wendy Staples. You said your witness was a he. Is it this guy, John?"

"His son," Parker said. "Corey. He was spending a couple of weeks with his grandparents in Wendell when it happened."

"His grandparents." She looked over at the house, a two-story with yellow-painted siding. Old, but well maintained. A manicured lawn with a pair of late-model SUVs in the driveway. "How old is Corey?"

"Fifteen."

"Jesus," she whispered. "How did you find him?"

"It's complicated."

"Okay . . . so you came out here to interview him?"

"No. I interviewed him over the phone. I came here because I wanted to convince him to let me talk to his parents."

"Because he's a minor?"

"More because I wanted to verify what I could about his story." She looked at him, and he shrugged. "But yeah, the minor thing too."

"So what happened?"

Parker looked outside and thought for a few seconds. Then he pointed across the street and said, "See that big tree over there?"

"Yeah?"

"He told me to park next to it. Just out of sight of his house. So I did, and he came out to talk to me just like we agreed on the phone. He told me his dad wasn't home yet. His mom was, but he wanted to talk to his dad first. He said his mom would freak out if she knew he'd seen someone get killed. And especially if she knew he was talking to a reporter about it."

"Can't say I'd blame her for that."

"Yeah." He stared at the massive oak. "I waited for a while. It started to get dark. After about thirty minutes or so, this truck pulled up behind me. Its lights were on. I couldn't see much in my mirrors, but a guy got out. A big guy. He walked up to my window. I still had it rolled down because it was so hot. He asked me something . . . something about who I was waiting for. I thought maybe he lived in that house behind the tree. I was going to answer him, but then my phone rang. I looked over at it and . . ."

"What?" she asked. "What happened?"

His throat suddenly felt dry. He swallowed and said, "He grabbed me."

Parker could hear the man's voice, even and polite. Then his phone rang and he took his eyes away, just for a moment. The hand seized his throat and yanked him toward the window. Up and out of his seat. He flailed, he thought. The beginning of a fight. An instinctive response, as his body seemed to recognize the danger, though his mind never had time to catch up.

Ramirez watched him struggle with his memory. After a few seconds passed, she asked, "Did you get a good look at him?"

He shook his head. "Just a big white guy. Tall and muscular, I think. I remember trying to look up at him, but I couldn't see his face. It was in the dark, like a shadow . . . a silhouette from the truck's headlights. But I think he had on a baseball cap." He looked at her and felt a rush of embarrassment. "It sounds stupid to say this, but it all happened really fast. And I was preoccupied, trying to think of a good reason for being there. I didn't want to tell him the truth. I mean, I didn't want anyone to know about Corey."

"I understand," she said, looking back at the house. "My God. You really were kidnapped, weren't you?"

"Yeah." He slumped in his seat as the full weight of his ordeal seemed to finally settle on him. "Crazy, right?"

"Yes, it is," she said. "You're lucky to be alive. Did you tell Detective Hughes any of this?"

He closed his eyes and wiped a bead of sweat from his temple. "No."

"You need to. You have no idea who this guy is. He might come after you again."

"Good thing I have police protection," he said, forcing a grin.

"Uh-huh." She shook her head, looking a little annoyed. "At least you're starting to feel better. What do you want to do?"

"I need to talk to Rachel."

She nodded toward the Staples' house. "Don't you think we should go talk to them? Ask them if they saw anything the other night?"

"No. Not until I talk to Rachel first."

She gave him a confused look. "We're right here."

"I don't want to get them involved. Not yet. For all I know, the kid could be in on it."

"You think he could've set you up?"

"I don't know." He rubbed his eyes and sighed. The frustration was getting hard to contain. "Maybe. I hope not."

"You really need to talk to Chad," she said. "Detective Hughes. I can take you to see him now if—"

"No," he snapped. He took a breath and tried to calm himself. "Please. Can we just go?"

She kept her eyes forward, staring through the windshield. She looked like she was entertaining the idea of kicking him out of her car.

"I'm sorry," he said. "I know you're just trying to help."

"Don't worry about it." She shifted into gear. "Where do you want to go?"

"Anywhere but here. And, if it's okay, I need to borrow your phone."

throughout your time together. He was taking pills all six months you two were dating?"

"Mm-hmm."

"So he was using at the same time he was in rehab?"

"Yeah."

"Help me understand that," Rachel said. "Why bother going if he wasn't trying to quit?"

"I mean, he *was* trying, but like, you know, it just wasn't working."

"I see."

"But that's not all he was going there for anyway."

"What do you mean?" Rachel asked.

She shrugged and looked away. "He was dealing with stuff."

"What kind of stuff?"

"You know, like, from his time in the Army. He didn't ever want to talk to me about it, but he said he'd seen stuff while he was over there. In Afghanistan. Things that gave him nightmares and everything. That's part of why he kept taking the pills. He said they helped. But he said he didn't need them as much when he went to therapy."

"Did he ever tell you about a friend of his named Tyler Larson?"

"No."

"Ever say anything at all about friends he had from his time in the Army?"

"Not really." Bianca glanced past Rachel toward the door. Her attention span appeared to be waning. "Like I said, he didn't like talking to me about it."

"Did he ever mention that he had been contacted by a reporter? A guy from the *Raleigh Herald* named Bryce Parker?"

THIRTEEN

According to the police reports, Hubbard's girlfriend was a young woman named Bianca Dwyer who worked at a coffee-and-doughnut shop on Jefferson Street. Rachel found her there tending the drive-through window. She looked like she could still be in high school, too young to have been dating a man in his twenties.

When Rachel finally got her attention, Bianca agreed to talk. She told the manager she was taking a break and went out back, even though the man looked like he wanted to protest. Rachel followed her out and said, "Thank you. I hope I'm not getting you into any trouble."

"Don't worry about it," she said, flicking her straight blonde hair over her shoulder. "I mean, I always want to do what I can to help, so whatever."

"I appreciate that. How long were you and Adam dating?"

"About six and a half months."

"I have to ask you about a touchy subject, if you don't mind. About Adam's drug use. Are you okay talking about that?"

She nodded. "Yeah, sure."

Rachel said, "You told the police that he was using

Her attention focused back on Rachel, and she looked hesitant, like she was afraid of saying the wrong thing. "No. I mean, he didn't *say* anything about it, but . . ."

"But what?"

"Well, I don't know if it's the same guy or not, but . . . one time, I was with Adam, and he got a phone call from someone. He got up and walked out of the room to talk to them. A few minutes later, I heard him say, 'No, I told you, I don't want none of this stuff showing up in the papers.' Then I guess he must've hung up on whoever it was, 'cause when he came back, he wasn't on the phone no more."

"And he didn't explain it? Didn't give you any clue what it was about?"

She shook her head.

"I see." Rachel thought for a few seconds and asked, "Do you know Kyle Strickland?"

"Mm-hmm."

"What can you tell me about him?"

The manager leaned out the back door and said, "Come on, Bianca. You're not supposed to be on break for another hour."

"Okay, Jake, I'll be right there."

He rolled his eyes and went back inside.

"Sorry about that," she said. "But yeah, Kyle . . . I know him a little. Adam brought him around a few times."

"Did you ever see them take pills together? Or know of a time when they did?"

"No, I don't think so. I mean, Adam didn't always like to take them around me, so I just might not have seen it."

"Did you ever see Adam and Kyle argue or get into a fight?"

She shook her head.

"Does Kyle have a bad temper?"

"Not that I know of."

"Okay." Rachel looked back at the door, knowing she was running out of time. "One last question. Can you think of anything the police might not know about concerning Adam's death? Anything strange about the circumstances surrounding it?"

"Not really." She brushed her fingers through her hair. "I mean, I thought it was a little weird that he went to that store to meet his dealer, but I told them that already."

"Why was that weird?"

"Well . . . he always bought from the same guy. He never told me who it was, but the guy always came over to Adam's. Usually he'd do it while I was at work. Or sometimes, he'd say, 'Hey, I need you to stay away today until I call you. I got my guy coming over for a while.' As far as I know, he never went anywhere to meet him."

The manager yelled for Bianca, so Rachel thanked her and decided to leave. When she got to her car, she checked her phone. There was a missed call and a text from a number she didn't recognize. She unlocked the screen and read it: RACHEL THIS IS BRYCE CALL ME AS SOON AS U CAN AT THIS NUMBER.

She called him back.

He answered with a sigh and said, "Thank God."

"You sound a lot better," she said. "Are you still at the hospital?"

"No, I checked myself out."

"Already?"

"Yeah, listen. I need to see you. Right away. How fast can you get here?"

"Get where? Are you home?"

"No. I'm still in Siler City. I'm with a police officer. The one who found me yesterday. I'm at her house."

"Her house?" Rachel's mind was still on Hubbard. She was having a hard time switching her train of thought. "What are you—"

"Rachel, I found a witness. Someone who saw Tyler Larson's murder. It wasn't Lauren Bailey. You were right."

"Holy shit . . ."

"Yeah. He's a kid. A teenager. I was outside his house waiting to talk to his father when I was taken."

"Jesus, Bryce."

"I know. We've got a lot to talk about. You gotta get your butt over here. I'm thinking we should go see this detective from the Siler City PD and tell him everything. Then we can all go and talk to the kid and his parents together."

Rachel knew it wouldn't happen like that, but Parker didn't seem to be thinking clearly. His voice was getting shaky. Some of it was probably the withdrawal. The rest was his excitement, and it was infectious. Rachel could feel her heart racing.

She put him on speaker and opened the Maps app. "Give me the address."

He told her and she typed it in, waited for the blue route to appear, and said, "I can be there in two hours."

"Two? Where the hell are you?"

"Take it easy, Bryce," she said, starting the engine. "I'm on my way."

FOURTEEN

Parker looked pale and gaunt. His hands were clammy, and he had a hard time standing. Rachel gave him a quick hug and helped ease him back down onto the plush leather sofa in Ramirez's living room. Then she sat across from him and listened to his story.

Ramirez was on the arm of the love seat a few feet away, watching Parker recount the kidnapping with compassion in her eyes. Rachel sensed that something was building between them. She wondered if it was some version of the Florence Nightingale effect, sympathy evolving into attraction.

The thought passed as soon as Parker started telling her about the teenager, Corey Staples. The boy had sneaked out of his grandparents' house in the middle of the night to meet a friend. He had cut across a public park and was climbing a fence when he heard a gunshot. Not the resounding report of a weapon fired in the open, but a muffled pop.

Corey hopped off the fence and jogged to the corner, looked up the street, and saw a car sitting about fifty yards away. There was movement inside. Corey ducked down behind a bush, knowing that something bad had happened. A moment later, a man got out of the passenger side. A large man. He wiped his face with his shirt and looked around. Then he turned and ran to another car parked further up the street, got in, and took off.

"Corey was scared," Parker said. "He ran back home and spent the night worrying that someone might have seen him. The next morning, his grandparents were talking about the murder, but he couldn't bring himself to tell them what he'd seen. He said he had nightmares every night after that. Kept seeing the man coming after him. Breaking into the house in the middle of the night and making Corey watch while he killed his grandparents."

"Poor kid," Rachel said, but she couldn't stop herself from feeling resentful. If only the boy could have found the courage to tell his story at the time. She tried to imagine how different her life would be. How different *everything* would be. And she heard Lauren Bailey's son screaming. The piercing cries, seared into her brain as she carried him away from his dying mother. "How did you find him?"

"A tip," Parker said, "from one of the Wake County detectives who worked with you on the case. I originally interviewed him for the story back in March. He called me a couple of weeks ago and said he'd just been to Siler City. Apparently, when Corey got back from visiting his grandparents, he told a friend what he saw. That friend told his older brother, and he called it in. But when the detective showed up to investigate, Corey stonewalled him. He wanted to keep trying, but Corey's mom wouldn't have it."

"And he thought you could get around that little roadblock?"

"Parental consent is more of a guideline in my business."

"Lucky for you," Ramirez said.

"And for me," Rachel said.

Finally, there was an eyewitness. Someone to confirm her belief—her certainty—that Lauren Bailey had not killed Tyler Larson. She felt vindicated, but that feeling evaporated when she thought about Parker.

He was a victim now. Based on Parker's description, the man who had kidnapped him was likely the same man who had killed Larson. The heroin overdose had been an attempt to make the story go away. A creative solution, perhaps less obvious, if not a lot cleaner, than another body with a gunshot wound to the head.

"So?" Parker asked. "What do you think?"

Rachel was staring at the floor. She looked up and said, "I think I should talk to Corey."

"Shouldn't we go see Detective Hughes first?"

"No. Not yet." Rachel tried to think of a justification for not getting the locals involved, but the truth was that she wanted to talk to Corey herself. Hughes would try to shut her out, and there was no way she was going to let that happen. "This was my case. I know it better than anyone. I don't think we should get him involved until I'm sure the kid's being straight with us."

"You think he could be making it up?" Ramirez asked. "That doesn't make any sense." She pointed at Parker. "If the boy's lying, then *he's* got to be lying about being kidnapped. Is that what you think?"

"Did I say that?" Rachel glared at her. "I don't think for a second that Bryce would make any of this up. On the other hand, I would like to know if the kid is hiding anything. Maybe he saw more than he's willing to admit. Or maybe he wasn't alone. He was sneaking out to meet a friend, right? Maybe he's not the only witness. Have you ever worked a homicide investigation, Officer Ramirez? Ever questioned a teenager who was an eyewitness to a murder?"

Parker said, "Okay, Rachel. We get it."

Ramirez was red.

Rachel softened her tone and said, "All I'm trying to say is that teenagers lie. Even when they're telling the truth. And I think I'm in the best position to get the whole story out of this kid before we hand him over to Hughes."

"Makes sense to me," Parker said. "Ashley, are you okay with that?"

"Fine," Ramirez said. "But you're not going alone. You may be the expert here, but this is *my* town."

"I agree," Rachel said. "It'll be good for you to be there."

Parker slid toward the edge of the sofa. "Perfect. It's settled, then."

"Not quite." Rachel stood and walked to the door. "You're staying put."

"What?"

"You heard me."

"She's right," Ramirez said, following her. "Stay here and rest. Watch TV. Make yourself something to eat. Whatever you want, except the chocolate chip cookie dough ice cream. That belongs to my girl."

Parker looked wounded by the command but didn't protest. He leaned back and said, "Corey's ready to talk, but you've got to go through his dad first. His mom won't let you anywhere near him."

Rachel put her hand on the knob and turned it, then paused, looked back, and said, "Oh, and by the way, at some point we're going to need to talk about Adam Hubbard."

"Shit," he said, looking like he might try to stand up. "I forgot to tell you about him."

"Don't worry," she said. "There'll be plenty of time for that later. Just rest up, and we'll be back before you know it."

She saw him nod and smile. She smiled back, and then the door slammed into her side, knocking her into Ramirez. She caught her balance and turned to see the motion of an arm swinging toward her head. There was a brief sensation . . . something resembling pain . . . and everything turned black.

★ ★ ★

Confusion. Commotion. Yelling.

Rachel tried to focus. Caught sight of Ramirez standing sideways with her hand at her hip. She was pulling at something. Then there was a deafening burst, followed by ringing.

Ramirez fell, the way a high rise falls during a controlled demolition, the whole thing dropping on top of itself, as if everything that had been holding it up was taken away in an instant. Knees, then hips, then limp arms crashing down. Her bloody face smacked the floor, and she lay perfectly still, like someone had simply turned her off by flipping a switch.

Rachel suddenly realized that she too was lying on the floor. She tried to sit up, her eyes searching wildly. She put her hand out to prop herself, but it slipped. She was back on her side, trying to hold her head up when she saw a pair of legs floating by her.

No, they were stepping *over* her.

She shook her head, desperate for clarity, searched again

and found the legs moving away. They belonged to a man, or some exaggerated version of a man. Impossibly tall and powerfully built. The more of him that came into view, the more he seemed to smear at the edges. The hazy image of some monstrous figure.

A distressed voice called in the distance. Rachel tried to answer it, but her words were mush in her own ears. The ringing was slowly dying, and the voice started to sound more and more like Bryce Parker's.

"Wait," it yelled. "Just wait!"

A crack in her ear, and the ringing was back. Dizzy and disorienting. Her senses were useless. She tried to sit up again, knowing that she should be doing something. Fighting or fleeing or calling for help.

Survive.

It was her first clear thought, but it left her as soon as she saw the monster turn around. He was coming back for her.

FIFTEEN

Rachel moved, just an inch or two, and felt agony. It was her neck, twisted and kinked. She was sitting with her torso leaning forward, her head lying against something hard. She reached up to brace against it, pushed away, and slowly straightened herself.

It was a dashboard.

Her dashboard.

She was in the passenger seat of her Camry, she realized.

She looked outside. The sky beyond the windshield was purple with a band of black clouds hiding the setting sun. Beneath, a line of trees marked the border of a dense forest that seemed to swallow the light from above.

She turned to look around and felt pain shoot through her neck. She rubbed it, and when it died down a dull throbbing above her ear took its place. She reached up and found a bump. A tender spot, crusted with dried blood that matted a lock of her hair.

Trying to spare her neck, she turned slowly in her seat to look behind her and felt something hard shift in her lap. It started to slide off her leg, and she reached down reflexively to catch it.

It was a pistol—a Glock 19.

She turned it in her hand to examine it and recognized a tiny scratch by the rear sight.

Her Glock 19.

There was the distinct smell of burnt powder. Her finger touched the indicator tab by the port and found that it was raised. That told her there was a round in the chamber. She ejected the magazine and checked the tiny holes on the back.

She counted twelve more rounds.

That meant two were missing. Two had been fired.

Memories flooded. A torrent of blurred images and indistinct sounds. She could hear Parker's voice above it all, screaming.

Pleading.

Rachel stared at the gun, shaking in her hand, and started to understand what had happened. She dropped it in the driver seat and threw the door open and jumped out. Standing on a grassy rise, she looked around and found herself at the end of a dirt road. It curved into the distance, leaving her no hint of what lay beyond.

She started walking, just to get away. Just to get clear and think straight. Her hands rose to her head, shaking even more now and clenching fistfuls of her hair. Her eyes welled, and her breathing became convulsive. She was on the verge of sobbing.

Parker was dead.

Ramirez was dead.

And she had watched it all happen. She had been powerless to stop it. Made worthless by a single hit. All of her training . . . all of her experience . . . had counted for nothing.

The killer, whoever he was, had shot two people with

Rachel's gun. Then he'd dropped her off in the middle of nowhere, leaving the murder weapon in her lap. For any cop trying to solve the case, she would be the prime suspect.

Tears fell in streams. Her entire body trembled. She felt like she was losing control of herself. Fear and frustration and rage and sorrow . . . it was too much to contain. She could have exploded with the raw power of it all.

But there was no use in that. No utility in breaking down. Rachel had a choice to make—she could give up or she could fight. And she had always thought of herself as a fighter.

Useless phrases of encouragement sprouted in her mind. Things she had seen on TV or heard people say. Social media memes with motivational messages meant to coax someone through a difficult work week.

You got this.

Stay strong.

You can make excuses, or you can make it happen.

She could have laughed at how absurd they all sounded now, but she needed something to cling to. Just some thought or image to inspire a little strength.

Suddenly, she remembered her friend, Diane. A jiu-jitsu classmate who was always posting those inspirational memes on Facebook. She thought about how Diane had helped her in the early days of her training, when she'd had no idea what she was doing. There was this rotund white belt named Chauncey who would get on top of her. He'd smother her with his overwhelming mass, not letting her move. No matter how hard she fought, there was nothing she could do to defend herself. He was just too big and too heavy. Rachel would panic, start hyperventilating, and quickly tap out.

"You have to calm down," Diane had said. "You're flailing because you're frustrated. You feel trapped. Claustrophobic. Nothing you try will work when your mind is all messed up like that. You have to accept that you're in a bad spot, and that it's going to suck. Slow down and work one thing at a time. And always start with your breathing."

Eventually, Rachel had learned how to get away from Chauncey. Then she had learned to keep him from getting on top of her in the first place. The day she finally beat him was the last class he ever attended.

Start with your breathing.

Rachel closed her eyes and pulled in a long, slow breath, fighting the sobs that made her spasm. Another breath, and she saw herself on the mats, sliding and rolling and changing position, always searching for better leverage, ways to beat opponents who were superior in size and strength. Defying the odds.

You're in a bad spot, and it sucks. Work one thing at a time.

Rachel reached for her back pocket and felt her phone there. Her first bit of good luck. She took it out and unlocked it, opened the Maps app, and tapped the location finder. Once the blue dot appeared, she pinched the screen to zoom out, then scrolled around until she found a landmark she recognized. She was just off a two-lane county road, about four miles from Ramirez's house.

Thinking about the house brought back images of being inside, talking about the case. Getting up to leave and seeing Parker's smile. Then the violence that followed.

She forced it away and thought for a moment, figured the smart thing would be to tell Dunn. She called him, but it went straight to voicemail.

"Mr. Dunn, this is Rachel. Something bad has happened . . . I think I need a lawyer. Please call me back as soon as you can."

She hung up and stood quietly for a moment. A shock of fear ran through her. She was alone, facing an opponent that was too many steps ahead of her. She'd gone up against killers before—smart ones, devious and cunning and ruthless—but none of them had ever targeted her like this.

She needed to get away from here. To find someplace safe where she could think, get her head straight, and come up with a plan. And she needed someone she could trust.

Only one name came to her. Her thumb seemed to find his number and touch it on its own.

"Hey, Rachel. How's it going?"

"Not good," she said, relieved to hear his voice. "I know this is short notice, but I'm coming to see you."

"You're . . . wow. Okay. What's going on?"

"I just . . ." Her voice cracked. She sniffed hard and took a beat to keep her breathing steady. "I need your help, Danny. I'm on my way. I'll be there in four hours."

SIXTEEN

There were cops all over the crime scene. Some stood in the yard, blank-faced from shock. Others kept circling near the front door, sticking their heads inside every so often to steal a quick look. A young hothead had punched the garage door and now paced the driveway, refusing to let anyone inspect his hand, which was puffy and red and most likely broken.

Hughes got out of his car and chased them off with a tirade of curses. He had to physically escort a couple of stragglers. Ramirez was their colleague. Their friend. A sister in their hallowed order. It was understandable that they had lost some of their professionalism. But Hughes had a duty to protect the scene. To preserve it for the tech, who was on the way.

If ever there was a time to take that duty seriously, it was now.

He stopped at the doorway and stared at Ramirez's body. A short movie overtook his mind, playing without his permission. Ramirez was in a pair of shorts and a football jersey, her little girl standing on the tops of her feet, hugging her tan legs. Their faces were alight with joy. A young mother and her daughter. In that moment, they were all that existed in their world.

It took him a moment to place that memory—a barbecue fund raiser put on by the department. Two years ago. It might as well have been yesterday.

He took out his phone, opened the camera app, and took several photos. Then he crossed the threshold, scanning the floor to make sure he didn't step on anything important. A shell casing, a drop of blood, a hair . . . all of it mattered in a homicide investigation.

He approached Ramirez, knelt down beside her, and studied her face. Blood trailed from a small entry wound in her forehead, much of it already dry. Her eyes were half-open and her mouth was contorted, pulled tight by her cheek pressing against the hardwood floor.

It didn't look like her, and he was grateful for that.

He took a couple of close-ups and then stood and turned away. He walked over to the reporter's body and stared at it for a minute. Parker was on the floor on his back next to the sofa. He had a bloody bullet wound of his own beside his nose, just below the tear duct. Hughes captured it all on his phone.

"Oh, Jesus," came a voice from the doorway.

Hughes turned to see the tech standing there, holding his kit. His eyes were fixed on Ramirez.

"Shake it off, Paul," Hughes said. "I need you to focus."

"Sorry, Chad." He set his kit down and opened it, took out a pair of nitrile gloves, and pulled them on. "Julie's outside looking for you. I think she might have found someone who saw something. You want me to start on the victims?"

"Yeah," Hughes said, stepping around him. "Why don't you work on the male first?"

"Okay."

Outside, Hughes found Detective Julie Morrison in her unmarked, looking over her notes from the canvass.

"I talked to a woman," she said, "three doors down, who says she saw a white sedan sitting in the driveway. She says she saw it there about fifteen or twenty minutes before she heard the gunfire."

"White sedan," he said, pinching his bottom lip.

"Yeah, like a Sonata or a Camry, maybe."

Hughes glanced over at the house. "Any chance she saw the person who was driving it?"

"Nope. She said she was coming home from the grocery store and noticed it parked there behind Ashley's car. But that's it. She didn't think anything of it. Then, a little later, she heard the shots but thought they came from somewhere else. She stayed inside while she called us."

He looked around, surveying the neighborhood. All of the houses were set back from the road. Ramirez's was tucked in between rows of trees and hedges. There was a tall privacy fence that did its job limiting visibility. The only house with a good view of the scene was directly across the street.

"Anyone home over there?" he asked.

She shook her head. "Sorry, Chad."

"Damn."

Morrison stepped out of her car and looked over at the open front door, now barricaded with red tape. "I haven't been inside yet."

"Best you don't put yourself through that," he said.

"Yeah." She lowered her eyes to the ground and kicked

a pebble on the rough asphalt. "She was a good woman, you know. A good cop."

"Damn straight, she was."

"We're gonna catch the sorry shitbag that did this, aren't we?"

"You bet your ass we are." He put his hand on her shoulder. "And we're gonna start by finding out who the hell was driving that white sedan."

SEVENTEEN

It was a long drive with the radio off and nothing to distract her, immersed in her thoughts. She had wanted the time to think, but it was too hard to concentrate. At least on anything productive.

Doubts and insecurities plagued her. Darkness brought uncertainty. Every pair of headlights in the rearview was a state trooper checking her license plate, calling it in, and preparing to stop her.

A suspected killer.

There would be no reasoning with them. No chance to explain. She would be forced to the ground at gunpoint, handcuffed, and carried away. Perhaps she would get lucky and they would just shoot her. Maybe they would see the gun in the passenger seat and feel threatened, spare her the trouble of having to tell her story, over and over again, as some investigator searched for holes and inconsistencies.

The way she always did.

Rachel was on the other side now. There was no telling whether or not they were actually looking for her yet, but they would be. A dead journalist. A dead *cop*. The entire state would be after her.

It didn't matter that she had been a cop. That she'd been a special agent with the SBI. With no evidence to offer in her defense and no other suspects, she would be presumed guilty. At least by the police and the prosecutors. As for trying to convince them that some giant had busted in and knocked her out while shooting the victims with her gun . . . there was no chance they would take her seriously. If the Larson case had taught her anything, it was how quickly an investigator could zero in on the most likely suspect to the exclusion of any alternative theories.

Her phone rang. She took it out and checked the screen. It was Dunn. She answered and told him everything. When she finished, he said, "My God . . . I don't . . . I'm sorry, I'm just . . ."

"Yeah, me too," she said.

"Where are you now?"

"I'm on the road. I'm going to stay with a friend."

"Okay. Will you be safe there?"

"Yes."

"Good. Okay. That's good. Damn . . . I need to think about this. Can I call you back?"

"Not at this number. I'm turning my phone off." She gave him Danny Braddock's number and an ETA. "Please call me back."

"I will," he said. "You can count on it."

A half hour past Asheville, Rachel got off I-40 and picked up on the Great Smoky Mountains Expressway. The traffic thinned out and the way ahead was shrouded in black. Rachel felt like a child under heavy bedding, pushing up at the sky and aiming a light to see a few feet at a time. The road snaked through the mountains, each turn slowing her pace, but she felt safer here. Burrowing into the valleys, shielded from the world out to get her.

She saw the sign for Dillard City and took the exit, headed to Main Street, then turned and followed the Tuckasegee River away from the center of town. She couldn't see it, but she knew it was there, flowing right alongside her.

A few minutes later, she turned left, coasted down a hill, and spotted the little craftsman at the end of the street. She pulled into the driveway, illuminating the front of the house. On the porch, seated on a bench by the front door, Danny Braddock was waiting. She shut the engine off and got out of the car. He stood up and met her at the bottom step.

Neither of them said a word. She walked right to him and hugged him, pressed her face against his chest and wept. He was tall and long-limbed, and when he wrapped her up in his arms she felt like she had come home.

★ ★ ★

Rachel sat at Braddock's kitchen table and held a handful of ice cubes wrapped in a dish towel against the side of her head. She was calmer now, able to explain everything with a cool detachment that made her feel like she was back in control. At least until she thought about Parker's smiling face. That had her voice quivering again.

Braddock sat quietly, processing. There was no suspicion in his wide eyes. He trusted her completely. It had been more than seven years since they had been partners in the Raleigh Police Department, but they had remained close. Good friends who were always there for each other, even with three hundred miles between them.

His divorce. Her resignation after the Larson case. They had leaned on each other in difficult times. And five months ago, when Braddock had been faced with the toughest case of his career, he'd turned to Rachel for help. The Lowry County murders had impacted everyone in the area, especially Rachel and Braddock. And their relationship was forever changed.

Still reeling from the Larson case and her decision to quit the SBI, Rachel had found comfort in working with Braddock again. Too much comfort, as it turned out, leading her to test what had felt like a growing attraction between them by seducing him in her hotel room.

He gladly gave in, and a couple of blissful days followed, but then the killer turned his sights on a pair of deputies, ambushing them with a hail of gunfire. Their deaths shook the community to its core. The stress of that loss caused Braddock to push her away, which put a sudden stop to their burgeoning romance. In the end, they had remained friends, but there were still feelings left to resolve. Raw emotions that had yet to find words.

Tonight wouldn't change that.

"Let me make sure I got this," Braddock said. "This big giant guy kills Larson a year ago but gets away with it 'cause everyone believes it was the girlfriend. At least until you give Parker the interview, telling him you think the real killer is still out there. So Parker starts his own investigation, talking to people who knew Larson, one of whom was this guy Adam Hubbard. Then Hubbard turns up dead, what, a month ago?"

"Something like that," Rachel said, suddenly feeling weak.

"But that doesn't stop Parker. He ends up finding a witness, but before he can convince the witness to go on the record, he gets kidnapped and drugged. He survives the overdose, so the giant guy decides to step up his game."

"Pretty much."

"Jesus." He stared at her for a moment, looking like he might reach out to hold her again. "I can't believe this is happening to you. What are you gonna do?"

She shrugged. "I don't know."

He stood and walked over to a cabinet next to the refrigerator. Opened it and took out a pair of Old Fashioned glasses and a bottle of bourbon. He put a few ice cubes in each glass and carried them back to the table.

He uncapped the bottle, started to pour, and said, "I don't know if this is a good idea or not."

"It is," she said, accepting one and drinking nearly half of it in a single draw.

"We're gonna figure this out," he said. "Someway, somehow. Whatever it takes."

"Yeah." She finished her drink and held her glass out for another. As he filled it, she looked at him and said, "I'm sorry, Danny."

"For what?"

"I've put you in a bad spot coming here."

"Why do you say that?"

"I imagine it won't be long before your office gets a BOLO with my name on it."

"Yeah, you're probably right." His mouth formed a half smile. "I'm gonna look like a hero bringing you in."

She chuckled, had another sip, and sat quietly for a couple of minutes, willing herself to come up with a plan.

Trying not to see Ramirez fall or the monster step over her. Or hear Parker's voice, silenced by gunfire.

★   ★   ★

It was after midnight when Dunn called back. Rachel was still at the kitchen table with Braddock, who had forced her to switch to water after her third glass of bourbon.

"So, this happened in Chatham County, correct?"

Dunn's voice was low, as if he was trying not to wake someone.

"Yes," she said.

"And you haven't spoken to the local authorities? Who would that be? The sheriff's office or the Siler City PD?"

She didn't know if Ramirez's house was within the city limits. "I'm not sure. But, no, I haven't spoken to either one of them yet."

"Okay." He sighed. "Legally, you have no duty to report what you saw. Or . . . what you experienced, I should say. But, given the situation, it obviously doesn't look good that you haven't."

"Yeah."

"If you thought better of it, I could contact them for you."

"Right."

"It's up to you. For now, anyway." He was quiet for a moment. Then he said, "Actually, if you have physical evidence the police will need as part of their investigation . . . I mean, if you're really sure your gun is the murder weapon . . . Yeah, you and I need to meet. In person, so we can go through all of this in more detail. I need to chew on it tonight, come up with some questions once I get a chance to think it over for a while. Maybe tomorrow you can come to the office."

Rachel considered that. The idea scared her. She would be putting her fate entirely in Dunn's hands as he tried to develop some legal strategy for her defense. Eventually, he would sit her down in front of an investigator. There was a good chance that might end up being Hughes. She would have to explain herself to him, explain how she had run away to the mountains while one of his fellow officers lay dead on a living room floor.

Meanwhile, the killer would remain free, safe in the knowledge that his plan had worked. Once Rachel surrendered, there would be no way of catching him. All of her attention would be focused on defending herself from prosecution.

Surrender.

The thought made her sick to her stomach. Made her blood boil. She could imagine herself in a courtroom, on trial for a double homicide. The news media would be all over it, and the killer would be somewhere watching it all on TV. *Laughing* at her. Knowing that he had beaten her at every turn. Larson. Bailey. Ramirez. Parker. They were all his. And so was she. His fifth victim.

"I don't think I can do that."

"What?" Dunn sounded shocked, almost angry. "What are you talking about?"

"Not yet. I've got to work this out on my own for a while."

"Rachel—"

"I'll call you back when I figure out what I'm going to do." She ended the call and stood up, handed the phone to

Braddock, and thought for a moment. Then, slowly, she walked to the door and opened it. "I need to get some fresh air."

Braddock rose from his chair, unsure of whether to follow her or stay behind. Before he could ask, she went outside, closed the door, and walked away from the house.

Rachel should have been overwhelmed by frustration. Paralyzed by it. But there was something strangely reassuring about her decision not to give in to Dunn's order.

Solve the murders, she thought.

It made sense to her, once it settled in. It was what she did. What she was best at. *Find the killer. Exonerate yourself.*

It felt desperate, but she couldn't see any other way. She was in a deep hole, half-buried by the killer's scheme. It was up to her to dig herself out.

Rachel crossed Main Street and followed the sound of churning water to a sandy bank. The Tuckasegee cascaded over a run of smooth boulders. Tiny whitecaps reflected the moonlight. She felt herself relax, and tension began to leave her back and her neck.

Her hands.

She hadn't realized they'd been balled into fists. It seemed like the river was drawing out her anxiety. A plan started to form in her mind. She kicked it around a few minutes, considering all her options. Then she walked back to Braddock's house.

When she came through the door, he was on a leather chair in the living area. He rose to his feet, looking worried.

Rachel said, "I know what I need to do."

That surprised him. "Really?"

"Yeah. I need to borrow some clothes."

"All right."

"You have a notepad handy?"

"Yeah," he said, motioning toward the guest bedroom. "In the desk in my office."

"You're going to take my statement."

"I am?"

"Yes. And then we're going to call Carly. I have a crime scene for her to process."

EIGHTEEN

Carly Brewer, the Lowry County Sheriff's Office crime scene technician, made an imposing silhouette in the gray moonlight. She was five nine and muscular, with broad shoulders and long legs. Her short black hair was swept to one side, brushing her cheek as she climbed the steps to Braddock's porch.

Braddock opened the door and invited her inside. The light struck her face and she squinted a little, still not quite awake, though half an hour had passed since he called her.

"All right, boss," she said. "You got me here. Now wha—" She saw Rachel and her face lit up. She yelled, "Oh my God," and ran up to hug her.

Rachel recoiled and put her hands up. "Wait!"

Carly took a step back, looking wounded. "What's going on?"

"My clothes," Rachel said. "And me, actually. We're evidence."

"Evidence of what?"

Rachel explained. Carly took it in, looking astonished, then upset, and finally determined.

"I need you to photograph me," Rachel said. "Especially

the wound on my head. And I think I might have some bruises on my side too. From where I fell."

"I can do that." Carly said. "I'll go get my camera."

"And a bag for my clothes. You'll need to take them with you and search them. Look for hairs or fibers . . . anything that might have transferred while he was carrying me." She glanced at Braddock, suddenly wishing she had thought of all this before she hugged him and made herself at home in his house. "You'll need samples from Danny too. For elimination."

"Are you sure about this?" Braddock asked. "Once we start down this road—"

"I'm sure."

Carly looked to Braddock, and he nodded. "Okay," she said. "I'll be right back."

She went outside to her SUV and returned with a digital SLR camera and a light mounted to a fold-up tripod. She set up the light and took several photos of Rachel with her clothes on. Then she said, "Boss, maybe you should . . ."

"Right," he said, and stepped out to the porch.

Rachel undressed. Carly put on a pair of blue nitrile gloves, collected the clothes, and placed them gingerly into a brown-paper evidence bag. She sealed the bag and continued taking photos. When she finished, Rachel put on a pair of baggy gym shorts and an oversized T-shirt Braddock had left for her. Then they went outside.

Standing in front of the Camry, Carly said, "I shouldn't process this thing here. At least not the interior. Can we use the garage?"

The Lowry County Sheriff's Office didn't have a facility for housing vehicles. The few times Carly had needed to scour a car or a truck for physical evidence, they had rented a bay from the local mechanic who serviced the office's fleet. He also had a flatbed for transporting them.

"Yeah," Braddock said. "Give him a call first thing in the morning and get him to come pick it up."

"Cool," Carly said. "In the meantime, I can photograph it and work on the exterior. What all do you want?"

Rachel said, "He put me in the passenger side . . ." She felt a moment of disgust, imagining the monster stuffing her into the seat. "Then he drove me for about four miles. So definitely examine those doors and the seats, the areas around them. Give the back seat a once over, but I'd focus your attention up front. Swab for DNA, look for prints on all the usual surfaces . . . I'd love it if you found a hair."

Carly's eyes were on the passenger side. She turned and gave Rachel a sympathetic look. The kind that should've been reserved for a patient suffering some terminal illness.

Rachel ignored it. "There's something else too. You might want to go ahead and get your kit."

"What is it?"

"My gun. I want you to swab the whole thing for touch DNA. Especially on the edges of the slide near the muzzle."

Carly gave Rachel a curious look but didn't question the request. She went to her SUV, and Braddock asked, "What can I do to help?"

"Mind going to Raleigh tomorrow?"

"Not at all."

"Thanks," she said. "I want to know how this asshole got my gun."

"What are you gonna do?"

"I'm going to Fayetteville. I need to see Larson's sister."

"What about the boy? The witness? You gonna talk to him?"

She shook her head. "I don't want to risk it. Might put him in danger. For now, I'll just assume he told Bryce everything he knows."

"Probably a good call." He thought for a moment, staring at the Camry, and said, "Wait . . . what are you gonna drive?"

"I was thinking I'd borrow your Explorer?"

"It's all I've got. I won't be able to get to Raleigh without it."

"What happened to the unmarked you had when I was here in March?"

"Had to give it to the new detective we just hired."

"Shit."

"Yeah." A little smile emerged. "I used to have this nice department-issued Tahoe, but somebody went and wrecked it."

"Try not to live in the past, Danny."

"Mm-hmm."

Carly walked up the driveway carrying her kit. Rachel looked past her at the SUV, marked with yellow stripes and the sheriff's office logo. It was assigned to Carly exclusively, which meant she would have the freedom to use it if Rachel commandeered her personal vehicle. She whispered to Braddock, "You think she'd mind if I borrowed her Civic?"

Braddock said, "Hey, Carly, didn't you just trade your Civic in for a new truck?"

"Sure did." She set her kit on the ground and gave Braddock a wary look. "A Tacoma. She's my baby."

"Nice," Rachel said. "That'll do just fine."

NINETEEN

Carly worked through the night, first on the gun, then on the exterior of the Camry. When she finished, she called the mechanic and waited around for him to show up with the flatbed. He loaded up the car, and she followed him back to his shop to maintain the chain of custody. It was destined for an isolated bay in his garage, one with doors that Carly could padlock when she wasn't there collecting evidence.

Rachel managed a few hours of sleep. Braddock had given her his bed and camped out on the sofa. She woke just before sunup and stared at the ceiling until she heard him stirring in the kitchen. She got up and took a quick shower, put on another one of his T-shirts and a pair of shorts, and went out to see him.

"I checked the news this morning," he said, cracking eggs into a frying pan. "They reported on the shooting, but no mention of you yet."

Rachel helped herself to a cup of coffee and settled in at the kitchen table. While Braddock finished cooking breakfast, she powered up her laptop and took a few minutes to study her notes from the Larson case.

"What are you hoping to get from the sister?" he asked, sliding a plate of scrambled eggs and sausage in front of her.

"Larson kept journals during his deployments," she said. "We turned them over to her after the investigation. I'm betting she still has them."

"What do you think you'll find in them?"

"I have no idea. I didn't have a lot of time to go through them the first time around. Once we got settled on Bailey as the suspect . . ." She bit off the tip of a sausage link. "Anyway, who knows what I'll find. Could be anything. Or nothing. All I know for sure is that Larson and Hubbard were in the same unit, so it seems like a good place to start."

"Makes sense."

"The only thing is, Larson's sister is convinced Bailey was guilty. She won't be happy to see me."

After they ate, Braddock drove Rachel to a thrift shop near the center of town. She bought sneakers and a pair of jeans, a couple of loose-fitting V-necks, and a sports bra that had her tugging at the elastic band squeezing her ribcage.

"Sorry," Braddock said. "It's the best we've got around here. Unless you want to try the Walmart over in Franklin."

"It'll do."

Their next stop was a convenience store on the edge of town. Rachel paid cash for a prepaid smartphone and hoped the technology for tracking them hadn't changed since she was an agent. She had considered disposing of hers during the drive last night, but there was still information and apps on it that she might need. As long as she kept it turned off, it shouldn't communicate with any cell towers. That meant local and state law enforcement agencies wouldn't be able to get her location from the service provider. There had been talk that Apple was creating a "zombie" mode for iPhones, enabling them to continue transmitting location data while powered down. As far as she knew, that hadn't happened yet. She programmed in a few contacts and texted her new number to Braddock and Carly.

When she finished shopping, Braddock took her to Carly's latest rental, an A-frame log cabin that was in need of a major renovation. It was perched on a hillside and provided a stunning view of the river below, but getting up to it was a challenge. Braddock had to switch his Explorer over to four-wheel drive to make the ascent.

Carly was still at the garage working on the Camry, but her charcoal-gray Tacoma was sitting right out front. She had given Rachel her keys the night before, unable to hide the fear in her eyes.

"I'll bring her back in one piece," Rachel had promised.

She loaded her briefcase and clothes in the passenger side, then gave Braddock a hug.

"You sure you're ready for this?" he asked.

"Not really," she said, forcing herself to smile. "Thank you, Danny. For everything."

He hugged her again, then said, "Damn, I almost forgot," and ran back to his open door. He reached inside the center console and returned with a tiny handgun, a Smith & Wesson .380 that he usually carried on his ankle as a backup. He unhooked the strap and handed it to Rachel. "Just in case."

She clipped the holster onto her waistband and pulled her shirt over it to make sure it was hidden. North Carolina was an open-carry state, but displaying a firearm on her hip would bring unwanted attention. She stretched her shirt a little lower and said, "That could work. Hopefully I won't need it." She took it off and stowed it under the Tacoma's driver seat.

"I've got a few things to do at the office before I can leave," Braddock said. "But I'll call you as soon as I get to your apartment. You be careful out there."

"You too."

She climbed in the truck and adjusted the seat and the mirrors. Watched in the rearview for a moment as Braddock backed down the gravel driveway. When she could no longer see him, a wave of apprehension washed over her. Once again, she was alone.

★ ★ ★

The drive to Fayetteville took Rachel east across the state, descending the mountains and crossing the rolling hills of the Piedmont until she reached the western edge of the Coastal Plain. A patchwork of farmland and untamed pine forests gave way to industrial parks and strip malls and neighborhoods.

After more than five hours, Rachel turned onto a road lined with two-story town homes. They were new and indistinguishable from one another. Each unit was identical to the next, facing its mirror image across the street.

She counted the numbers above the garage doors until she found the right address. Then she parked on the street and looked around. She decided to leave the little pistol under the seat as she got out and went to ring the doorbell.

Kristy Romano came to the door yelling. There were children in the background, noisy and defiant. She opened the door with a scowl and said, "Can I help you?"

"I'm sorry to bother you, Mrs. Romano . . . I don't know if you remember me or not. I used to be with the SBI."

Romano's face deadened.

Rachel said, "I was the agent assigned to your brother's case. My name's—"

"I know who you are. What are you doing here?"

"I was hoping I could talk to you."

"About what? Tyler?" She shook her head. "I've read the papers, Miss Carver. I know you're not an agent anymore. And I know you think everything the SBI told us is a damn lie, but I can't go through this again. I'm sorry. I just don't have it in me."

She moved back and started to close the door.

"Wait," Rachel said, reaching out to stop her. "Please. I don't blame you for being upset with me. And I know it's a shitty thing for me to just show up here like this, but it's important. Something's happened. Something bad. I really need your help. I promise you, I wouldn't be here if I didn't."

There was a scream and a thud, like something heavy had fallen upstairs. A child started to cry.

"Shit." She glared at Rachel, looked like she was trying to decide what to do. There was another scream. She rolled her eyes and turned toward a set of stairs. She said, "Fine, come in, but close the door behind you," as she stomped her way up to the second floor.

Rachel stepped inside and closed the door, listening to Romano's disembodied voice go from concern to exasperation as she interrogated her children. A pair of boys, Rachel remembered. Eight and ten. Their toys were strewn over the floor, as were their dirty dishes from a recent lunch. Sweating cans of soda stood on a wooden TV stand, certain to leave a pair of rings in the red-stained finish. A bag of Doritos had been torn open, its contents disseminated in a swath across the carpet.

For all that Rachel had dealt with in her life, few things terrified her more than the idea of motherhood.

Romano came downstairs, seemingly oblivious to the state of her home, and invited Rachel to sit with her in the living area. "Sorry about that. I got 'em playing PlayStation, so they should be good for a little while."

Rachel stepped over the stripe of Cool Ranch crumbs and settled on a couch. "Thank you for letting me in. I know it's difficult—"

"You said something happened?" Romano sat with her arms folded. She had a round face that defaulted to a sweet expression. She was trying her best to look stern.

"Yes. A friend of mine was killed."

That made Romano's eyebrows go up. Some of the tension left her pursed lips. "I'm sorry to hear that. Who was it?"

Rachel saw Parker's face, weak but determined, anxious to do his part to uncover the truth. She felt her throat tighten. She swallowed and said, "He was a reporter, investigating your brother's murder. I think he was killed because of what he found."

Romano looked away. It seemed like a reflexive act. An involuntary response to what she was hearing. "You know, when you went to arrest Lauren . . . when you shot her . . . I thought this was all over. I thought we were gonna have some kind of resolution. Some peace of mind. Or some justice, at least. Then you went and started saying all that stuff in the papers." Her eyes welled. She rubbed the puffy skin beneath them. "I hated you for taking that away from us."

"I can understand that. But I'm here now, trying to get you the justice you deserve."

She laughed, sniffed hard, and said, "Right. And what about Lauren's family? What're you gonna do for them?"

Rachel couldn't answer. She didn't have the courage to admit that there was nothing she could do for them. Nothing that would matter.

"I'm sorry," Romano said. "I shouldn't be such a bitch."

"It's okay. With everything you've been through . . ."

"Yeah, well . . . look, I'm not trying to be rude, but what is it that you want from me?"

Rachel thought it best not to come right out and ask for the journals. She said, "I know you and Tyler were close. Do you think there's anything at all we might have missed during the investigation? Anything that might have occurred to you since then?"

"Like what?"

"Can you think of anyone who would've wanted to hurt him? Or anything he might have been into?"

Romano suddenly looked offended. "Are you asking me if he was doing anything illegal?"

"No. That's not exactly what—"

"Good. 'Cause that's the kind of question that would really piss me off right now." Romano was getting agitated. She shifted in her seat and took a breath. "You know, you haven't told me why you think Lauren was innocent. I know she found out Tyler was still cheating on her. Hell, he was only staying with her because he loved that little boy so much. Don't you think she could've been mad enough to do it when she found out?"

"No. After Miss Bailey died . . ." Rachel hated saying it that way, as if she was trying to make it sound like some freak accident or sudden illness, like Bailey had been struck by falling plane wreckage or consumed by flesh-eating bacteria. Anything other than Rachel shooting her eight times in the chest. ". . . a friend of hers came forward. She had a number of private messages they had shared on Facebook. It seems Lauren was cheating on Tyler as well. With more than one person. She wanted to break up with him, but she was dragging it out. Trying to get as much money out of him as she could. But she said that was starting to get old. She said it wasn't worth the money anymore, and she had fallen in love with one of the other guys she was seeing."

Romano started to cry. She wiped her eyes, and the look of annoyance vanished from them.

Rachel said, "We thought she was angry and jealous. We thought that gave her motive. We were wrong."

"Yeah. I guess you were."

Rachel decided it was time to try for the journals. "Kristy, do you remember the notebooks Tyler kept? The ones where he wrote things down about his deployments?"

She nodded.

"Do you still have them?"

Romano sat quietly for a moment, as if considering whether or not she wanted to answer. Then she stood up and walked away, disappearing into a bedroom. Rachel heard closet doors being opened. The sound of boxes being pulled from shelves and dropped to the floor. When Romano came back a few minutes later, she was carrying one. She laid it on the coffee table, opened it, and withdrew five composition notebooks. She eased herself back onto the love seat, holding them against her chest.

"I read through them, you know." She sniffed and wiped her eyes again. "There's things in here . . . awful things. The kind of stuff you hear soldiers talk about and you're glad you never have to see it for yourself." She looked up as if struck by some horrible thought. "You don't think he could've . . ."

"What?" Rachel asked.

Romano looked like she was about to burst into a crying fit. "What if he . . . ?"

"It's okay." She tried to sound reassuring, hoping Romano could hold it together. "What if he what?"

"What if he killed himself?"

Rachel shook her head. "That's not what happened."

"Are you sure? I mean, I know you think he was murdered, but you hear about soldiers doing it all the time. I've seen it on Facebook. They say twenty-two vets kill themselves every day. Twenty-two. You don't think there's even a chance?"

"No." Rachel's mind started recalling the evidence. Proof that Larson had been the victim of a homicide. There was the lack of powder burns or a star-shaped wound on his temple, which told her that the gun had not been held directly against his head. There was a gap in the back-spatter pattern, where the blood from the entry wound had sprayed whoever had been sitting in the passenger seat. Then there was Corey Staples, the witness Parker had discovered. And, of course, Parker's kidnapping and murder, which only made sense if someone was desperate to cover up the crime. "Trust me. Your brother didn't take his own life."

Romano looked relieved. She took a deep breath, wiped her cheeks and patted her eyes. "And your friend . . . you're sure whoever killed him is the one that . . . ?"

"Whoever it was, I'm sure they're involved."

"Well . . ." She leaned forward and handed Rachel the notebooks. "I don't know what you're looking for, but whatever it is, I hope you find it."

Rachel opened one and read the inside of the front cover. Larson's name and rank and unit number. The writing triggered something in her mind. Some thought or memory that didn't make sense.

"I can't imagine who would've wanted to hurt Tyler," Romano said. "He never had any enemies as far as I know."

Rachel closed the book and gave Romano a sympathetic look. "Thank you, Kristy. I'll get these back to you as soon as I can."

"Don't," she said, eyeing them. "I'll be too tempted to read them again if you do. I'd rather not do that. You keep them. Or throw them away, if you want to. Just don't bring them back here."

TWENTY

Rachel was sitting in a gas station parking lot, sipping on a Monster Energy and reading one of Larson's journals, when Braddock called.

"Someone kicked the hell outta your front door," he said. "No one seems to have seen anything, though. The neighbors didn't even know you had a break-in."

"Figures," she said. "My gun safe?"

"Gone. He must've just taken it someplace where he could cut it open."

"That's what I thought." Rachel was relieved that she hadn't simply left it unlocked, though it didn't really matter at this point.

"I got through to one of the guys on the burglary team. He says he knows me from our patrol days, but I can't remember him to save my life. Anyway, he's on his way over with a tech. You know he'll wanna talk to you."

"Give him my number."

"Have you thought about talking to anyone in homicide? We still have a few friends there. Might not be a bad idea to get them on your side."

"I've thought about it," she said. "I'm not ready yet."

"All right."

There was concern in his voice. She could tell he was worried, afraid that she was making a mistake, though he wasn't ready to say so just yet.

He asked, "What are you up to?"

She told him about her visit with Romano and the notebooks.

"You're reading them now?"

"Yeah."

"Find anything good?"

"Not yet," she said with a sigh.

"Well, keep me posted."

"Are you heading back?"

"I'll wait around for a bit. See if the tech happens to find anything interesting."

"Thanks, Danny."

She went back to the journal. The oldest of the five, written during Larson's first summer in Afghanistan, from June to September 2012. Most of the days had passed uneventfully. Training exercises and patrols and frustrating encounters with local tribesmen. Weeks of boredom in harsh living conditions, surrounded by teenagers who were expected to do the kind of work that older men shied away from.

Suddenly, there would be an incident. Mortars fired from some hill in the distance. A grenade lobbed over a wall. A sniper that no one could pinpoint. "Asymmetrical warfare" was the term. Attacks that got men injured, sometimes killed, but too often went unanswered.

Larson had been a staff sergeant back then. A squad leader in charge of eight soldiers. His boys, as he had called them. The hardest part of his job seemed to be keeping their morale up and their frustration in check. Especially near the midway point of their tour, when the attacks became more frequent.

It wasn't until mid-August that they finally got some payback. While patrolling a village in the Guldara District, Larson's squad had come under attack. A fire team, four of his boys on the other side of the village, reported contact. Bursts from an assault rifle. Then came a grenade that, luckily, didn't go off.

Larson had rushed to their position. By the time he got there, it was over. No one was hit except the Afghan boy who had attacked them. He couldn't have been more than sixteen, but that hadn't made him any less dangerous. When they approached his riddled body, they found an AK-47, a spare magazine, and another grenade.

Morale improved after that.

Rachel counted seven more attacks before Larson went home. Three of those ended with dead enemy combatants. Taliban or al-Qaeda militants hidden among villagers. To Larson and his boys, they were all starting to look the same.

The villagers never bothered to warn their American protectors. Perhaps they stayed quiet out of fear. Fear of retribution from the terrorists, against themselves or their families. It was understandable, at least in the beginning. But there's only so much understanding in a soldier living under constant threat from an unseen enemy. Months in Afghanistan wore it paper-thin.

Larson's journals were light on commentary. For the most part, they were concise descriptions of events, with only the essential details listed along with the names of those involved. There was little in the way of sentiment or reflection. The only words that betrayed his personal feelings came near the end. On more than one occasion, he referred to the Afghan civilians as *savages*.

TWENTY-ONE

Hughes dialed the number again—his third attempt in the last hour—and groaned when he heard the voicemail greeting.

"Hi, Ms. Carver," he said after the beep, "this is Chad Hughes with the Siler City Police Department. We met at the hospital the other day. I need to talk to you regarding your friend, Mr. Parker. Could you give me a call back, please? As soon as possible, if you don't mind? Thanks."

He hung up the phone, leaned back in his chair, and tried to think of what to do next. He had spoken to Ramirez's neighbors, her family, and her friends. None of them had been able to shed any light on what had happened. Parker had lived in Raleigh, so the police chief had requested assistance from that department's homicide unit. They were still waiting for them to call back.

There was only so much a municipal detective could do. Hughes didn't have the authority to run all over the state and question whomever he wanted, which meant the investigation was starting to get out of his hands. On top of that, the chief was cautious when it came to homicides. He'd already insisted on asking the SBI for help with the crime scene process, which probably wasn't a bad idea, but it certainly slowed the works. It was only a matter of time before he called them and asked for an investigator to be assigned to the case.

But Hughes wanted this one for himself. It wasn't a matter of pride; he felt responsible. The reporter had been into something bad, and that's what had gotten him and Ramirez killed. If only Hughes had stayed at the hospital, stuck it out until the sorry bastard woke up from his heroin-induced coma . . .

Hughes wasn't the type to let his emotions get out of control. Anger didn't make him a better detective, but he couldn't shake the feeling that there was something he could have done differently. Or better. Or that he could have done anything at all rather than just leaving. Rather than ignoring the fact that a man was claiming to have been kidnapped and drugged against his will.

He stared at his desk and chewed on the dead end of a ballpoint pen. He nudged his chair into a gentle rock and let his mind wander. It didn't take it long to drift back to Rachel Carver.

There was something about her that bothered him. More than just the attitude she had given him. The look of condescension. Something that didn't make sense about her relationship with Parker.

He stood and strolled over to Morrison's desk. She was on her computer, punching away at the keys, most likely typing up her report about the morning's follow-up canvass. She'd gone back to Ramirez's street to question a few neighbors who had not been home the first time around. She paused to glance up at him and said, "You're not coming over here looking for a sounding board, are you?"

He was pacing between her and a wall of filing cabinets. "Huh? No . . . I'm just thinking."

"That's not possible," she said, getting back to her report. "Your mouth's not moving."

"Uh-huh." He stared at the floor as he took a few more turns. "So this guy ODs on heroin . . ."

"Here we go."

". . . and the first person he wants us to call is an ex-cop?"

"Yep."

"And not just any ex-cop. A freakin' SBI agent."

"Right," she said with an absent nod.

"I mean, this woman's supposedly a goddamn hero. She saved a Wake County deputy's life, for cryin' out loud."

"That's something."

"And she just comes running over. Straight to the hospital to see him." He stopped and leaned against a cabinet. "Almost like she wanted to make sure she was the first one to talk to him."

Morrison sighed and stopped typing. "Let me guess. You haven't done a background check on her yet, have you?"

"You know how I feel about the new computer system."

"One of these days, I'm gonna stop enabling your lazy butt." She moved her mouse around and made a few clicks, then asked, "What's her name?"

"Rachel Carver."

She typed it in and started scrolling through the results.

Hughes went back to thinking, staring into space, mumbling whatever came to mind. "It might make sense if he was an old informant or something. And if she was still an agent. But a reporter? On heroin?"

"Oh, damn," Morrison said under her breath.

"And what the hell did Ramirez have to do with any of this?"

"Chad, you need to see this."

"Huh?"

She was staring at the screen. "Come here and have a look."

He walked behind her and bent down to look over her shoulder. "What is it?"

She pointed her index finger at a block of text. It was the return from the DMV database—a vehicle registered in Rachel Carver's name. It was a white Toyota Camry.

"Holy mother of God," Hughes said. "Looks like we got ourselves a suspect."

TWENTY-TWO

Rachel finished skimming the last few pages and went back to the beginning, hoping something might jump out at her. But nothing did. She was starting to think the journals were a waste of her time.

She closed the oldest of the set and stared at its cover for a moment. Suddenly, she remembered the uneasy feeling she'd had when she'd opened it in Romano's living room. As if something inside it hadn't made sense to her.

She opened it again and studied the inside of the front cover where Larson had written his name, rank, and unit number. The formality of those details made Rachel wonder if the journals had been a requirement. Something Larson's superiors had demanded in case there was ever a need to review the actions of his unit.

Tyler Larson.
Staff Sergeant.
B—2/525 PIR.

She understood the nomenclature of the last line. She had learned the format during the original investigation. It meant that Larson had been assigned to Bravo Company in the 2nd Battalion of the 525th Parachute Infantry Regiment.

But that didn't look right.

Rachel straightened in her seat. She stared at it for a moment, realizing why it had bothered her. At the time Larson was murdered, he had been a platoon sergeant for a different unit—the 508th.

Larson's promotion to sergeant first class must have come with a transfer. During the original investigation, Rachel had spoken to several of his fellow soldiers. Searching for any hint of hostility or ill will. Any kind of grudge that might have gotten him killed. She hadn't found anything, but only one of the people she'd interviewed had served with Larson in the 525th.

PFC Adam Hubbard.

If Larson had been killed because of something that had happened during his time as the leader of Hubbard's squad, Rachel would've had no way of knowing about it. Aside from Hubbard, she had been talking to the wrong people.

She flipped through the pages again, this time looking for names. They were peppered throughout. Each time she found one, she jotted it down in her steno pad. When she got to the end, she dropped the journal in the passenger seat and stepped out to stretch.

A gray blanket was drawing west across the sky, leaving a thin band of blue stretching over the horizon. The cloud cover brought a respite from the sun, but the damp air clung to her skin. It was thick and suffocating. She tugged on her shirt and felt it sticking to her back.

Frustration engulfed her. She was grasping at straws in the most important fight of her life. The memory of her history professor explaining that phrase popped into her mind. "A drowning man will reach for any object to save himself," he had said, "even a straw, floating on top of the water."

In that moment, she thought about Calvin Grant. About the anonymous tipster he was protecting. Would they be willing to help her out? If she called Grant, would he be willing to go to his client and ask for more information? Some new clue that might point her in the right direction?

Rachel heard the prepaid ringing in her car. She ran back to grab it and read the screen. CARLY BREWER.

"Hey Carly. You find anything?"

"Yeah, I did, actually. By accident."

"What do you mean?"

"I was searching the driver side floorboard and I dropped my light. It fell out on the ground and rolled under your car. I had to lay down on my side to look for it, and I saw this thing stuck under there . . . almost looks like a hockey puck. It's magnetic, and there's a little switch on it. I'd bet you anything it's some kind of GPS tracker."

"Holy shit."

"Yeah, for real. It's got me kinda freaked out right now."

"Did you get anything else? Hairs or prints?"

"Got a few of each," Carly said. "Along with the swabs I took for touch DNA and the samples for comparison. I'll leave first thing Monday morning to take them in. The prints can go to the Asheville lab. That'll be the quickest turnaround. But the DNA tests have to be done in Raleigh. I wouldn't get too excited about the hairs, though. They look like they're probably all yours."

"Okay."

"There's something else I need to tell you." Her voice

lowered. "The BOLO came in. For you and your car. You're wanted for questioning, but I don't think there's an arrest warrant yet."

"Damn." Rachel looked around instinctively, then held her head a little lower. "Was only a matter of time, I guess."

"Yeah . . . take care of yourself, okay?"

"I will." She climbed back into the Tacoma. "Thanks, Carly."

It felt like the world was closing in on her. Time was running out. She had to move. Had to make something happen.

She turned her iPhone on and typed Grant a text message, giving him the prepaid number and asking him to call her. She sent it, then thumbed her way to the app she used to run quick background checks. When the search screen came up, she typed ADAM HUBBARD, MONROE, NORTH CAROLINA, 24 YEARS OLD.

The app was a paid subscription service. It could dig through thousands of public records in a matter of seconds, an invaluable tool for a private investigator. She had signed up for the premium version, which wasn't cheap but often proved its worth.

The little wheel that told Rachel her phone was thinking or processing spun at the top of her screen, testing her patience. It didn't help that she knew it was also transmitting her location to the nearest cell towers.

"Come on," she growled.

On command, the results appeared, displaying the top six returns based on her search criteria. The first name seemed to be the best fit. She touched it, and the profile opened. A menu with several options: Overview, Contact Info, Address History, Relatives, Employment History, Criminal Records, Associates . . .

She touched the Associates tab and compared the results with the list of names she'd copied from Larson's journal. There were two matches: Seth Martin and Austin Buckley. They had shared an address with Hubbard back in 2014. It was an apartment. Apparently, the three of them had been roommates for a year after getting out of the Army.

Rachel ran a search on both men and checked their most recent addresses. They still lived in Fayetteville. She decided to try Martin first, entering his address into her navigation app. The route came back a second later showing a ten-minute drive. She wrote the directions on her steno pad, then plotted the course from there to Buckley's apartment. She copied those directions as well, then turned off her phone, downed the last of her Monster Energy, and started the Tacoma.

★ ★ ★

Martin lived in a new apartment complex not far from Fort Bragg. He shared his two-bedroom with a roommate, who said he was at a pool party behind the next building over. Rachel went down to find a group of twenty-somethings in board shorts and bikinis, tossing each other into the water and yelling over loud country music as a heavyset man in a tank top cooked hamburgers on the community grill.

Rachel went to the cook first.

"Hi there," she said. "Mind telling me where I can find Seth Martin?"

"What do you want with that asshole?" he asked playfully.

"He knew a friend of mine in the Army."

"In the Army?" He waved smoke away from his face and yelled, "Yo, Seth. This chick says you were in the Army. Say it ain't so."

Rachel looked toward the pool and saw a man look back and say, "What?" He was short, maybe an inch taller than Rachel, with a barrel chest and heavy arms. When he spotted Rachel, his mouth formed a little smirk, and he strolled over.

He slapped the cook on the butt and said, "Is this guy bothering you?"

"Not at all," Rachel said. "He's actually been quite helpful."

Martin sipped on a can of Busch Light, taking a second to examine Rachel's figure. He seemed pleased with what he was seeing. "I can be helpful too."

The big man in the tank top put a towel to his mouth and snickered.

Martin punched him in the arm with an expression of mock indignation. "Hey, show some fuckin' respect, bro." He leaned toward Rachel. "Never mind this heathen."

"Do you mind if we have a word in private?" Rachel asked.

"Why not?"

They walked away from the crowd and stood at the edge of the concrete deck behind a row of metal lounge chairs.

"I'm sorry to pull you away from your friends," she said. "I won't keep you long."

"No worries. How can I help?"

"I've been hired by a law firm in Monroe to investigate the death of one of your former squad mates. Adam Hubbard."

His expression changed. Some of his cockiness disappeared. "Little Adam. I miss that guy."

"Were you two close?"

He shrugged. "For a while. We lived together after we got out. He was too serious, though. And then he got into the pills, and that just wasn't my thing."

"Would you say his addiction was out of control?"

"Well, yeah. When you think about it, that's what got him killed. The guy did two tours in Afghanistan, dodging bullets and IEDs and shit. Then he comes home to get beat down by some fuckin' junkie."

"You think that's really what happened?"

"Hell yeah, I do."

His answer seemed a little too forceful. He looked like he was starting to get agitated. He shifted his weight and took a large gulp of his beer. It must have gotten too warm. He spit some out and poured what was left in the can on the grass.

Rachel asked, "Do you know if Adam spent any time with Sergeant Larson after he got out?"

He looked down. "No, I wouldn't know anything about that." His mood had changed completely now, and he seemed to recognize it. He put on a smile and said, "Look, I hate to cut this short, but it looks like those burgers are just about ready, and I could use another beer. You're welcome to join us if you want."

"I'm fine, thanks."

He started to turn away.

Rachel reached out to block his path. "Sorry, I hate to keep you, but this is really important. Just a couple more questions?"

He stopped but kept his eyes fixed on his friends, who were forming a line for food. "Yeah?"

"Did you happen to have any contact with Sergeant Larson before he was killed?"

He shook his head. "Nope."

"Would you happen to know why anyone would want him dead?"

"You mean aside from the fact that he was cheating on his girlfriend?"

"Yeah. Aside from that."

He took a step closer to her and lowered his voice. "I don't know why you're asking me all these questions, and I don't care. All I know is, these are my friends you're talking about. It was hard enough when they died. I don't need to keep reliving the shit."

He went back to the grill, where the cook was waiting with a hamburger and a fresh beer. Rachel wondered if she had just seen genuine pain, or if Martin had something to hide. Either way, she wasn't getting anywhere with him. It was time to try Austin Buckley.

★ ★ ★

The woman answered the door in a brown T-shirt and a pair of pink panties. She had red sores on her shins and looked too skinny for her own good. Sucking on a vaporizer, she looked Rachel up and down, exhaled a cloud, and said, "You lookin' for Austin?"

"Yes, ma'am."

"Ain't gonna find him here. Not at this time of the evenin'."

"Any idea where I *could* find him?"

She stuck the end of the tube back in her mouth while she considered the question. Then she took it out and asked, "Whatcha want with him?"

Rachel adopted a conciliatory tone. "Oh, I'm actually trying to find an old friend. He was in the Army with Austin. I thought he might be able to help me out."

"Hmph." She pointed across the street. "Well, he'll be sittin' over there at the bar. Just like he always is. When you see him, tell him not to forget to bring me home some chicken fingers."

Rachel thanked her and walked over, stopping at the edge of the parking lot to think about who or what she might find inside.

The bar was called Chappy's. The sign out front advertised billiards and darts, chicken wings and cheap beer. The windows were blacked out, but the door was propped open, inviting her in.

She suddenly felt vulnerable. Unsure of herself. Alone, with no one to call for backup. She wasn't going to let that stop her, though. She just needed a little extra security.

She turned and went back to the Tacoma. She opened the door, reached under the driver seat, and grabbed the .380. Leaning into the cab, she ejected the magazine and checked it. It was full. She slid it back into place with a click, drew back on the slide to chamber a round, and flicked the safety up with her thumb.

She shoved the weapon into the holster and looked around to make sure there were no eyes on her. It was all clear. She stood and lifted her shirt, clipped it to the waistband of her jeans and took a second to make sure it was hidden. Then she locked up the truck and headed for the bar.

TWENTY-THREE

It said NO SMOKING on the door, but the interior smelled like cigarettes. The wooden floor was dull and caked with layers of grime, sealed to its surface by the residue of spilled beer, wine, and mixed drinks. It grabbed at the soles of Rachel's shoes, forcing her to rip them free with each step into the dank space.

There were a dozen or so patrons seated at the bar. All but two of them were men. Rachel walked to the corner and looked toward each end. She spotted two candidates that fit her preconceived image of Austin Buckley, mostly because they were the right age.

She walked behind one and leaned in. "Austin?"

He turned slowly, looking confused.

"Are you Austin?" she asked.

He shook his head.

"Sorry."

She moved on. The other candidate was at the far end, rocking on the front legs of his stool and trying to get the bartender's attention. He saw Rachel approach and flashed a crooked grin.

"Hey, pretty girl," he said. "Ain't seen you in here before."

Rachel gave him a demure smile, acting like she wanted to walk past him.

He rocked back, blocking her way. "You're not leavin', are you?"

She glanced at the floor and giggled, trying to look embarrassed. Pointed at the door to the lady's room.

"Well, hurry on back, now. I'll save you a seat."

"Leave her alone, Austin."

Rachel turned to see the bartender, a large woman with curly hair, glaring at him.

"I ain't done nothin'. We're just talkin'."

"He botherin' you, hon?"

Rachel shook her head.

"Well, let me know if he does," the woman said with a wink. "I'll put him out on his skinny ass. Won't be the first time, neither."

"I love you too, Missy," Buckley said. Then he blew her a kiss.

Rachel eased past him and went into the restroom. She stood by the door and waited for a minute, liking the idea that he had engaged her instead of the other way around. His guard would be down, at least in the beginning. When she went back to the bar, he was waiting.

He hopped off his stool and grabbed the next one over. He pulled it closer to his and invited her to sit. "My lady," he said with a little bow.

Rachel offered a playful smile as she accepted. The bartender was eyeing him. He put his hands up and said, "Just talkin', Missy. Nothin' to see here."

She shook her head with disdain and asked Rachel, "What can I get ya?"

"Maker's, please. On the rocks."

Missy went to the bourbon shelf, and Buckley, looking impressed, said, "A woman after my own heart."

"What did you expect me to get?" Rachel asked.

"Well, you know, pretty girls like you usually order wine. Like some sorta pinot something or other."

She leaned toward him, put her cheek to her shoulder. "You think I'm pretty?"

"Hell yeah. You're about the prettiest thing to walk into this joint in ages."

Missy poured the drink, set it down on a short stack of square napkins, and said, "Behave, Austin."

He waved her away and whispered to Rachel, "She acts like I'm a damn child molester or some shit. But I'm just a nice guy is all. I can't help it that I like to talk to people. Everybody that comes in here is just grumpy as hell all the time."

"I know what you mean," Rachel said. "This looks like the kind of place my ex would hang out at. He was always so serious all the time. I think he spent too much time in the Army."

"I was in the Army. Didn't let 'em break me, though."

"You served?" she asked with a skeptical look.

"Damn right, I did. One tour in Iraq and two in Afghanistan."

"Shut up!" she said. "What unit?"

He straightened up. "Badgers, baby. Five-twenty-fifth Parachute Infantry Regiment."

Rachel's eyes widened. She slapped his arm and said, "No way. My ex's best friend was one of you guys."

"For real? What's his name? Maybe I know him."

"Tyler Larson."

His face changed, like something had stolen his spirit. He stared at the beer between his hands and said, "Nah. Don't think I ever heard of him."

"You haven't?"

He shook his head. "Lot of guys in the five-twenty-fifth."

"Yeah, but it's kinda strange. I think he may have mentioned you before."

He glanced at her, then looked around. "I don't think so."

She leaned a little closer. "Yeah, now that I think about it . . . he definitely mentioned you. Austin Buckley, right?"

He looked around again. His expression became tense. He shifted away from her, kept his voice low, and said, "Look, I don't know who you are, but you're full of shit. And we're done talkin'."

Missy was a few feet away, washing glasses. She hadn't heard the exchange. Rachel decided it was time to change the playing field. She stood, grabbed Buckley's beer, and dumped it in his lap.

"What the fuck?" he yelled.

As soon as Missy looked over, Rachel slammed the empty mug on the bar and said, "Suck your own dick, you freaking pervert." Then she turned and stormed for the exit, catching a glimpse of Missy's irate face as she got to the door.

Outside, Rachel moved to the side of the building, opened her jeans, and tucked in her shirt. She zipped and buttoned them back, making sure the pistol was visible on her hip, and waited.

Buckley came outside a minute later and yelled, "To hell with this place, man." He stuck his head back through the doorway. "Fuck all y'all." He turned to walk back to his apartment, then saw Rachel and started for her. "I oughta backhand your sorry ass for this, you fuckin' bitch."

Rachel put her hand on the gun. "I wouldn't recommend that, Specialist Buckley."

That stopped him in his tracks. "Aw, shit. What the hell?" His eyes moved between her face and the gun. "You undercover CID or some shit?"

Army Criminal Investigations, Rachel thought. That told her something. "Not exactly," she said. "Why don't we take a walk. I just have a few questions for you. Shouldn't take long."

He hesitated. It looked like he was thinking about running.

"I know where you live," she said. "You're not in any trouble. I just want to talk."

"Whatever. Ain't like I got nothin' better to do now."

She led him away from the door and toward the corner of the building. He leaned against the wall and pulled at the crotch of his jeans. "Better not have ruined my smokes," he mumbled. He took a pack of cigarettes and a lighter out of his pocket. He lit one with a smirk and asked, "So? What do you want?"

"What made you think I was CID?" she asked.

He shrugged. "I dunno."

"You haven't had any run-ins with them lately?"

"Maybe. Why should I tell you? I thought the whole thing was . . . Shit, you're from Counterintel, ain't you?"

She smiled, deciding there was no harm in misleading him.

He said, "I knew this wasn't just gonna go away."

She wanted to pounce. Wanted to ask him what he was

talking about, but she had to restrain herself. Establishing a position of authority over him required her to pretend she already had the information she wanted. She had to work her way around the edges. Make him feel like he wasn't giving away anything valuable. Pry it from him without letting him realize she was hearing it all for the first time. "When was the last time you spoke to CID?"

"Not since the whole thing started," he said, exhaling a puff of smoke. "I only talked to that warrant officer one time."

"But you didn't tell him everything you know, did you?"

"Yes, hell, I did," he said indignantly.

"Then why am I still chasing my tail over this?" She let a little of her frustration show, and suddenly found it hard to contain. "Private Hubbard and Sergeant Larson aren't the only people who've died. A reporter and a cop were killed over it. Just yesterday."

"Hey, I don't know nothin' about that, all right?"

"Then tell me what you do know. Because right now, every member of your squad is in my crosshairs until I get to the truth."

"Man, this is some bullshit. I wasn't even there when it happened."

"Convince me." She took out the prepaid phone and opened the voice-recording app. She touched the red button and said, "Let's go through it. From the beginning."

★ ★ ★

Missy was stacking glasses when she heard someone yell for her. It was Roach—one of the regulars. His eyes were fixed on the TV above the liquor shelves.

"Jesus American Christ, Missy. You gotta see this."

She wanted to ignore him. It was just about time for his daily rant, and she wasn't in the mood. He liked to show up every day, right before the news came on. He'd drink Blue Moon and read the captions in silence until he had a good buzz going. Then he'd start in with his political commentary, which often turned into conspiracy-laced tirades about the federal government. Some of it was entertaining, but most of the time it was just plain annoying. The other regulars had taken to calling him Roach after he spent a solid week lecturing everyone about bug-out bags and doomsday prepping and how, despite everyone else's faith in modern institutions, he'd be the only one left standing when the shit went down.

"Missy, get over here." His hand was waving furiously. "I'm serious, girl. You gotta see this."

"What is it, Roach?" she asked.

He kept waving at her. A few of the other patrons were now staring at the TV as well. She sighed and walked over.

"What are you all worked up about?"

He pointed at the screen. "You can tell me I'm a damn fool, but don't that look exactly like the woman that just went and dumped a beer in Austin's lap?"

"You're a damn fool," she said.

Then she looked up.

TWENTY-FOUR

"We was way on the other side of the village when it started," Buckley said.

"So I've heard," Rachel lied. "Be more specific. I'm going to check your story against what you told CID. You'd better hope it hasn't changed."

He rolled his eyes and flicked ash off his cigarette. "It was August eighteenth. We was in Guldara."

He paused and gave her a look that asked if she was satisfied.

"That's better," she said, remembering the incident she'd read about in Larson's journal. "Keep going."

"We was there lookin' for a weapons cache. The village elders said some kids had found it hidden behind a ridge near a tree line to the south. The lieutenant took a squad to go check it out. We stayed behind to secure the village. Sergeant Larson sent four guys over to watch the road headin' north into the hills. We'd heard some trucks had been spotted out there earlier that mornin'. Villagers said they was Taliban."

He took a long drag and slowly exhaled the smoke

through his nose. It drifted up around his eyes, making him squint.

"Couldn't have been more than fifteen minutes or so later," he said. "All of a sudden, we heard shots comin' from the north. Then we got the call. Seth came over the radio and said they had contact. Then we heard 'em returnin' fire. Sergeant Larson was all like, 'Fuckin' move it, boys. Let's go.' And we hauled ass. But, by the time we got there . . ." He dropped the cigarette on the pavement and stamped it out. "They'd done shot that little bastard full of holes."

He stood silent and stared at the ground, and Rachel realized he was done with his story. Apparently, the CID investigation had been about the attack. Or the fire team's response. There was something perfunctory about the way Buckley had said "little bastard." A lack of indignation that she would've expected to hear in his voice. He seemed to be using those words out of habit, even though he was talking about a militant who had ambushed his friends. There was no anger. No sense that the shooter had gotten what he deserved. Perhaps Buckley doubted that was the case.

"When you got there, what did you see, exactly?" Rachel asked.

"They was all out in a field behind one of them mud farm huts, standin' around the body."

"In the middle of a field? The attacker wasn't behind cover?"

He shook his head. "Sergeant Stoller said he just came across that field firin' at 'em. Like he wasn't afraid of shit. We all figured he was tryin' to martyr himself."

"And who else was there?" Rachel knew she could look it up in Larson's journal, but she wanted to keep Buckley talking. "Besides Sergeant Stoller?"

"Just Seth and Riley and Adam."

She pulled the steno pad from her pocket and checked the list of names. "As in Seth Martin, Riley Gordon, and Adam Hubbard?"

He nodded and said, "Yeah, Little Adam."

"Little Adam's dead, you know."

He had to look away.

"Same with Sergeant Larson," she said. "Any idea who might be responsible for that?"

He shrugged, refusing to make eye contact. "I heard his girlfriend done it."

"Yeah, and your buddy Adam was killed in a drug deal gone bad. Two out of nine people murdered in less than a year."

Rachel heard scuffling steps and turned to see a man exit the bar. He glanced over and saw her, did a double-take and froze. He stared for a second, then turned around and hurried back inside.

She looked at Buckley and said, "I'd be careful, if I were you. Those aren't very good odds."

She turned and walked away, rounded the corner, and crossed behind the building. Buckley shouted, "That's it?" She ignored him, pulled her shirt free from her jeans, and covered the pistol on her hip.

The road was clear when she emerged on the other side of the building. She started across it toward the Tacoma, still parked at Buckley's apartment complex. She was halfway there when she heard a man's voice yell, "Hey! You! Stop right there!"

She picked up her pace, but the man was determined to catch her. She heard his footsteps grow louder as he jogged up behind her. A hand seized her shoulder and spun her around. She used the momentum to her advantage, letting her arms swing with the turn. Her left forearm knocked the man's hand off her shoulder while her right hand shot up toward his nose. The heel of her palm found it with a crunch, and he staggered back, cupping his face in his hands.

Blood seeped between the man's fingers. He looked at them, spit a red splotch on the pavement, and growled, "Crazy fuckin' bitch." He reared back, like he might try to hit her, but stopped short when he saw the gun pointed at his chest.

"Walk away," Rachel said, dropping the safety with a flick of her thumb. "Turn around and walk away."

He stood his ground. His eyes were fixed on hers. They seemed to be questioning whether she had the nerve to pull the trigger.

Missy ran up with her hands in the air. "Whoa now, everybody just calm down." She grabbed the man's shirt and pulled him back. "Come on, Roach. It ain't worth it." Then to Rachel, she said, "You ought to go on and get outta here. I done called the cops. They're on the way."

Rachel glanced past them. A crowd had gathered by the entrance to the bar. Buckley was among them. She looked at Missy, then at Roach, and kept her gun leveled on his chest as she backed away. She reached the edge of the road, turned, and ran for the truck, shoving the pistol back in its holster as she got to the driver's side. She jumped in, started the engine, and tore out of the parking lot.

Once she was on the road, she checked the rearview. People were gathering around Missy and Roach. She turned at the next intersection, went two blocks, and turned again.

In the distance, a siren blared.

TWENTY-FIVE

Rachel was speeding down a residential street when Braddock called. He was still at her apartment with the Raleigh PD crime scene tech, who, apparently, was on the verge of losing his mind.

"I've got him printing every square inch of this place," Braddock said. "I can see it in his eyes. This guy wants to kill me."

Rachel was hoping to find a highway soon. She turned a blind corner and nearly spun out. She put Braddock on speaker and set the phone down so she could grip the wheel with both hands. Then she told him about her interviews with Martin and Buckley, though she chose to leave out the part where she had smashed a guy's face and threatened him with Braddock's gun.

There was a long silence, and she asked, "You still there?"

"Yeah," he said with a sigh. "Sorry, I'm just . . . I mean, damn, Rachel, what the hell is this? Army CID and Counterintelligence?"

Rachel came to a dead end and slammed on the brakes, cursed, and threw it in reverse. She backed up until she saw a road leading into a different neighborhood. It curved out of view, hidden by lines of brick houses that looked like they had been built in the 1970s. She had no way of knowing if there was a way out on the other side but hated the idea of doubling back.

She put it in drive and made the turn.

"I don't know," she said, exasperation heavy in her voice. "It's starting to feel like this is too much for me. I'm running around like a freakin' chicken with its head cut off . . . What I do know is that Buckley told me Hubbard was involved in the incident in Afghanistan, along with Martin and two others."

"You gonna try to talk to them?"

"Not yet. Now that my face is on TV, I can't just keep going back and forth between these guys and comparing stories. I might only get one shot to question each of them. If that. I need to get some idea of what the hell this is all about first."

"Yeah." He was quiet for a moment, then said, "Well, I hate to be the one who's always thinking everything is drug related, but have you considered it? I heard a story once about a group of soldiers that made a deal with some Afghani warlord for raw opium. They were shipping it back to the states and selling it to some other guys, who were turning it into heroin."

The road opened up. The houses came to an end. There was a school and a convenience store, then a Burger King just ahead of a stoplight.

"That's a thought," she said, easing into a right turn.

"Maybe that's what the Army's investigating. And you got Parker turning up in a hospital after OD'ing. This guy, Hubbard, was in rehab."

"All true." Rachel felt better being on a four-lane road, surrounded by traffic. She relaxed a little and allowed herself to consider his point. The more she thought about it, the more it began to make sense. "Damn, Danny. I knew I kept you around for a reason."

"Yeah?"

"Yeah."

"So where are you headed now?"

"Back to Monroe," she said. "I think I know who I need to talk to."

As she touched the button to end the call, she saw a notification for a text message. It was from Grant: I'M SORRY, MISS CARVER, BUT I'M AFRAID THAT, GIVEN YOUR SITUATION, IT WOULD NOT BE APPROPRIATE FOR ME TO CALL YOU. PLEASE CONSIDER THIS OUR LAST CORRESPONDENCE. I HAVE ALSO RECOMMENDED TO MY CLIENT THAT HE NOT SEEK ANY ALTERNATE MEANS OF CONTACTING YOU.

"Mother . . . !" Rachel nearly threw the phone out the window. She tossed it in the passenger seat instead, gripped the steering wheel, and tried to calm herself.

She was tempted to drive to Raleigh and confront him face-to-face, but there was no time for that. There was also a high probability that, upon seeing the impeccably tied Windsor knot at the base of his throat, she might seize the length of cloth dangling beneath it and use it to strangle the life out of him. As satisfying as that image was, it didn't help. So she fixed her eyes on the road and put Grant out of her mind.

★ ★ ★

Two hours later, Rachel was back in the heart of the Piedmont. Thunderheads roiled on the horizon, silhouetting the distant hills with flashes of pale blue. The road leading to Monroe was slick and exhaling steam, the storm having doused the entire town on its westward sweep.

Rachel left the highway and found the turn into Manish Gulani's neighborhood a moment later. She had risked turning her iPhone on during the drive, just long enough to run a background check on him and get his address. As far as she could tell, he was single. She hoped the rain had convinced him to stay home for the evening.

She parked on the street in front of his house and went to knock on his door. It took a few tries before he finally answered.

"I should not be talking to you," he said, standing with the door cracked just enough to show one of his eyes.

"Did Dr. LeMay tell you that?" she asked, hoping he hadn't seen her face on TV.

"Yes, she did."

His eye moved to the floor, reflexively. He looked back at her, perhaps a little embarrassed that the gesture had betrayed him, and Rachel knew she had caught a glimpse into his past. She had seen it before—a bullied child grown into a weak man, unable to stand up for himself. And it bothered him that he had never outgrown that weakness.

Self-loathing could be a useful tool. Rachel had to find a way to take advantage of it. She needed to empower him, to make him feel like he was doing something to conquer the part of himself he hated most.

"I wouldn't blame you for listening to her," she said, "but, before you slam this door in my face, you should know that things have changed since we talked yesterday. Two more people have died. You may have information that could help. Information that could help me stop this killer before he hurts anyone else. I'm sorry to put it on you like this, Manish, but you have a choice to make. You can be a good little boy and do whatever LeMay tells you, or you can man up and help me."

His eyes went back to the floor as he considered. Then he smiled, shook his head as if admonishing himself, and drew the door open to let her in. She followed him to his tiny kitchen and leaned against the counter while he went to the fridge and took out a pitcher of water. He got a glass from a cabinet and filled it.

"Would you like some? I'm afraid it's all I have to offer."

"I'm fine," she said.

He drank half the glass, put it down, and stared at it for a moment. "A good little boy." He chuckled. "They say people become therapists out of a desire to fix themselves. But listening to patients complain all day has obviously not made me any stronger." He took another sip and turned to face her. "You are smarter than I thought you were, Miss Carver. What is it that you want from me?"

There was no point in being coy. Rachel said, "I need to know why Adam Hubbard was killed."

"You are convinced it was not over drugs?"

"It might have been drugs, but it sure as hell wasn't because of a few Percocet."

"And you are convinced it was not Kyle Strickland?"

"I am."

"That's what I thought, too." He set the glass in the sink. "But I'm afraid I have no idea why he was killed or who did it."

"Did you know that Adam was being investigated by the Army?"

His brow creased, a look of genuine surprise. "No, I did not."

"His entire squad, actually. For something that happened in Afghanistan. Did he ever talk to you about his time over there?"

"Is that why you came here? To convince me to betray Mr. Hubbard's confidence?"

"I know it's asking a lot—"

"It is asking me to jeopardize my career."

"To bring a killer to justice," she said. "And maybe save lives. Doesn't that matter to you?"

"It does. But I wonder why I'm talking to you about it and not a police officer."

"I was an agent with the SBI when I started this case."

"But you are not one anymore." He looked past her into the living room and nodded at the TV. "You have been on the news tonight. They say you are suspected of killing two people. Would those be the people you mentioned?"

She didn't answer. Tried to think of a way to explain.

He said, "It seems that you are here, most of all, to help yourself. Assuming you were not the one who killed the officer and the reporter?"

"I'm not," she said.

"You must be desperate to prove that." He moved closer and peered into her eyes. "I see it in you. You have the look of a wild animal. One that's been trapped. Ready to lash out at whoever gets in the way of your escape."

Rachel's hand moved closer to her hip, stopping just beneath the gun.

Gulani turned and went back to the front door, pulled it open, and said, "I am not as motivated as you, I'm afraid. I will not betray the trust of my patients to help you."

She opened her mouth to protest, but he raised his hand to stop her.

"You will find, Miss Carver, that I take my job very seriously. Every aspect of it. For instance, if I were to take you to my office, you would see that I keep detailed notes about my patients. I document every interaction that I have with them. It's a pity, of course, because I could never show them to you. But the files are . . . quite extensive."

"I see." Rachel walked past him and through the doorway, paused on the stoop, and turned back to look at him. "I may have underestimated you, Manish. I'm sorry for that."

He gave her a little smile and closed the door.

TWENTY-SIX

"Well, why in the hell am I just hearing about this now?" Lester Arnold, the Siler City Police chief, was red-faced and yelling into the handset. "Jesus H. Christmas, that was almost three hours ago."

Hughes was in the doorway, waiting for an invitation. Arnold leaned back in his black leather office chair and waved him in. He stepped in quietly and eased into a seat facing Arnold's desk.

"It doesn't matter if you weren't sure it was her." Arnold looked over and shook his head with annoyance. "Let me tell you something. I have never, in all my years, seen this kind of incompetence. Your office needs a lesson in interagency cooperation. God forbid you ever want a little help from our end someday." He slammed the handset down and dropped against the seat back. "Sorry sons o' bitches."

"What was that all about?" Hughes asked.

"That was the assistant chief of the damn Fayetteville PD. He says they responded to a call about your suspect today. Says a bar full of people saw her come in and pour a beer in some guy's lap and leave."

"She dumped a beer in a guy's lap?"

"Yep."

"And then just took off?"

"That's what he said. He also said one of the regulars tried to stop her out in the street, and she popped him one good in the nose and pulled a gun on him."

"No shit?"

"That's what he said."

Hughes slid to the edge of his chair. "That's our girl. I know it is."

"Well then, you'd best get on the phone with him and see what more he can tell you about it. I don't think he'll want to speak to me anymore."

"Did he say what bar it was?"

"I think he said it was called Chappy's."

"In Fayetteville . . ." Hughes glanced at his watch. "I can probably be there by nine thirty."

"Just check in with Assistant Chief Dipshit over there. Maybe he can loan you somebody."

"You know I'd rather not."

"Aw come on, Chad . . ."

"Seriously, boss. You gotta let me off this leash."

Arnold leaned his head back and cast his eyes up to the ceiling.

Hughes asked, "You heard anything more from Raleigh?" Arnold didn't bother to answer. They both knew things were moving too slow on that end. "That's 'cause they're stalling. I'm telling you, she worked there for years. She's probably still friends with everyone in their homicide unit. You think they're going to be in any hurry to help us?"

"What's that got to do with these assholes in Fayette-ville?" Arnold asked.

"Same deal," Hughes said. "I bet she's worked with them too. Back when she was an SBI agent. They probably think we're crazy as hell for going after her."

"Yeah . . ." He rubbed his eyes with his thumb and forefinger and pinched the bridge of his nose.

Hughes sensed that he was wearing Arnold down. He said, "Let me run over there and talk to those people myself. See if I can find out what she was doing at that bar. Maybe I can get a lead on where she's going next."

"You get more than a mile outside of this town, you're a civilian. You know that."

"I'll call Dipshit as soon as I figure out what she was up to."

Arnold took a deep breath, let it out slowly, and said, "Ah, what the hell? All right, Chad. Do what you gotta do."

TWENTY-SEVEN

Rachel stopped at a little hardware store just off Main Street to buy a hammer and a flashlight. She had a story ready, in case the cashier wanted to make conversation, but the teenage girl's only interest appeared to be counting the seconds until she could close up and enjoy what remained of her Saturday.

Outside, the air was heavy and cool. The sky was solid black, and the streetlights seemed to glow too brightly. Rachel kept close to the trees lining the sidewalk, avoiding the eyes of a couple walking hand in hand, lazily browsing the storefronts and debating where to stop for a few after-dinner cocktails.

The Tacoma was parked on the street. Rachel hopped in and dropped the bag in the passenger seat. Then she sat still and took some time to think, to reconsider her decision.

She thought about buying another phone and trying to call Grant, to see if she could trick him into answering a number he wouldn't recognize. Maybe if she was able to actually talk to him, to get a few words in before he tried to hang up on her, she might be able to convince him to help. To allow her to speak directly to his client.

In all likelihood, that would be a wasted effort, and thinking about it only made her angry. Made her revisit her fantasy of throwing him to the ground and choking him out. For now, she had to push that aside. It was time to focus. She took the prepaid out and started typing Braddock a message.

I'M GOING TO DO SOMETHING STUPID. I CAN'T TELL YOU WHAT IT IS, BUT, IN CASE ANYTHING HAPPENS . . . SETH MARTIN, RILEY GORDON, COLIN STOLLER. THEY WERE IN LARSON'S SQUAD WITH ADAM HUBBARD. THEY WERE THERE WHEN THE SHOOTING HAPPENED IN AFGHANISTAN. THANKS AGAIN.

She hit send and dropped the phone in the cup holder, started the truck, and wheeled onto the road. The phone rang a minute later. It was Braddock, but she didn't want him talking her down. She switched the ringer to mute and did her best to ignore the light from the screen. It came on every few seconds as she made her way through town.

The Monroe Outpatient Treatment Center appeared on the right, and Rachel slowed to study it as she passed by. There were no cars in the parking lot and no lights on inside. She sped up and made the next turn, looking for a good spot to park. It was a curvy road, flanked by single-story offices tucked into wooded parcels. The types of buildings that were usually occupied by doctors or lawyers, architects or engineers.

She found a parking lot with a gap between the circles of light shining on the pavement, the void left by a broken lamp overhead. The Tacoma fit nicely in the space. She shut it down and collected her tools. The flashlight went into her pocket, along with the keys. She slid the prepaid into another pocket and decided to leave her iPhone behind. She carried the hammer in her hands as she stepped out, shut the door, and spun in a circle to scan her surroundings.

Satisfied that no one was around, she moved toward the nearest office, staying in the void as she slipped around to the back. Once behind the buildings, she started to jog toward the highway. She was less than a hundred feet from it when she spotted a break in the trees that lined the border of the treatment center's property.

Rachel crouched behind a bush and surveyed the grounds. The space between the tree line and the building was wide open on this side. There would be nothing to hide her. The building itself seemed much larger than she remembered. Landscape lights shined faint yellow on the walls. A bank of floor-to-ceiling windows told her she was looking at a large room, perhaps a meeting room for group sessions.

Whatever it was, it didn't appear to be Gulani's office. She rose and moved among the trees until she could see the back side, then crouched and looked it over. The nearest wall was much closer here, and there was a series of smaller windows, evenly spaced. It looked like a row of offices, though she had no way to tell from here which was the right one.

She took the flashlight out of her pocket and ran her eyes along the wall near the roof, searching for a camera. There didn't appear to be one. She moved into the clearing, her head panning side to side as she went from a timid walk to a jog. By the time she was halfway there, she was in a full sprint.

She reached the first window and looked inside. A red speck of light seemed to be floating in the blackness. She clicked on the flashlight and aimed it inside. The speck was coming from a laptop charging on a desk. There were pictures on a credenza. She cupped her hand around her eyes for a better view. The images were of children, one of whom looked old enough to be in high school.

It was the wrong office. Rachel moved to the next window and shined the light. A mirror image of the first office, with identical furniture facing the opposite direction. Rachel moved to the edge of the window and ran the light over the wall behind the desk. As soon as she did, the beam hit a framed diploma. A master's degree from the University of South Carolina. She squinted to read the name, ornately scribed in the center. After a moment, she was certain it said MANISH GULANI.

She passed the beam around the room again, looking for a motion detector or a glass-break sensor. There didn't appear to be one. Examining the window frame, she spotted a magnetic switch on the bottom. As long as she didn't try to lift the sash, the little sensor would not trip the alarm.

She stepped back to give herself room for a big swing and raised the hammer.

"Whatever you're looking for . . ."

Rachel spun and shined the light on a figure standing a few yards behind her.

He put a hand up to shield his eyes and said, "I don't think you're going to find it in there."

He looked young—perhaps in his midtwenties. He was lean, stood just under six feet, and was dressed in jeans and a T-shirt.

Rachel dropped the hammer, lifted her shirt, and put her hand on the gun, ready to draw and fire should the need arise.

"Who are you?" she asked with a shaky voice. Her heart was thundering, and the adrenaline spike was making it hard to stand still. She wanted to run for the trees.

"Take it easy," he said, raising his hands to calm her. "My name's Riley."

"Riley Gordon?"

"Yes, ma'am."

"What are you doing here? How did you find me?"

"Manish called me. He told me you'd probably be coming here. He also told me you were someone I could trust. That you're trying to figure out what happened to Adam."

"That's right," she said, trying to control her breathing.

"And you think it's got something to do with what we did in Afghanistan?"

"Why don't you tell me?"

He looked around and shook his head. "Not here. You want my help, you'll have to come with me. I got a place nearby where we can go. It's safe there."

"Why should I trust you?"

He shrugged. "You don't have to. We can go our separate ways, and I'd be good with that. But if you want to know what happened in Guldara, you're just going to have to take a leap of faith. I'm on your side, whether you believe it or not."

Rachel had no way of knowing whether or not he was telling the truth, but she was certain of one thing—he was not the monster that had attacked her. The giant that had killed Ramirez and Parker.

"Give me an address," she said. "I'll meet you there."

"That's not going to work. There's no address where

we're going. Besides, the cops are after you, and they know what kind of truck you're driving. The last thing I need is for them to see that thing turn onto my property. It's been all over the news, and, to be honest with you, I wouldn't be surprised if Manish called them on you after he talked to me."

"Shit." She tried to think of a different plan. Something that didn't involve getting in his car.

He started to back away. "Either come with me right now or don't. It's up to you, but I'm not hanging around here anymore."

She looked to her left. Beyond the trees, Carly's Tacoma sat in the empty lot, waiting for her. She could make a run for it and be gone in under a minute, hopefully before any cops showed up. But that would come at a price. She would lose her best chance to get the answers she needed.

"You can keep the gun, if it'll make you feel safer," he said.

It did. She made up her mind, said, "Screw it," and followed him.

★ ★ ★

Gordon's car was a red Dodge Charger. It was loud, and he drove it too fast. The wheels screeched as he turned onto the highway heading away from town. As the road slid between wooded slopes, he seemed to relax a little. Rachel spent most of the ride turning in her seat, constantly searching for patrol cars.

"We're far enough away now," he said. "You can relax. We're almost there."

She faced the front and made herself sit still. "How do you know Manish?"

"I was a patient at the center for a while."

"You and Adam both?"

"Yeah. I was first. I talked him into going there once I found out he had a problem with pills."

The landscape leveled out and opened up to farmland. On a curve, the headlights swept into emptiness. With nothing to reflect the beams, Rachel knew she was seeing a vast field. The road straightened, and Gordon slowed the Charger. A dirt road appeared on the right. Gordon made the turn and pushed into a cut separating smooth seas of green that dimmed to black in the distance.

"My family used to own all of this," he said. "We've sold most of it. We're down to just a couple hundred acres now."

The headlights hit a line of trees. The road squeezed through them, emerging into another field. A gray structure stood on the left. An old barn, clad in weatherworn planks. Gordon parked in front of it and killed the engine.

"This is it," he said.

"You live here?"

"Sometimes. It's a lot nicer on the inside."

They got out, and she followed him to the side where a bare bulb lit a door. He unlocked it, pushed it open, and stepped in, disappearing into the darkness.

Rachel hesitated. "Riley?" Her hand moved instinctively to her hip.

A light came on, and he was there, standing closer than she had expected. She took a step back and said, "Shit."

"Sorry," he said, stifling a laugh. "Come on in."

She went inside and looked around quickly. The room was small for what it held, resembling a studio apartment with a kitchen, a living area, and a queen-sized bed all sharing the space.

"I'll leave the door open," he said, moving past her. "It gets a little stuffy in here."

Rachel kept her eyes on him as he stepped toward the kitchen area.

"A couple years back, I turned this into a hunting camp. It also makes for a nice spot to get away from everyone for a night or two." He opened a cabinet door and reached inside. "Can I make you a drink? I've got Jack in here and a few Cokes in the fridge."

He was trying too hard to put Rachel at ease. She was growing more suspicious of him by the second.

"I didn't come for cocktails," she said. "How about we just get on with why you brought me here."

"Suit yourself."

He withdrew his hand from the cabinet, and it was holding a black semiauto. She spotted it immediately and had the .380 out of its holster and leveled on his torso before he could turn to face her.

"Drop it!" she yelled. "Put it down! Now!"

He held it low and smiled. "You might want to look behind you."

Rachel didn't have to. She felt the hard ring of a muzzle pressed against the back of her head. A man's voice said, "Checkmate, bitch."

TWENTY-EIGHT

The man had sneaked up behind Rachel, through the open door, while she was preoccupied with watching Gordon. She cursed to herself and let go of her gun. As soon as it hit the floor, Gordon stepped forward and picked it up, turned it over in his hand, and said, "Isn't this cute?"

The other man circled into view, keeping his pistol aimed at Rachel's head.

It was Seth Martin. He glanced at Gordon and said, "All right, you got her. Now what are you gonna do?"

Gordon's smirk grew a little wider as he said, "It's time to get high."

He went to the cabinets and laid both of the guns on the counter. Then he opened another door and took out a plastic bag, dug through it until he found a pair of zip ties. He made a loop with one, fed the other one through, and made a second loop. Then he approached her and said, "Give me your hands."

She stared at him for a moment, not wanting to comply. His jaw tensed. He squeezed the zip ties in his fist, turning his knuckles white.

Martin said, "My boy Flash has a bit of a temper. I'd do what he says, if I were you."

She held her hands out. He slid the loops over them and cinched them tight, pinching her skin and binding her wrists together. She winced, and Gordon smiled again.

"Don't worry. In a little while, you won't feel a thing." He stuck his hand inside each one of her pockets and dug out her phone, the flashlight, and the keys. "And you definitely won't be needing these."

He walked back to the counter and continued sifting through the bag.

Martin glanced over his shoulder and said, "Dude, what are we doing? Where's Stoller?"

"Stoller fucked up with the reporter," Gordon said. "He's not gonna mess this up too."

"Are you kidding me?" Martin asked. "You seriously haven't called him? He's gonna fuckin' kill you."

Gordon was taking items out of the bag and laying them on the counter. There was a blue strip of rubber, a box of syringes, and a tiny bag of white powder.

"It's all right, Seth," Rachel said. "He looks like he knows what he's doing."

Martin gave her an incredulous look. "Dude, let's just smoke this bitch. This is stupid."

Gordon sighed, turned, and tossed him the keys he had gotten from Rachel's pocket. "Go get her truck and bring it back here. It's parked at one of the offices around the corner from the center. It's a gray Tacoma."

He looked annoyed. "What the hell for?"

"We're gonna put her in it after I give her the first dose.

I know a good spot. We'll take her there and give her a couple more. Make sure it's done right this time."

"Why didn't you just let her drive her truck here in the first place?"

"Because I didn't want her out of my sight, dumbass. I wanted to know if she was going to text or call someone to tell them where she was going."

"Whatever, man. This is fucked." He studied Rachel for a second. "You can handle her on your own?"

"I got this. Hurry up."

Martin shook his head in frustration and stormed out.

Gordon picked up his gun and turned to Rachel. He waved it toward the bed. "Have a seat. And don't be stupid enough to think you can make a run for it."

She walked over and sat down. Tried to think of a way to get him talking. Maybe she could reason with him. Or at least get him to lower his guard so she could find a way to escape.

"He called you Flash," she said. "Flash Gordon. It's not the worst nickname, I guess. Is it because you're so quick to lose your temper?"

He put the gun down and opened a drawer, took out a large spoon, and then went to another drawer for a cigarette lighter. "Nope. It's about me being fast at something else, actually."

"What would that be?"

He looked at her. His smiling eyes turned inquisitive, wondering what she was up to. He walked over and crouched down beside her.

"You really want to know?" He put a hand on her knee.

"One weekend, we were on leave. Seth and I took a trip down to Savannah and partied our asses off all Friday night. The next day, I'm too hungover to drink. So Seth goes out on his own. A few hours go by, and he shows up back at the hotel with this girl. Just some drunk sorority chick, but she had a kick-ass little body. Kinda like yours."

His fingers started to massage her thigh.

"Seth starts taking her clothes off, telling me he's already done her out in the parking lot. Now she's talking like she wants a threesome. He looks at me and says, 'Dude, you gotta hit this.'"

He slid his hand up. Rachel pinned her forearms to the top of her thighs, blocking him.

He chuckled, stood up, and went back to the counter. "So I did. But I didn't last very long. I was done in a couple of seconds. Of course, Seth wasn't going to just keep something like that to himself. Pretty soon after that, the guys started calling me Flash."

Rachel was searching the room, looking for something heavy she could use to hit him with, but there was nothing. "Seems like a strange thing to brag about."

"Oh, it used to piss me off in the beginning." Gordon went to the sink and turned on the faucet. "But if you act like it bothers you, they'll just fuck with you even more."

He caught some water with the tablespoon, then dropped a few pinches of the white powder in and used a syringe to stir it. He grabbed the lighter, flicked it on, and held the flame under the spoon. Once the solution was heated enough, he stirred it again and sucked it up into the syringe. "Besides, it's not like you're going to be telling anyone."

He laid the utensils on the counter, picked up the blue

strip of rubber, and walked over to Rachel. He grabbed her by the wrist and pulled her arm straight.

"No." She wrenched free. "Please. You don't have to do this—"

He struck her with the back of his fist. It caught her on the cheek just below her right eye. She was dazed. Black spots appeared in her vision.

He yanked her wrists again and wrapped the rubber strip around her upper arm. He tied it tightly, then seized her throat and growled, "Don't make this any harder on yourself. It's either this, or I beat you to death with my bare fucking hands."

Her lip quivered. She nodded quickly, avoiding eye contact.

He let her go and went for the syringe. Holding it in his fingers, thumb on the plunger, he came back, ready to inject her. She recoiled, slid off the bed down to the floor. On her back, she kicked to get away from him.

"No, no, no, please." She held her arms tight to her chest. There was panic in her eyes.

He stepped over her and reached for her arm. Before he could grab it, she sat up, swung at his other hand, and knocked the syringe free. It flew across the room and hit the wall, disappearing on the other side of the bed.

"Fucking whore!"

He cocked back to punch her, but she was already moving. She rolled back and brought her hips up. Her left leg snaked around his right. Her other leg hooked behind his left knee. She kicked and he came crashing down.

Rachel kept her legs entwined with Gordon's. She shifted her hips closer to his and secured her hold on him.

His right leg was twisted awkwardly, and he was trapped. He flailed, pulling hard to free it, but Rachel had him locked in. She tucked his foot under her arm and hooked his heel with the crook of her elbow. It was one of the few jiu-jitsu techniques she could do with her hands bound.

With a grunt she twisted, using the power of her whole body against his ankle. She heard it pop, and he screamed in pain. But she wasn't finished. She straightened her legs on his contorted knee. She repositioned her hands and pushed on his shin to make it worse. Both of her hands and both of her legs worked against his cruciate ligaments. She felt them give, and he screamed even louder.

Pretending to be helpless, overcome by terror, had done the trick. He had underestimated her, and she had made him pay for that mistake.

She freed herself from his useless leg and got to her feet. He moaned and cursed as she ran to the far side of the bed and found the syringe. She came back and knelt beside him. "Don't worry, Flash. In a second, you won't feel a thing."

His eyes went wide as she stuck the needle into his neck and pushed on the plunger.

She wanted to give it all to him, but she didn't know how much he could take. She squeezed slowly until half of it was in his bloodstream. A second later, his eyes rolled back, and he was silent.

Rachel ran to the cabinets and pulled open the drawers until she found a knife. She held it like an icepick and carefully slid the blade between her wrist and the zip tie and started to saw. She kept checking the door and tried to think of how much time had passed since Martin had left to get the Tacoma.

"Come on," she said, working faster.

She sawed and pulled and sawed some more. The zip tie popped, and her hands were free. She dropped the knife, grabbed the .380, and slid it back into the holster. Then she grabbed Gordon's gun and checked to make sure a round was chambered.

She went to the door and peeked outside. The Charger was still there. Martin must have taken his own car, which had probably been hidden out back. She thought about taking off in the Charger, making her getaway before Martin returned. She was turning to go back for the keys when something caught her attention.

Through the trees, headlights bounced up the dirt road.

★ ★ ★

Martin stepped inside, spotted Gordon on the floor, and froze. "What the . . . ?" He pulled the gun from his waistband and quickly scanned the room. There was no sign of the woman. She must have made a run for it.

He approached Gordon, looked him over, and said, "Dude, your leg is fucked, bro."

Gordon moaned and exhaled white froth onto his lips.

Martin saw the syringe lying next to him and said, "Oh shit. Stoller's gonna be so pissed. I'm sorry, man, but I had to call him. He's on his—"

The hard ring of a muzzle tapped the back of his head. A woman's voice said, "Checkmate, bitch."

TWENTY-NINE

Rachel made Martin lay his gun on the floor and move away from it. She kicked it under the bed and said, "Where are my keys?"

He dug them out of his pocket and tossed them to her.

"Let's step outside," she said.

"Why? What are you gonna do?" His voice was taunting, but there was fear in it. "You gonna take me for a ride?"

"Maybe." She started backing toward the door. "I haven't made up my mind yet. If I were you, I'd be praying I don't decide to just shoot you."

"So you can be charged with another murder? Face it, you're in over your head."

"Shut up and start walking."

He followed her through the doorway. She glanced over her shoulder and spotted the Tacoma. Then she heard a sound coming from the field beyond the trees. The low roar of an engine. She looked over and saw headlights coming in fast.

"That'll be my buddy, Stoller," Martin said. "You're so fucked."

"Turn around."

He smirked. "You're not gonna shoot me."

"Do it!" she yelled.

He raised his hands and spun around slowly. "Tick tock, sweetheart. You're almost out of time."

"Tell me about it."

She aimed the gun at the back of his calf and fired. He dropped to the ground and rolled to his side, screaming and holding his leg.

Rachel turned and ran for the Tacoma. She jumped in and started the engine but left it in park. Outside, the flickering headlights became solid beams as they emerged from the trees. Rachel ducked down and waited.

The approaching vehicle came into view. It was a black F-150. It slid to a stop with its lights shining on the barn. The door opened and a large figure stepped out.

It was *him*.

Rachel felt herself trembling. The monster was coming for her. But he didn't know exactly where she was. The sound of the F-150's engine was masking the Tacoma's. He started for the barn, crossing directly in front of her.

He spotted Martin on the ground, heard him yelling something, and stopped. Suddenly, he turned to face her truck.

Rachel threw it in gear and slammed on the accelerator. The Tacoma shot forward and barreled straight for him. He stood his ground, and she braced herself to hit him. With only a few feet to spare, he jumped clear, landing just out of her path.

She turned and headed for the dirt road, flicking on the lights so she could maneuver through the trees. Behind her, Stoller was up and running for the F-150. She rounded a pair of tight turns, sliding into the grass and almost spinning out. When the road became a straight run to the clearing, she checked the rearview. A pair of sweeping beams told her Stoller was wheeling around in pursuit.

The Tacoma burst into the field. Rachel turned off the lights and banked hard to the left. She kicked the brake with both feet, skidding to a stop, then let off it and pushed the shifter into neutral, hoping Stoller hadn't seen her taillights make the turn.

In the side-view mirror, she could see that he was just entering the path through the trees. She spun to look through the back window and saw his headlights approaching quickly. In her head, she was working out the timing. It had to be perfect if she was to catch him.

The F-150 drew near the clearing, and Rachel shifted into reverse.

"Sorry, Carly."

She floored it, launching backward toward the road. The F-150 passed the last few trees and suddenly lurched to a stop, as if Stoller had seen her coming. But he was too late.

The back of the Tacoma slammed into the front corner of the F-150.

Rachel turned and searched the passenger seat for the gun, but couldn't find it. In the jolt of the impact, it had been thrown off. She remembered the .380 on her hip, jumped out, and drew it. She leveled it on Stoller's back tire and fired twice. Both shots hit the sidewall, and air hissed out.

Inside the cab, Stoller was fighting the airbag. He forced it aside enough to see out the window and caught sight of

Rachel. Their eyes locked. She pointed the gun at him and held it there, wanting to shoot him dead.

There was no fear in his eyes. He stared at her with cold resolve, a look that sent a shudder through her. She turned and ran back to the Tacoma, hopped in and put it in drive. She punched it, but it rolled forward only a foot before the tires lost traction, trying to drag Stoller's truck with it.

"Shit!" She turned on four-wheel drive and tried again.

The Tacoma broke free with a loud snap as the F-150's bumper tore off and dropped to the ground. Rachel hit the lights and steered onto the dirt road, speeding toward the highway. She kept checking the rearview, veering into the grass each time. The lights behind her grew dimmer as she made her escape.

★ ★ ★

Stoller forced his way out of the cab and examined his truck. It would drive once he changed the tire, but there was no sense in rushing. The woman was long gone now.

He walked back to the barn.

Martin was sitting up, still holding his leg and groaning in pain. Stoller walked past him and went inside to look around. Gordon was there on the floor, dizzy and confused. He looked like he was coming down from a good high. The lower half of his right leg was pointing the wrong way, like it was dislocated at the knee. He wouldn't be happy when the drugs wore off.

Stoller went back outside to talk to Martin.

"Looks like you boys got your asses handed to you."

"Dude," Martin said through gritted teeth, "my fuckin' leg, man. Bitch shot me."

Stoller had heard it as he was making his way across the field. He had worried that Gordon had lost his cool and shot the woman. But this was worse.

"You gotta get me to a hospital."

Much worse, Stoller thought. "I don't think I can do that."

"What the fuck are you talkin' about, man?"

"If I take you to the hospital with a gunshot wound, they'll call the cops." He reached around to the small of his back and withdrew a .40-caliber Sig Sauer.

"Wait! No, don't!"

He aimed the gun at Martin's forehead.

THIRTY

The bartender was quick to tell Hughes where he could find the regular who'd ended up wearing the Bud Light. She also gave him a name and a unit number—Austin Buckley, 201. Hughes walked across the street to Buckley's apartment and knocked on the door.

Buckley answered and rolled his eyes. "Don't tell me. Another damn cop."

He stepped back and let Hughes in, asked his skinny girlfriend to excuse herself to the bedroom, and dropped onto the sofa.

"My name's Chad Hughes. I'm a detective with the Siler City Police Department."

Buckley picked up a remote control and started flipping through the channels. "What can I do you for, Detective?"

"I hear you had an interesting encounter today. Mind telling me about it?"

"Not much to tell, really. A psycho woman went and poured my beer on me. Turns out, she's a damn murderer, according to y'all."

"Well, we're still trying to figure that out. Can I ask you why she did it? Pour the beer on you, I mean."

"I don't know." He settled on a fishing show and dropped the remote on the coffee table, sat back and put his feet up. "I guess she was trying to get me outside, away from everyone, so she could grill me."

"Grill you about what?"

"About some shit that happened in Afghanistan."

"Afghanistan," Hughes said, scratching his chin. He sat down in the love seat and leaned in with his elbows on his knees. "You were in the military?"

Buckley nodded, keeping his eyes on the screen. "Army."

"Okay. So what happened in Afghanistan that she was so curious about?"

The look on Buckley's face said he was tired of telling the story. "We was in this village looking for weapons, and some of our guys got shot at. So they killed the shooter, and it turned out to be a damn teenager."

"I'm sure that happens a lot over there."

"Damn straight, it does."

"Then what was so special about this time?"

"I don't know."

The man on the TV was holding a large wriggling bass by the mouth. He raised it up to the camera, struggling to maintain his grip.

Buckley said, "Damn, I need to catch me one of them."

Hughes reached over, grabbed the remote, and turned the TV off. "It occurs to me that I might not have your undivided attention."

"Hey, come on, man."

"Listen to me," he said, raising his voice, "one of my friends was killed yesterday. She was a good cop and an even better mother. Now she's dead, and I need to know why. So how about you take a break from the goddamn TV for a minute and tell me what the hell's going on."

"All right, man," Buckley said, putting his hands up. "Take it easy." He stood and went to the kitchen, grabbed a cigarette and a lighter, and came back. He lit up and took a puff. "Look, I wasn't there right when it happened, so I don't know what's true and what's not."

Hughes motioned with his hand, encouraging him to continue. "Go on."

"You hear things, you know. Guys talkin' shit and what-not. Some of the fellas in the platoon said they heard the kid was unarmed when they shot him. Just out in the field, mindin' his own business. Some even said he was out there kickin' a soccer ball. They said Sergeant Stoller found the AK and the grenade hidden under a blanket next to a mud hut. Then they saw the kid out there and came up with this idea to just shoot his ass and plant the weapons on him."

"Why shoot an innocent kid?"

Buckley shrugged. "For fun, I guess."

THIRTY-ONE

Rachel spotted an abandoned gas station ten miles outside Monroe and parked behind it. With the engine and the lights turned off, the darkness consumed everything. Only her breath disturbed the silence. Her heart raced, and her hands shook as she tried to wrap her mind around what she had been through.

There wasn't just one killer; there were three.

Luckily, there had been some discord between them. Apparently, Gordon and Stoller weren't seeing eye to eye. Had all three of them worked together to abduct her, she never would have made it out alive.

She turned on the overhead light and searched for Gordon's gun. It was lying on the floorboard on the passenger side. She picked it up and slid it under the driver's seat. Her iPhone was in the cup holder, but she had lost the prepaid. It was still at the barn.

She turned the phone on and called Braddock. When he answered, she was almost afraid to tell him what had happened, fearful that he would be furious with her for attempting a break-in. For getting in the Charger with

Gordon, which, in hindsight, was beyond stupid. But most of all, for not talking to Braddock about her plan beforehand.

It took some effort, but she finally got it out. He was speechless for a minute. Then he asked, "Are you somewhere safe?"

"Yes."

"You sure?"

"I'm sure."

"All right. I'm on my way there now. I left as soon as you sent me that text. I've got about an hour and a half left till I'm there. Stay put."

"I will. I promise."

It felt good to know that he would be there soon. She relaxed a little, turned off the light, and stepped out of the cab. She went around to the back and lit up the flashlight app on her phone to inspect the damage.

The bumper and the tailgate were crushed into a wide V. The end of the bed was rippled, and the taillights were broken on one side. If a cop had gotten behind her, she would've been pulled over.

Carly was going to be devastated. She would understand, of course, but that wouldn't make the Tacoma any easier to look at. Between this and the sheriff's office Tahoe she had destroyed a few months earlier, the citizens of Lowry County would never trust her with one of their vehicles again.

She climbed into the bed and lay back, putting her feet up on the lip of the bent tailgate. The adrenaline was gone, taking her energy with it. She was exhausted, but there was no chance she would be able to sleep. So she lay there, waiting for Braddock to arrive, gazing into the starless night.

* * *

Braddock called earlier than she had expected. Or perhaps time had gotten away from her as she lay in the back of the truck, feeling like she had been immersed in some kind of sensory-deprivation chamber. The ringing came impossibly loud, jarring her away from her dazed meditation.

She sat up and answered. He was getting close. She gave him directions to the gas station, then hung up and climbed out of the bed. He pulled up a few minutes later.

"I think you've just about used up all of your lives, young lady," he said, hugging her.

He wanted to hear the story again, this time with more detail. She told him everything. Leaning against the side of the Tacoma, he took it all in, trying not to look too devastated about the fact that he'd nearly lost her.

She finished, and he said, "We should call it in. Have the locals raid the place. They probably rushed to the hospital, but your phone could still be there. Maybe even the heroin."

"They could make up any story they wanted to explain it all," she said. "It would be my word against theirs. And I'm a suspect in a homicide investigation. We just don't know enough yet. We've got to figure out what this is all about. What they're trying to hide."

"Hmph." He thought for a moment. "It's gotta be the drugs. Maybe Larson and Hubbard were in on it, and the others decided to cut them out."

"Maybe." She thought about Gulani, and a surge of anger came over her. "There's definitely some connection to the therapist. He spends his days counseling addicts. Maybe he's helping them find customers. Or dealers. Either way, he sent Gordon after me. And just when I was starting to warm up to the guy. Kinda hurts my feelings, to be honest."

"I want to break his freakin' neck."

"Answers first," she said. "We can break his neck later."

"When do you want to go after him?"

She wanted to go right then, but she was still feeling shaky. She needed food and rest, though she didn't know if she'd be able to eat, and sleep seemed like an impossibility. But she had to try. "First thing in the morning. I don't want to go off half-cocked and risk running into Stoller again. He's probably pretty sore with me for wrecking his truck. Let's find some place to hole up for the night and come up with a plan of attack."

"Roger that. I saw a hotel on the highway a few miles—"

Rachel's phone rang. She checked the screen, then held it up to show Braddock. He gave her a look that asked what she was going to do.

She answered.

"Hello, Detective Hughes."

"Miss Carver," he said, sounding surprised that she had answered. "I've been trying to get ahold of you all day."

"Sorry about that. I've been a little busy."

"So I've heard. I met a friend of yours this evening."

"Yeah? Who would that be?"

"Austin Buckley. He told me an interesting story, though I don't know quite what to make of it. Any chance you'd be willing to come in and clear it up for me?"

"I'm still trying to figure it out for myself."

"Well, you and I still need to meet, regardless. Face-to-face. How about you come to the station in Siler City and talk to me about what happened yesterday?"

"Not yet," she said. "But you have my word, when this is all over, I'll come see you."

"You're in a lot of trouble, Miss Carver. And you're not doing yourself any favors by avoiding me. This will all go a lot easier if we can sit down together and sort this out."

"Take care, Detective."

She ended the call and turned off her phone.

Braddock said, "I'm surprised you answered that. Unless he's a complete idiot, he's gonna track you here."

"I can't hide from him forever. Besides, I think I might have an idea."

★ ★ ★

Hughes was on the edge of Fayetteville, heading back to Siler City. He wheeled his unmarked Crown Victoria into a shopping center and called Morrison, who was still at the office.

"I got her."

"What do you mean?" Morrison asked.

"I called her, and she actually answered her phone."

"Seriously? I figured she was too smart to even turn it on."

"So did I. I guess it never hurts to try."

There were the sounds of mouse clicks and typing on a keyboard. "I'm putting her number into the carrier search website . . . hang on . . . she uses AT&T."

"Perfect. Mind calling them for me?"

"I'm on it," she said. "I'll call you back in a few."

Morrison would be able to get the phone's GPS location from the service provider. They charged a fee for the information, but it would happen quickly. The state of North Carolina didn't even require that she get a warrant before asking.

A half hour had passed when Morrison called back. "She's in Union County. Just outside Monroe."

"That's a couple hours away," Hughes said, starting the engine. "I'll probably have to stay the night there."

"Want me to book you a hotel?"

"Nah, I'll take care of that. But if you don't mind, I'd love it if you could call over to the Union County Sheriff's Office and let them know I'm on the way. See if they can send a deputy or two to hold her until I get there."

"You got it. Good hunting, Chad."

★ ★ ★

Rachel left the Tacoma at the abandoned gas station and rode with Braddock. They stopped at a Walmart, and Braddock went inside to buy Rachel some clothes and toiletries while she waited in the Explorer. When he got back, they picked up cheeseburgers from McDonald's and drove to a nearby Holiday Inn, where they got a room with two queen beds.

Once they were settled in and had finished eating, Rachel took a long shower. Braddock scanned the local channels for any news about her but didn't find anything. She came out of the bathroom wearing the sweat pants and an oversized T-shirt he had intended as makeshift pajamas. The shirt was sky blue, and the front was covered with a picture of Dale Earnhardt Jr.'s race car. She pointed at it and said, "Seriously?"

He laughed.

She eased herself onto the bed and lay back, staring at the ceiling. "I think I know how to kill two birds with one stone."

Braddock turned the volume down on the TV. "Let's hear it."

"Hughes is chasing me around the state. He was in Fayetteville today, talking to Buckley. He won't be content with calling the locals and telling them I'm here. He's coming for me himself."

"All right. So how does that help us?"

"I think I'm going to let him do some of our work for us."

THIRTY-TWO

Stoller decided it was a bad idea to leave Martin's body lying around while he changed the tire on his truck. He needed to get rid of it quickly in case the woman decided to go to the cops. He didn't think she would, given her circumstances, but he couldn't be sure.

He went into the barn and tore the blanket off the bed. Got a flashlight from a drawer and left his phone on the counter. Then he went outside and wrapped up the body and loaded it into the trunk of Gordon's Charger. He threw a shovel in and went back to check on Gordon.

"I gotta borrow your car, Flash."

Gordon turned his head in Stoller's direction but looked right through him.

"All right, then," Stoller said. "Take it easy. I'll be back in a couple of hours."

He hopped into the Charger and drove to a remote spot on the other end of town. He saw the gated entrance and sped past it, slowing once he found the best spot to traverse the swale beyond the shoulder. He left the road and dropped down, then turned up and climbed a gentle rise, stopping at the edge of a pine grove. With no light from above, he couldn't see through to the other side of it, but he knew what was there.

A large plantation house stood in the center of a sprawling field. The Union County Historic Preservation Commission had designated the property a protected site. They had also spent a good bit of money landscaping the grounds. The work had been completed just a few days earlier.

Stoller popped the trunk, pulled Martin out, and hefted him onto his shoulder. He grabbed the shovel and started his march through the woods. Emerging on the other side, he needed his flashlight to orient himself. He set Martin down on the ground and started pulling up pieces of the freshly laid sod. When he had exposed a large enough area, he started digging.

Excavation was forbidden on historical sites. There would be no construction here for the foreseeable future. No one to disturb the grounds and discover the remains that Stoller was putting to rest.

When he started, he was planning to go six feet deep, but he got too tired and had to stop short. Standing in the hole, the ground level was at the center of his chest, and he decided that was good enough. He climbed out and pushed Martin in, then filled in the hole and smoothed it out. Once he thought the ground looked even enough, he started replacing the sod rectangles, a jigsaw puzzle of grass. He hoped it would look right in the daylight. In a few days, the roots would take hold, and no one would be able to tell that he'd been there.

Stoller clicked off his flashlight, stared at the wet grass, and said, "Good-bye, brother."

In the Army, your fellow soldiers were your family. You

depended on them for your survival. You loved and hated one another, but protected each other all the same. It was a bond more powerful, more real, than shared genetics. And Stoller had just broken it.

When he'd killed Larson, he'd felt justified. CID had been investigating the shooting in Guldara, and Larson was working with them to betray his brothers. Stoller had been happy to do the job. But since then, he'd found something even more important to protect. Regardless of his duty to his squad, Martin's gunshot wound had put that in danger.

So he had fired without hesitation. The cold calculus of minimizing risk had demanded such action. Swift and dispassionate. But now, standing at Martin's graveside, he allowed himself to feel it. And the weight of his emotions overcame him. He fell to his knees and wept, even though he knew, no matter how much it hurt, he had done what was necessary.

★ ★ ★

Stoller went back to the barn and cleaned himself up. Gordon had managed to climb onto the bed before passing out again. He woke up and started complaining about his leg. Stoller offered to set it back in place, but Gordon refused.

"I need a hospital," he said.

Stoller examined the twisted limb. "Yeah, it looks pretty fucked up."

"Bitch did a number on me, man."

"That's what you get for trying to do this shit without me. Now hang on, and I'll bring the car around."

Gordon mumbled something unintelligible and nodded off.

Stoller went out to the Charger and drove it right up to the door. He opened the passenger side and laid the seat back down, then went inside and collected Gordon. As he carried him out, Gordon's leg dangled loosely. It bumped the doorjamb, and Gordon woke with a yell.

"Sorry, Flash," Stoller said. "We're almost there."

He set him in the seat gingerly and buckled him up. Then he got in and drove him to the emergency room at the Carolinas Medical Center on the east end of town.

The admitting nurse came out to the car and stared at Gordon's leg with wide eyes. "What happened to him?"

"He fell in a hole and twisted it."

She looked at him in disbelief, then made a note on a clipboard. She knelt down and said, "Just sit tight, baby; we're going to have to put you in a gurney."

He moaned and mumbled.

She stood and leaned toward Stoller and whispered, "Is he on anything?"

"I think he might've taken some old painkillers he had lying around."

She made another note and went inside.

Gordon opened his eyes and said, "Stoller . . . you gotta call my mom. You gotta tell her I'm here."

"You sure about that?"

"Yeah, man. Please."

"If that's what you want," he said, "I'll do it. But you know she's not going to be happy."

THIRTY-THREE

Hughes turned into the parking lot of the abandoned gas station and went around to the back. A Union County sheriff's deputy was sitting in his patrol car with the door open and his leg hanging out. As Hughes approached, he asked, "You the detective from Siler City?"

"That's me."

"Well, sorry to tell you, but your girl was long gone by the time we got here."

"Figures." Hughes clicked on a tiny flashlight and started looking over the Tacoma.

The deputy climbed out of his patrol car and shuffled over. "Looks like someone rear-ended her pretty good."

He aimed the light at the bent license plate and took a picture with his smartphone. "Any calls about it?"

"Nope. 'Course, I guess that makes sense when you think about it."

"Yeah? How so?"

"Well . . . whoever hit her wouldn't have wanted us to get involved. And she sure as hell wasn't gonna call."

"Mm-hmm." Hughes crouched down to get a closer

look at the tailgate. "Let me ask you something. Have you worked a lot of traffic accidents?"

"I seen my share. Why?"

"It seems to me that an impact like this would have to come from an angle." He stood and motioned with his hand. "If she was hit from behind, that is."

"Yeah? So?"

"So a vehicle moving fast enough to do that kind of damage, striking at that angle, wouldn't have just stopped in its tracks. Both vehicles would've bounced away from each other." He used both hands to demonstrate. "Sort of like when you're playing pool and the cue ball hits one of the other balls at an angle."

"Okay?"

"That would've left horizontal scratches as the other vehicle tore away." He shined the light on the tailgate and the bumper. "See any of those here?"

The deputy clicked on his own flashlight, ran it over the back of the truck, and said, "All right, so what do you think did this?"

Hughes moved around to the driver's side and scanned the bed, then looked inside the cab. "I'd say she was probably running in reverse and hit something that was sitting still. There's a few flecks of paint in the tailgate and some chrome on the bumper, so it was most likely another vehicle."

"Well, hell," the deputy said, crouching down and squinting, "if she'd have hit me like that, I definitely would've called it in."

Hughes came back around and saw the deputy reaching out to flick a chip off the bumper. "Please don't touch that."

He stood and backed away, looking embarrassed. "I guess you want me to call in our crime scene unit?"

"No, actually, I'd just like you to sit here and make sure no one touches this thing until the SBI crime scene search unit I called shows up."

Hughes stepped away and called Morrison to let her know what he'd found. She was home now, getting ready for bed. She asked, "Any idea whose truck it is?"

"Not yet," he said. "I'll get them to run the plate for me."

"Not if you don't play nice, you won't."

★ ★ ★

A half hour later, the Union County sheriff was sitting on the corner of his desk, looking down at Hughes as he said, "I hear you were kinda short with my deputy out there."

Hughes gave him his best conciliatory smile and said, "I'm sorry, Sheriff. It's been a long day. I feel like I've been running all over the state of North Carolina trying to figure out why my friend was shot and killed yesterday."

The sheriff looked down and changed his tone. "Well, I'm real sorry about that, Detective." He went back to his chair. "Obviously, we want to assist you in any way we can."

"Thank you, Sheriff. Can you spare a deputy to escort me around while I do some digging?"

He gave a deep nod. "Absolutely. What kind of digging, if you don't mind me asking?"

"Not at all," he said. "My suspect questioned a guy at a bar in Fayetteville, then took off and headed this way. Turns out a few names came up. Two of them, a gentleman named Riley Gordon and a gentleman named Colin Stoller; both live in this area. I'd like to talk to them, if I can?"

"All right," he said with another nod. "Let's see if we can't dig 'em up for you. I'll get one of my boys to carry you around town."

★ ★ ★

It turned out to be a frustrating night for Hughes. He rode with the deputy to Stoller's house first. No one was home, and the neighbors said he was gone a lot. Whenever he was there, he kept to himself. They didn't know much about him except that he was quiet and could intimidate the hell out of someone by just glancing at them.

Next, they drove to Gordon's apartment in the heart of Monroe. He had a better reputation with his neighbors, but none of them knew where he was. They said during hunting season, he would take off and stay at some property he had just outside of town. It was too early for hunting, but maybe he had gone there.

With the deputy yawning and Hughes feeling spent, they gave up and went back to the sheriff's office. Hughes wanted to try again in the morning after a good night's sleep. The deputy agreed, and they parted ways.

A few miles outside of town, Hughes found a Hampton Inn and got a room. He'd brought his toothbrush and a change of clothes with him when he'd left for Fayetteville, just in case. He was grateful he didn't have to go shopping. He had a hot shower and put on a late-night talk show as he lounged in bed. It seemed like he had just started to fall asleep when the phone woke him in the morning.

He opened one eye and checked the time on the alarm clock. It was a little after 9 AM. He fumbled for his phone on the nightstand, then held it up to read the screen.

Rachel Carver.

He sat up and answered, suddenly wide awake.

"Hello, Detective," she said. "Is there any chance you're in Monroe this fine morning?"

"Um . . . well . . ."

"I'll take that as a yes. If you feel like having a nice breakfast, I'd recommend the Skinny Hen Diner on Main Street. But you'd better hurry. You've got ten minutes. Come alone."

"Ten minutes? I don't even know where it is. Hello . . . ?"

She was gone. He jumped up and scrambled to get dressed. Then he typed the name of the diner into Google Maps and checked the directions as he slid on his shoes. He was out the door with eight minutes to spare.

THIRTY-FOUR

Rachel was standing on the corner of Windsor and Beasley, two blocks away from the Skinny Hen. She couldn't see it, but she had Braddock on the phone. He was inside, seated at the bar, sipping coffee and keeping an eye on Gulani. They had followed him there from his house, then split up as he'd gone inside for a table.

"Hughes should be there any minute now," she said.

"Good," Braddock said in a low voice. "Sigmund just got his order in."

Braddock had chosen the code name. Sigmund Freud wasn't the most creative reference for a therapist under surveillance, but it was adequate for their needs.

"I gotta tell you," he said, "this guy sure as hell doesn't look like any kind of drug kingpin I've ever seen."

"Who did you expect him to look like? Tony Montana?"

"Hey, there's a code name."

"It is better than Sigmund."

"Yeah . . . wait. I got something. I think our detective friend is here. He just rushed in. He's looking around for you. Now he's going back outside."

"I'll call you back." She got off the phone with Braddock and called Hughes. He answered, and she said, "Glad you could make it."

"I don't see you," he said.

"That's because I'm not there."

She heard him exhale sharply into the phone. "I'm not in the mood to play games, Miss Carver."

"I don't blame you, Detective. You lost a fellow officer, and I lost a friend. I promise you, we're on the same side. If you want to figure this out, then let me help you."

"I'm listening."

"The man you're looking for is named Colin Stoller. He killed Bryce and Ramirez and set me up. But he's not working alone. There are at least three others involved."

"Let me guess, Seth Martin, Riley Gordon, and who? Austin Buckley?"

"Not Buckley, but you're right about the other two. They abducted me last night. They were going to dose me, just like they tried to do with Bryce, but I managed to escape."

"That's quite a story," he said. "Can you prove any of it?"

"I'm working on it, but I could use some help, if you don't mind."

He laughed. "Miss Carver, I'm more inclined to arrest you than to help you at this point."

"That's understandable. So how about we make a deal. You question my third suspect in this conspiracy, and I'll tell you exactly where you can find the gun Stoller used to kill Bryce and Officer Ramirez."

"Okay," he said, sounding cautiously intrigued by the

idea. "Are you telling me you have the murder weapon and you've been keeping it from the law enforcement officers investigating this case?"

"It's not quite that simple."

"Jesus." He was quiet while he considered her offer. "All right, Miss Carver, I'll bite. Who's your third suspect, and where do I find him?"

"His name is Manish Gulani, and he's sitting in the diner, by himself in the third booth on the right when you walk through the door."

"Manish Gulani . . ." She got the sense that he was walking inside to look for him. His voice was lower when he asked, "What exactly am I supposed to ask him?"

"I went to see him last night. I wanted to know about a murder victim who was a former patient of his. That victim also served in the Army with our other suspects. He told me where to find the information I was looking for, but when I got there, Gordon was waiting for me. He told me Gulani sent him."

"So . . . you want me to just walk up to him and ask if he arranged to have you kidnapped and murdered last night?"

"I'll trust you to figure that out, Detective. You've gotten this far."

She hung up. A few seconds later, she got a text from Braddock. HE'S SITTING DOWN.

★ ★ ★

Hughes slid into the booth, holding up his badge and ID.

"Good morning, Mr. Gulani. Mind if I join you?"

Gulani had a forkful of food an inch away from his

mouth. He froze and stared wide-eyed at the badge. A wedge of wet egg fell and slapped the edge of his plate before tumbling into his lap. He put his utensils down, grabbed a napkin, and tried to clean it up. But his eyes kept darting up to Hughes and the ID.

"Um . . . what can I do for you, Officer?"

"Detective," Hughes said, stuffing his wallet back into his pocket. "I need to know if you've had any contact with a woman named Rachel Carver."

He looked around quickly. "I suppose I have, yes."

"And when was that, exactly?"

His eyes went to the table. "It was the day before yesterday."

"Friday?"

"Yes, sir. She came to the treatment center where I work. She wanted to talk to me about a former patient of mine."

"Uh-huh." Hughes was studying Gulani's expression. "And you haven't seen her since?"

Gulani looked around again, glanced at Hughes, and then put his eyes back on the table. He was trying to think of something to say.

"I already know she came to see you last night. So you might want to think carefully about what you say next, in case you're thinking of lying to me."

"I don't think I should be talking to you," he said.

"You don't think so, huh?" Hughes smelled blood. He decided to try a gambit. "Well, that's up to you, but I gotta tell you, silence might not be your best option right now. You see, Miss Carver turned up dead this morning, and as far as I can tell, you might've been the last one to see her alive."

Gulani looked shocked. His head started shaking. "What? No . . . I don't . . . I don't know anything about what you are saying."

Hughes reached over to his plate and grabbed a sausage link. "You have a good day, Mr. Gulani. We'll be in touch."

He took a bite of the sausage and stood from the booth.

"Wait," Gulani said.

Hughes was headed for the door. Gulani jumped up and dug his wallet out of his pocket, dropped a twenty on the table, and hurried after him.

★ ★ ★

Rachel answered her phone, and Braddock said, "That was interesting."

"What happened?"

"They talked for a minute, then Hughes got up to leave, and Gulani ran after him. They're outside now."

Rachel wanted to start walking that way to see for herself, but she knew that would be a bad idea. She didn't want to risk Hughes spotting her. "Are they talking?"

"Yep. Looks like Gulani's desperate to set the record straight about something."

There was a scream.

Braddock said, "What the . . . shit!"

"Danny? Danny, what is it?"

The line was dead. In the direction of the diner, Rachel heard the pop and roar of a gunshot.

THIRTY-FIVE

Screams and gunfire. People running from the vicinity of the diner. A minivan sped up the street, the terrified woman behind the wheel trying desperately to maneuver it away from danger while yelling at a child to get down.

Rachel was running toward the shots. She squeezed her way through a group of churchgoers fleeing the chaos and pulled the .380 from her hip. She got to the corner of Main and went straight for a black sedan parked on the side of the street, crouching down next to the front wheel on the passenger side.

The screams had stopped. There was a moment of calm, and Rachel peeked over the hood to see if she could spot the shooter. Directly across the street, a man was crawling beneath a large pickup truck. A couple was huddled in the recessed entrance of a store. A woman, sitting on the curb with a child in her arms, scrambled to her feet and ran for the corner.

A shot made Rachel duck. There was a sharp crack, followed by the echo of the report as it reverberated off the buildings. She realized it had come from further up the street. The violence had shifted away from the front of the diner.

She stayed low and moved to the rear wheel and carefully looked over the trunk.

Across the street, less than thirty yards away, Stoller moved behind a silver SUV. Through the windows of the car behind it, she could see him with his arms outstretched. He held a black semiauto, and it looked like he had it trained on another car somewhere further ahead. He fired a pair of shots and stepped around the SUV before sprinting to get behind the next car in the line.

He was moving in on his target, firing a couple of rounds at a time to keep their heads down while he advanced on them. Rachel had to halt his advance before he got there, but he was out of sight now. She looked up the sidewalk and found an oak tree that would give her cover. There was a gap, though, between it and the last car on this side of the street. She would be exposed, if only for a second.

She ran to the last car and huddled by the rear wheel. The tree was directly in front of her. It couldn't have been more than thirty feet, but it might as well have been a mile, if Stoller caught her in the open.

She flinched before she registered that another shot had been fired. Then there were two more in quick succession. Stoller was making another run.

Rachel had to move. She backed up a few paces, hoping she could use the extra space to get up to full speed by the time she cleared the car. She took a couple of quick breaths and broke into a sprint. The cars across the street became a blur in her peripheral vision.

Somewhere in that haze of colored shapes, Stoller was behind cover, possibly taking aim, matching her pace as he prepared to fire. He wouldn't take the shot until she was just a step away from safety. The bullet would strike her in midstride and she would spill to the ground, dying on a sidewalk on a beautiful summer day in Monroe.

She skidded to a stop behind the tree and leaned against it for just a moment to steady herself. She had made it unscathed. And, as far as she could tell, she hadn't been spotted.

She extended her arms and braced her shooting hand against the trunk. Her feet edged sideways a few inches at a time, keeping her stance balanced as she circled to search for Stoller. She was adding a sliver to her visual field with each step. Then he appeared.

Leaning against the trunk of a car, he looked ready to make another run. She took aim, but he shifted away from her, moving to the corner on the passenger side. It was no longer a clean shot—she had missed her opportunity. She cursed at herself for not putting him down the night before. Her fear of being charged with another murder . . . her fear that he would somehow survive her attempt to gun him down in the cab of his truck . . . had kept her from pulling the trigger. She regretted that decision now. If anyone died today, it would be because she had failed to act when she'd had the chance.

Out of the corner of her eye, she saw Braddock. He was two cars away from Stoller, reaching around the hood, searching for a target. Hughes was doing the same on the other side.

Stoller fired, and Hughes ducked. Then he came back up and shot twice. He turned and looked at Braddock, yelled something and held up his pistol. It looked like he was out of ammo. Braddock moved to his side and fired a single shot.

Stoller had a fresh magazine in his hand. He fired, then ejected the spent magazine and slid the new one in.

Rachel took a deep breath and exhaled it slowly, aimed at the corner of the car window where she expected to see Stoller pass by, and waited.

Stoller rose, fired twice, and started to move.

Rachel squeezed her trigger and felt the gun pop in her hand. The window became a haze of shattered glass. From that distance, she couldn't see through it, but she knew he hadn't made it to the next car. Her shot had stopped him.

"Danny," she yelled, "he's on the sidewalk."

Stoller rose, blood streaming down his cheek on the left side of his face. She tried to aim at him, but he was too fast. Bark exploded off the oak as he fired a volley at her. She spun for cover and crouched down.

There were other shots—Braddock returning fire. Stoller fired back at him. She looked around the other side of the tree to see if she could help.

Stoller was moving away, firing a shot every few steps to cover his retreat. Sirens blared from several directions. Rachel stood and tried to get a sight picture, but Stoller was running hard now. He turned a corner and disappeared.

"Rachel," Braddock yelled. "Are you all right?"

"Yeah. You?"

"I'm good. But you better get over here."

She rushed across the street, staying low and keeping an eye toward the corner in case Stoller returned. When she got there, Braddock and Hughes were knelt over Gulani. He was on his back, unconscious. His shirt was blood-soaked and his lips were turning blue.

"He's losing blood too fast," Braddock said, pressing his hands against a spot on his shoulder.

Hughes was on his phone trying to guide an ambulance their way. Two Monroe PD patrol cars were stopped up the street by the diner. She could see one of the officers. He had his weapon out, held low as he talked to a hysterical woman pointing in their direction.

Rachel lifted Gulani's shirt and spotted a second wound seeping blood. It was in his abdomen, just under his ribcage. She dropped to her knees and covered the hole with her hands and pushed against it, trying to slow the bleeding.

"Where are they?" she asked Hughes.

He shook his head and started cursing at the 911 operator.

Gulani's breathing was rapid and shallow, and Rachel knew, no matter how much pressure they kept on the wounds, they wouldn't be able to stop them from bleeding internally.

Braddock looked at her and said, "He's not gonna make it."

THIRTY-SIX

Stoller turned into an industrial park on the north end of town and hid the F-150 between a pair of red cargo containers. He killed the engine and checked his face in the mirror. The woman had almost made a direct hit. Luckily, her bullet had struck the car's rear door at the base of the window, sending pieces of glass and metal flying after him.

There was a hole just beneath his cheekbone. Something was inside it—glass or a bullet fragment. He tried to dig it out, sucking a breath through clenched teeth as the pain grew. But it was deep, and his fingers were too large.

He gave up, knowing that it didn't matter anyway. In a few hours, he would be dead. He had accepted that now. There was no saving him. Duty demanded that he protect what was most important to him, and that required a sacrifice.

But first, he needed a car.

He grabbed his bag and got out, moved to the corner of the container, and looked around. The park housed a logistics center where tractor trailers were loaded with goods for delivery around the state. It was closed on Sunday, so the expanse of concrete surrounding the warehouse was barren. There was no one around.

He ran along a fence at the edge of the pavement. Overhanging trees on the adjacent property offered some cover. He got to the end of the fence and watched the road beyond, keeping an eye out for cops. Across the street, another fence separated the industrial area from a neighborhood.

A car approached. A large sedan with an old man behind the wheel. Stoller turned around and leaned against the fence, showing the driver his back and trying to look like he belonged there. After the car passed, he turned around and gave the street a final look. It was clear.

He dashed across and tossed his bag over the fence, then propped his foot and scaled it. When he cleared the top, he didn't bother trying to lower himself gently. He dropped to the ground, crashing on his side. It took some of his wind away, but he didn't mind. The pain made him feel alive. Soon enough, he wouldn't feel anything at all.

He jumped up and grabbed his bag, then ran to the side of the nearest house. Voices came through a window—a man and a woman. He listened for a minute, hoping he wouldn't hear children. They sounded older, perhaps in their sixties. If they had grandkids, they weren't around today.

He reached into the bag and took out his gun. There was a side door to the garage. He tested it and found that it was unlocked. He crept in and looked around.

A pair of SUVs were crammed into the space. A Nissan Pathfinder and a Hyundai Tucson. The Tucson looked newer. It was white and inconspicuous and probably belonged to the woman. He would take it and make his way north. After a quick stop, of course. He had to say good-bye.

The old couple would have to be detained. He had come prepared for that. Inside the bag, there was duct tape and the package of zip ties Gordon had bought for the woman. There was also some rope he could use to secure them to something heavy and rigid, like a bed frame. He would tie them up and destroy their phones and make his escape.

Eventually, someone would find them, and the car would become a target. But he was willing to bet that he could get where he needed to go and do what he needed to do before that happened. He only needed a few hours.

THIRTY-SEVEN

The emergency room doors opened up with a frenzy as the EMTs handed Gulani off to the doctor and his team of nurses. They wheeled him around a corner and through another pair of doors into a hall, making their way to a trauma bay. Rachel could hear the doctor yelling orders as the automatic doors drew to a close.

Then there was silence. The first instant of calm since the shooting had started. Downtown, things were different, Rachel knew. Monroe PD officers and Union County sheriff's deputies were scouring the streets, talking to witnesses, and searching every nook and cranny to make sure Stoller wasn't still there, wandering around on foot or hiding in some alley-way. A SWAT team had been dispatched to his house, but they had come up empty—no sign of him or his truck.

Rachel looked at her hands, coated with sticky blood, and tried to take stock of what had happened. And, more importantly, why. Her first thought was that Stoller had seen Gulani as a liability. He had come after him in an attempt to keep him from talking. But to gun him down in broad daylight in front of a hundred witnesses? What crime could he be trying to cover up? What could be worse than first-degree murder? He had to know that he would never get away with shooting Gulani dead in the street. Every cop in town was now after him. It didn't make any sense.

Unless it wasn't the crime that he was trying to hide.

A thought struck Rachel. She started for the admissions counter, but a hand stopped her. It was Hughes. He had been outside on his phone, but he was back now and he looked furious. He pushed her against the wall and put a finger in her face.

"Enough fucking around," he said.

Braddock yelled, "Hey," and started for Hughes. "Get off her."

Rachel put her hand up and said, "It's okay, Danny."

He stopped short, but his hands were clenched into fists. His eyes threatened violence.

Hughes didn't back down. He said, "I don't like getting shot at. I want to know what the hell is going on, and I want to know right now."

Rachel explained everything. She told him about her time on the Larson case as an SBI agent, how it seemed to be connected to the Hubbard murder, though she didn't know exactly how yet. She told him about Parker's story and how he had located a witness. When she described Stoller's attack on them at Ramirez's house, Hughes finally eased back, giving her some room.

Braddock, calmer now that Hughes was no longer in Rachel's face, chimed in. "We think it might be about the heroin. Could be, they got their hands on some raw opium in Afghanistan. And maybe that firefight in Larson's journal had something to do with it."

Hughes exhaled a deep breath and said, "Well, I don't know anything about heroin, but when I talked to Buckley, he said there was a rumor about that attack. He said he'd heard that they weren't attacked at all. Some of the guys in their platoon were saying that Stoller and the others just shot an innocent kid for the hell of it."

"Damn," Braddock said. "That's messed up. Doesn't really help us, though, does it?"

Rachel was staring at the floor, thinking. She felt the blood, dried and crusty on her palms, and said, "I need to go wash up."

Braddock looked at his own hands. "Yeah, me too."

She went to the restroom and scrubbed the blood off, left her fingers soaking under the running water as her mind shifted into high gear. The faces of the killers appeared to her. Stoller, cold and calm, a relentless force with no emotion. Martin, cautious and nervous, who hid his fear with curses and taunts. And Gordon, the man with the temper.

Then she thought about Hubbard.

She dried her hands and went out to find Braddock and Hughes seated in the waiting area. Hughes reached over, shook Braddock's hand, and said, "By the way, thanks for saving my ass."

Braddock had told Rachel the story on the ride to the hospital. He had heard a scream from outside, looked in its direction, and saw Stoller approaching with a gun. He had jumped up and run for the door, drawing his weapon along the way. Stoller shot Gulani twice, saw Hughes going for his service pistol, and took aim. Standing in the middle of the sidewalk, taken completely by surprise, Hughes was an easy target.

Braddock had come out shooting. He had missed, but it had been enough to get Stoller to dive behind a car. Then he'd helped Hughes pull Gulani to safety.

"Anytime," Braddock said.

"Mind if I interrupt this little love fest?" Rachel asked.

He looked up at her. "Shoot."

"Poor choice of words," Hughes said.

Rachel asked, "What are the chances that four homicidal maniacs would all find each other in the same squad in the Army?"

Braddock looked at her like he hadn't understood the question. "What are you thinking?"

"I'm thinking about living in constant fear and anger . . ." She paced in front of them. Her hands gestured as she spoke, as if they were urging the words up and out of her. ". . . and about wanting to get payback for being attacked all the time."

Hughes leaned back in his seat. "I can sympathize."

"And I'm thinking about peer pressure." She stopped walking and sat down. "Especially the kind of peer pressure that young soldiers can put on each other."

Braddock said, "You've got a theory?"

She nodded. "Larson's journal talks about the frustration of dealing with asymmetrical warfare. How they were always getting sniped at or hit with a grenade or an IED. But, for a while, they never got any payback. And they never got any warning from the villagers, so some of the guys started seeing all of them as Taliban or al-Qaeda sympathizers."

"You think they decided to take it out on this Afghani kid?" Hughes asked.

"Maybe some of them did. Imagine, you're a nineteen-year-old private. Your buddies are all talking trash about wanting to kill an enemy. They say they might as well just shoot a villager, because they're all terrorist sympathizers anyway. Savages, is what they called them. And you, as that nineteen-year-old kid, start to join in on the trash talking.

"Then one day, it's not just talk anymore. Three of your squad mates, all higher rank and a little older than you, decide it's time to act. They spot a target out in a field, and they want to take it out. They all aim their rifles and get ready to fire. And right up to that very instant, you've been acting like you're on the exact same page with them. You really just wanted to fit in, but now it's about to actually happen. What do you do?"

"You go along with it," Hughes said.

Braddock shook his head. "I wouldn't. I *couldn't*."

"But would you have the courage to stop them?" she asked. "Right then and there, with someone like Stoller in charge of you?"

His expression changed. He looked less certain, as if he was conceding that her narrative was plausible.

"You just became Adam Hubbard," she said. "Imagine how he must've felt, watching this teenager get murdered by his friends. Maybe even taking part in it. He's tortured by guilt. He gets pills for a back injury, but they're really to mask a different kind of pain."

"I'd buy that," Braddock said.

She looked at Hughes. "You said Buckley told you there was a rumor that Stoller and the others shot the teenager for the hell of it."

"Yeah?"

"What might you do if you were Larson and you got wind of that rumor?"

"I guess I might call CID," he said.

"Exactly. But it's a difficult thing to prove. A shooting

that's several years old. A crime scene that's half a world away. The investigators probably tell Larson they need a witness. Or perhaps one of the shooters to turn on the others."

Braddock said, "I know who I'd choose out of that bunch, if I were Larson."

"Which explains the phone calls leading up to Larson's death," she said. "He was trying to convince Hubbard to flip."

Hughes: "So they kill Larson, thinking that'll be enough to make it go away?"

Rachel nodded. "Killing both of them at the same time would've made the connection obvious. And without Larson to prod him, they probably expected Hubbard to just lose himself in a bottle of pills. Which is pretty much what happened until Parker came along asking questions. I think Hubbard's guilt started rearing its ugly head again, and Gordon had had enough. He decided Hubbard had to go."

"What makes you think it was Gordon?"

"He's the one with the temper. I've seen it myself. It doesn't take much to send him into a rage. Hubbard was beaten with a brick until half his face was caved in."

"Ouch," he said.

"Yeah. I've seen the autopsy photos. Ouch is right."

"But that wasn't the end of it," Braddock said.

"No. Poor Bryce just wouldn't let it go."

"You gotta admit, though," Hughes said, "the whole heroin overdose thing was pretty clever."

Something about that bothered Rachel. "Yeah. Almost a little *too* clever for these guys. It's not like they have a problem with shooting people. Then there's the heroin itself."

"You think they got it from Gulani?" Braddock asked.

"Since he knows all the addicts, maybe that's how he fits into this."

"Shit," Hughes said, as if struck by a memory. "I forgot to tell you. Gulani swore he didn't call Gordon."

"It had to be him," Rachel said. "He was the only one who knew I was going to his office. Gordon even said it was him."

"He didn't deny that he had called *someone*. He just swore it wasn't Gordon."

"He wouldn't tell you who?"

"I almost had it out of him. I could tell, he was gonna break. But then, of course, we were interrupted."

"Well," Braddock said, "he won't be telling us anytime soon."

Rachel suddenly remembered what she'd been about to do before Hughes stopped her. She jumped up and said, "They could be here."

Hughes asked, "Who?"

She ran for the admissions counter, and they jogged after her. Then it hit Braddock. "Damn, she's right. This is the only hospital in the area."

"Who are we talking about?"

"Gordon and Martin. She dislocated Gordon's knee and shot Martin in the calf."

"Jesus Christ."

Rachel put her hands on the counter and said, "Ma'am?"

The nurse looked up from her computer.

"I need to know if someone was admitted last night." She figured the gunshot wound would be a certainty. "His name's Seth Martin."

The nurse moved the mouse around, clicked it several

times, and studied the screen. Her eyes moved side to side as she said, "Nope. Sorry."

Rachel was stunned. "Are you sure?"

"I'm sure. There's no record of him here."

Braddock said, "Maybe they drove him to Charlotte."

She looked back at the nurse. "How about Riley Gordon?"

A few more clicks, and she said, "Yep. He checked in last night."

"Is he still here?"

The nurse eyed Rachel with suspicion. "Are you a family member?"

Braddock unclipped his badge from his belt and held it up for her to see. "We need to ask him a few questions."

"Good enough for me," she said. "He's scheduled for surgery this afternoon. He's on the third floor."

They started for the elevators, but a booming voice yelled, "Detective Hughes."

They stopped and turned to see a man in uniform entering from the double doors. He looked irate.

Hughes said, "That'll be the sheriff for me."

"I'd like a word with you about this goddamn gunfight you started in my town."

Hughes said, "You two go on. I'll handle this."

Rachel and Braddock didn't need to hear it again. They made for the elevator. As they waited for the door to open, Braddock leaned over and said, "I almost feel kinda sorry for him."

THIRTY-EIGHT

Gordon was asleep when Rachel and Braddock came into his room. His leg looked like it had been reset by the ER staff, though the surgery would be needed to fix the internal damage. Presently, it was splinted and wrapped with gauze and bandages to keep it immobile. Rachel walked up to the side of the bed and slapped his foot.

He woke with a start and growled, "Goddammit. What the . . . ?" He saw Rachel, then looked at Braddock, caught sight of the badge on his hip, and went quiet.

"Hi there, Flash," Rachel said. "Did we wake you?"

He looked at the ceiling.

"Aw, what's the matter? Not happy to see me?"

"You should leave," he said. "If I call my mother and tell her you're here harass—"

Rachel laughed. "Did you just threaten to call your mommy on me? You're even more pathetic than I thought you were, *Flash*. And don't forget, I know how you got that nickname."

"Fuck you!"

"Hey." She put her hand on top of his knee and pushed. "Watch your mouth."

He groaned, looked over at Braddock, and said, "Come on, man. You just gonna stand there and let her torture me?"

Braddock said, "I ain't seen a damn thing."

"You're in a lot of trouble, Flash. I know what you did in Afghanistan. I know you murdered that kid."

His eyes became defiant. "I don't know what you're talking about. And even if that was true, you couldn't arrest me for something that happened in another country. Much less a war zone. Hell, come to think of it, you can't arrest anyone for anything now. You're just some bullshit private eye."

"Oh, I won't be the one to arrest you. We'll let the Monroe police or the sheriff's office take care of that."

"For what?"

"How about for beating Adam Hubbard to death with a brick, you sadistic little shit."

His expression changed. He went back to staring at the ceiling.

"That's right," she said. "I know all about it. You found out he was talking to a reporter and decided to shut him up for good, didn't you?"

His eyes moved to hers for an instant, then looked away. A reflex that told her he had heard something that wasn't right. Some part of her narrative was wrong. Or maybe just incomplete. She made a mental note and pressed on.

"In case you haven't heard, Stoller tried to kill Manish Gulani today. But he blew it. Manish is going to live. He's here now, in surgery. As for Stoller, he's on the run, but it's only a matter of time before the cops catch up to him. Him and your buddy, Seth. When that happens, one of you is going to cut a deal for a lighter sentence. My money is on Seth, but you could prove me wrong and do yourself a favor."

"Yeah? And what kind of deal would I get?"

"That would be up to the cops and the DA, but I've been through this a thousand times before. Trust me when I tell you, it's your best option. And you can start by telling us who else is involved in this. We know Manish didn't call you to tell you I was going to his office, so who did? Who's Stoller trying to protect?"

His mouth formed a little smile, smug and fatalistic. "If you were so sure Manish was going to survive, you wouldn't be trying this hard to work me over. You want to know what Stoller's up to? Go ask him yourself."

★ ★ ★

Gordon refused to say anything else. Out in the hall, Braddock let out a sigh and said, "Well, at least we know he's not going anywhere."

Rachel was thinking about Gulani. How he had tried so hard to convince Hughes that he had not sent Gordon after Rachel. Hughes had thought that Gulani was on the verge of telling him who he had called. If he truly was a part of this conspiracy, he likely would have lawyered up when interrogated by a cop. The fact that he was willing to talk said otherwise, but he hadn't managed to get it out. He had hesitated, probably out of fear, giving Stoller just enough time to silence him.

So who was Gulani afraid of? Rachel knew of one person in particular that intimidated him. But that was because she held a position of authority over him, with the ability to ruin his career.

Suddenly, she heard Gordon's voice in her mind. *If I call my mother . . .*

It was more than just an infantile response induced by pain and heroin withdrawal. He knew his mother could protect him. Like she could exert some power or influence, particularly at this hospital.

Rachel ran back to Gordon's room and threw the door open. "Who's your mother, Flash?"

He looked away. His jaw muscles flexed as he gnashed his teeth.

She went back into the hall and pulled her phone from her back pocket, opened it, and tapped on the background check app.

"What was that all about?" Braddock asked.

"Hang on." She typed in Gordon's name. When the results came back, she scrolled down and touched the Relatives tab. "I'll be damned."

"What is it?"

"It's Gordon's mother. Looks like she used to work here at the hospital."

"And?"

Rachel looked at him with a half smile. "Now she runs the drug treatment center where Gulani works."

"Oh . . . shit. You think she's the one Gulani called?"

"Yep."

Near the nurse's station, Hughes stepped out of the elevator with the sheriff in tow. He looked around and spotted Rachel and Braddock and started walking toward them. The look on his face told them to brace themselves.

"Am I to understand," the sheriff boomed, "that there's a murder suspect in that room, and you two have been in there questioning him without talking to me first?"

"We're sorry, Sheriff," Braddock said, stepping forward. "We're just trying to do our part to help, seeing as how you've got a manhunt going on. I'm Danny Braddock, chief deputy of the Lowry—"

"I know who you are, Chief Braddock." He looked at Rachel. "And I know who you are too, Miss Carver. You've been in the news enough lately. Seems like whenever you two get together, people start dying. I should arrest you both on principle."

They looked at each other, and Rachel said, "Sheriff, I can explain everything."

"Save it." He pointed a thumb at Hughes. "He's already told me more about this mess than I ever wanted to know. If he says you're in the clear, I guess that'll have to do. For now, anyway." He nodded toward the door to Gordon's room. "Did he say anything?"

"Not much," Braddock said. "But Rachel managed to figure out that his mother runs the drug treatment center where the shooting victim works."

"The Monroe Outpatient Center?"

Rachel nodded. "We believe the victim called his boss, Pamela LeMay, to tell her I was . . ." She flushed. "Well . . . to tell her that I was planning to break into his office. She, in turn, must have told her son."

"And that's when he came and kidnapped you?"

"Yes, sir."

"Hmph." He seemed to study her for a few seconds. There was a hint of admiration in his expression. "Glad you got away."

"Thank you, Sheriff. So am I."

"Before he got there, did you manage to break in?"

"No, sir."

"Well, hell, I guess we can forgive you for that." He looked at Braddock and Hughes, pointed at Rachel, and asked, "Is there anyone around here who's got a better handle on this situation than she does?"

Both men shook their heads.

"All right then, Miss Carver. Congratulations. You are now, officially, a consultant for the Union County Sheriff's Office on this case. Assuming you still want to get to the bottom of it?"

"Bet your ass I do. Thank you, Sheriff."

"Don't thank me." He tipped his head toward Hughes. "It was his idea."

"I figure it'll be the best way to keep you out of trouble," Hughes said.

He smiled, but Rachel could see tension in his eyes. Some part of him still didn't trust her. Not completely. He'd spent too much time chasing her, seeing her as a suspect in Ramirez's murder. Rachel didn't blame him. It was a hard thing to shake off.

"So what's our next move?" the sheriff asked.

Rachel said, "We figure out exactly how Pamela LeMay fits into all this."

THIRTY-NINE

The sheriff sent a deputy along as an escort. He stopped on the street as Hughes turned his Crown Victoria into the driveway. LeMay's house, a small mansion sitting on the edge of a golf course, was covered in stone and gray brick. It had high-pitched gables and broad windows and was surrounded by immaculate landscaping.

Hughes whistled. "Curing drug addicts must be a lucrative business."

In the back of her mind, Rachel recalled Gordon telling her about his family's land, and how most of it had been sold off. She wondered if LeMay had used the money from that sale to buy this house. And maybe to purchase her one-third share of ownership in the treatment center.

They made their way to the front door, and Braddock rang the bell.

"I wonder if she'll actually answer."

Hughes, peering through a haze of frosted glass said, "Here comes someone."

Rachel could see a tall figure running toward them. The door burst open, and LeMay stood there with a phone in her hand, panting. There was panic on her face.

"Thank God you're here," she said, trying to catch her breath. "I was just trying to call you."

"Calm down, ma'am," Hughes said. "What's the matter?"

"It's Colin Stoller. He's the one who did the shooting this morning. Manish Gulani is my employee."

"We know all of that, Doctor," Rachel said. "We're searching for Mr. Stoller now. Do you have any idea where he might be?"

"He was just here!"

Hughes went wide-eyed. "Son of a . . ."

"How long ago?" Braddock asked.

"He just left a few minutes ago . . . maybe fifteen."

Braddock ran to the deputy's patrol car, yelling at him to get on the radio and call it in.

"Fifteen minutes?" Hughes said. "And you're just now getting ready to call someone?"

"I was locked in my room . . . I didn't know for sure he had left . . . I didn't have my phone on me—"

"Do you know where he's going?" Rachel asked.

LeMay nodded, swallowed hard with her hand on her chest, and said, "He's going after someone else. He said there's a witness. He said he was going to make sure the kid never talked to anyone again."

Rachel turned to Hughes. "He's going after Corey Staples."

"Dammit." Hughes pulled his phone out and hit a number on speed dial, listened for a second, then said, "Julie, we got a problem." He started running for his car. "The shooter from this morning is on his way to Siler City. He's going after Corey Staples. Yeah, Wendy's boy. You gotta find him. Get some units over to his house . . ."

Braddock was running for the car. Rachel grabbed LeMay by the wrist and said, "You're coming too."

"What? I'm not . . . What are you talking about?"

She was trying to fight her way back inside. Rachel yanked hard, looked her dead in the eyes, and said, "You've got a lot of explaining to do, Doctor. Right now, you look like a coconspirator in this nightmare. You either come along now and help us figure this out, or I'll have that deputy arrest your ass. What's it going to be?"

LeMay's expression changed, just for a moment, and Rachel glimpsed the harsh, intense woman she had met two days earlier. But she relented, following Rachel to Hughes's car. They jumped in the back seat, and Hughes backed out of the driveway and sped toward Siler City.

FORTY

Stoller was being cautious. No one would be looking for him in the Tucson, but he didn't want to chance that there might be a roadblock on the shortest route. So he took the long way, jumping on I-85 and heading to Greensboro, where he'd circle around and come into Siler City from the north. It would add ten minutes to the trip, but it was safer that way.

It was a shame that the boy had to die. If only the reporter had left things alone. After all, it was his fault that Stoller knew anything at all about Corey Staples.

When the article had come out speculating that Larson's real killer was still on the loose, Gordon had panicked. He had wanted to kill the reporter right then, but cooler heads had prevailed. Then the reporter had started talking to Hubbard, who suddenly seemed incapable of keeping his mouth shut. It became clear that the story wasn't going away on its own.

After Hubbard died, Stoller had suggested that they surveil the reporter. To see how close he might get to the truth. Martin had acquired bugs for his car and apartment. He'd gotten them from the same site where he'd purchased the

GPS tracker. And he'd installed them too—Martin had been good at that kind of work.

They spent the next few weeks monitoring him in shifts. But day after day, nothing happened. They started to think it might have been a waste of their time. They were all but ready to quit when a phone call came in that changed everything. A tip from a detective in the Wake County Sheriff's Office. A new lead for the reporter to run down.

As it turned out, that new lead had been a legitimate threat. As soon as Stoller heard the reporter interviewing the Staples kid over the phone, he knew it was for real. A witness who had actually seen Stoller kill Larson. Who had seen him get in the car with Gordon and take off.

If Stoller had done it by himself, he wouldn't have bothered making the trip. His fate was already sealed. But if the boy was able to testify that he had seen Gordon in the getaway car, Gordon would go to prison. And that would devastate LeMay.

Stoller couldn't let that happen.

Hughes had the siren blaring and the visor lights flashing as he pushed the Crown Victoria along Highway 49 at close to a hundred. Braddock was on the phone with the highway patrol and the various counties along the route, trying to see what could be done about setting up roadblocks and advising troopers to be on the lookout for a large white male, armed and dangerous, speeding toward Siler City in a black F-150.

Rachel turned to LeMay and said, "It's time to start talking, Doctor. Why did Stoller come to see you?"

There was sadness in her expression. A look of mourning. "He wanted to say good-bye."

"Good-bye? If that's all he wanted, why were you locked in your room?

"He told me he was going after the boy, and I tried to talk him out of it. He became angry . . . violent."

"So why would he want to say bye to you in the first place? How do you know him?"

"Colin was a patient of mine."

"Like Adam Hubbard and your son?"

"I never treated my son." LeMay's eyes fixed on the window, gazing into the wooded countryside.

"Come on, Doc. Keep talking. Help me understand what's happening."

She looked down at her hands, resting in her lap, then back out the window and said, "When Riley got out of the Army, he stayed close with the other members of his team. Adam and Colin both had problems. Adam had become dependent on prescription painkillers, and Colin was suffering from PTSD." She glanced at Rachel. "He was suicidal."

"You offered to treat them?"

She nodded. "We arranged for them to move to Monroe. I thought it was good for Riley, too. He had some issues adjusting to civilian life, and it helped to have them around."

"So what's Colin doing now? Why's he going after the boy?"

"I can't answer that."

"Can't or won't?"

LeMay didn't say.

"Why did he shoot Manish? Is it because he didn't want us to find out that Manish called you last night? And that you sent your son to kidnap and murder me?"

That got Braddock to turn around. Hughes stole a peek through the rearview mirror. LeMay had an incredulous look, like she was shocked that Rachel would suggest such a thing. Rachel didn't buy it. She wanted to smack that look off her face, but she also wanted to get whatever cooperation she could out of LeMay.

"Colin came to see you while he's on the run for attempted murder. Why would he do that? Why are you so important to him?"

"He's in love with me," she said. "Colin and I . . . developed a personal relationship."

"You're sleeping with your son's friend?"

Braddock and Hughes looked at each other. LeMay closed her eyes. Rachel regretted letting the question slip out. She searched for something else to say before LeMay had a chance to become indignant.

"It's obvious that Colin wants to protect you," she said. "I think it's because you did something to help your son. Something you shouldn't have. Maybe you helped him get his hands on the heroin they used on Bryce Parker. That they were going to use on me. Or maybe you just felt compelled to tell Riley that I was on my way to your office, and that I might find something that implicated Riley in Adam Hubbard's murder. Maybe you didn't know he was going to try to kill me. Maybe you didn't want to know. But whatever it is, he's doing this for you."

LeMay looked at her hands again and nodded.

"Right now, he's on a suicide mission," Rachel said.

"You've talked him out of killing himself before. If we can get to him in time, will you help us do it again?"

"Yes," she said, looking at Rachel with tears in her eyes. "I will."

★ ★ ★

Stoller reached into his bag and dug out Parker's phone, turned it on, and typed the password. He had forced it out of Parker after the first heroin injection, when he was coming out of the euphoria, still dazed and susceptible. Then he'd given him another dose, thinking that would do the trick, though it hadn't.

Not that it mattered now.

He touched the contacts app and scrolled down, searching.

Corey Staples.

He touched it and memorized the number. He didn't want to use Parker's phone to make the call, just in case the boy had stored the contact in his own phone. After all, he wasn't planning to impersonate the reporter.

★ ★ ★

Corey and his friend, Ryan, were playing *Gears of War 4* in co-op mode. Sitting on the floor in Ryan's living room, they had the volume on the sixty-five-inch TV as high as they could stand it. With no parents around, they wanted as much realism as they could get from the gunfire and the chainsaws.

They finished a chapter in the game, and Corey took a break to check his phone. It was loaded with missed calls, voicemails, and text messages.

"Oh shit."

"What is it," Ryan asked.

"My parents have been blowing my phone up."

He checked the latest voicemail. It was from his mom. "Honey, please, I need you to call me, okay? Please, it's an emergency. As soon as you get this. I need to know where you are."

She sounded distraught. He was about to call her back when the phone rang.

"Hello?"

"Corey, this is Detective Hughes with the Siler City Police. Are you at home right now?"

"No, sir, I'm at a friend's house."

"Is it safe there?"

"Uh . . . yes, sir. I guess."

"Good. I need you to listen to me very carefully, son. Someone has made a threat against you. Now, there's no need to worry; we're going to take care of it. But I need to know exactly where you are so I can send an officer to your location."

Corey gave him the address.

★ ★ ★

Stoller ended the call and turned his phone off, just in case the cops were trying to track him with it. He was coming down Highway 421, heading toward the center of town. He opened Parker's phone and typed the address into the Maps app. When the route came back, he touched the start button and followed the directions, making a right on 64.

The screen said he was six minutes away.

FORTY-ONE

It had taken Morrison too long to reach one of Corey's parents. His father was apparently out of town, and his mother worked as a massage therapist who made house calls on the weekends. When she was with a client, she kept her phone on silent. By the time Morrison spoke to her, she was beginning to fear they had been too late.

She stood with a pair of officers in front of the house, hoping Corey would turn up unharmed. If he was inside, he wasn't coming to the door. Staples suspected he was at one of his friends' houses. Morrison sent officers to each address Staples could remember and prayed that one of them found him before the gunman did.

When Staples called back, Morrison answered, asking, "Have you found him?"

"Yes, he just called me." She sounded breathless. "He's at Ryan Calloway's house. The house on Amherst."

"Okay, I've already got a unit on the way. I'm leaving now to go there myself."

She started for her car, waving at the other officers to follow. They fell in stride, looking confused. One of them said, "Where are we going?"

"We got him. Just follow me."

She jumped in and took off, made a screeching right, and floored it to speed out of the neighborhood. In her rearview, she saw the pair of patrol cars struggling to keep up.

★ ★ ★

Stoller turned onto Amherst and saw a Siler City police officer stepping out of his car three houses away. The officer looked like he was headed for the front door. He paused when he saw the Tucson, but Stoller kept his speed steady and cruised by.

The officer watched for a moment, then turned and continued on toward the door. Stoller slowed and pulled into the nearest driveway. He was four houses away now. He parked and grabbed his gun and a spare magazine from the bag and stepped out. He walked around to the far side of the house to get out of view and sprinted toward the rear corner. He took a quick look, then rounded it and ran through the row of backyards to get to the target house.

Once there, he eased up the side yard toward the front. The officer's voice met him as he paused at the corner of the house to scan the front yard and the road beyond, both of which were clear. The officer sounded confident and reassuring. There were two other voices answering him—Corey and his friend.

Stoller leaned around carefully until he caught sight of the officer. He was standing in front of the doorway, turned at an angle so that his back was facing Stoller. *Lucky break,* he thought. But then he noticed that the officer was wearing a ballistic vest, obviously anticipating a potential shootout. Stoller raised his gun and crept around the corner, looking for a clear shot at the back of the officer's head.

The roar of an engine caught Stoller's attention. He

looked and saw a black unmarked screech to a halt in front of the house. He turned his sights back on the officer, who had spotted him and was now backing into the house, drawing his service weapon with one hand and pushing the boys to safety with the other.

Stoller cursed and advanced on him, but the man had his weapon out. He yelled for Stoller to drop his but didn't finish the command before he started shooting. Stoller returned fire, making two hits on the officer's chest and one at the base of his neck, just above the clavicle.

The officer spun and stumbled inside. A female officer in plain clothes was yelling at Stoller from the road. He turned to take aim and felt his leg falter. He looked down and saw that he had been hit. Other police cars arrived. Stoller raised up and fired at the woman, but she was tucked in behind her open door, using the unmarked for cover. The front yard was large, at least twenty yards to the street, which made for a tough pistol shot under stress. The woman fired back, and her second shot caught him in the shoulder.

Stoller winced, saw the open front door of the house, and limped for it. The wounded officer was gone. There was no sign of the boys either. Stoller glanced back and fired a blind volley. Three shots. But more came his way. Another officer was out of his car and taking aim. Stoller caught a round in the back as he rushed through the door and slammed it shut.

★ ★ ★

"He's there already?" Hughes yelled into his phone. He looked at LeMay in the rearview. "Fifteen minutes, my ass."

Rachel asked, "Is Corey safe?"

Hughes listened for a moment and said, "Oh no. I can't believe this." He pulled his phone away from his ear. "They found Corey at a friend's house. Stoller's inside with him, the friend, and a wounded officer."

LeMay leaned forward. "He'll kill that boy as soon as he gets an opportunity."

"Damnit, did you hear that, Julie?" He was listening and shaking his head. He lowered the phone again and said, "They can't tell what's going on inside the house, but they haven't heard any more shots since Stoller went in."

Braddock asked, "How far out are we?"

"At least twenty minutes." To LeMay, he said, "Have you tried calling this asshole and talking him down?"

"I've tried," she said. "It goes straight to voicemail."

"Do you guys have megaphones or PAs in your cars?" Rachel asked.

"The newer ones do. There'll be one there."

Rachel looked at LeMay. "Would it help to tell him you're on the way there?"

LeMay thought for a moment. "It might. Tell him I need to see him one last time."

"What?" Braddock asked. "That makes it sound like you're condoning this whole murder-suicide thing."

"No," Rachel said. "She's right. He won't let anything stop him. But if he thinks she's not going to try, then maybe he'll hold off long enough to see her. It might buy us the time we need to get her there."

★ ★ ★

Stoller had taken three hits. One had gone through the muscle in his shoulder. Another had hit high on his back, but the angle had made it ricochet off his scapula. Together, they made his left arm useless. But the real disappointment was his leg. Despite his willingness to sacrifice himself, there had been the distant fantasy that he would get out of this alive. That he would finish the job quickly and make his getaway. Go on the run and make a new life in the wilderness of some remote place like Montana or Wyoming.

A bum leg made that impossible.

He pushed it out of his mind and started searching the house. The officer was likely still a threat. Stoller's first two shots had hit the ballistic vest. They might have been painful, but they wouldn't have killed him. The one above his collarbone was a different story. It was probably serious, but Stoller didn't know if it had been enough to put him down for good.

Not that he cared about killing the officer. It meant nothing to him one way or another. The man could live, for all he cared, so long as he stayed out of the way.

Stoller saw a closed door off the living area. There were drops of blood leading to it, a smeared handprint in red on the doorframe. He limped over to it and tested the handle. It was locked, but the privacy hardware of a bedroom door was hardly a challenge for him. Leaning against the frame, he twisted the lever until it popped. Then he pushed the door open, staying clear of the doorway in case the officer tried to take a shot at him.

He waited outside the room and listened. Hearing nothing, he suddenly feared that they had escaped through a window. He chanced a quick look. Back out of the doorway, he took stock of what he had seen. The three of them were huddled together between the foot of a bed and a dresser.

The officer was lying on his back on the floor. The boys were next to him on their knees. One of them held a towel to his neck. The other one held the officer's weapon, aiming it in a pair of shaking hands in the direction of the door.

"Throw the gun this way," Stoller said. "I want to see it come through this door."

"Screw you, man. If you come in here . . . I'm gonna shoot you. I swear."

Stoller laughed quietly. *Brave kid*, he thought. "Listen, son, I'm not going to hurt you. There are too many cops outside now. If I do anything to you, they'll come in here and take me out. All I want to do is make sure you don't make things worse by firing that thing off. Now throw it out here."

"No!"

Stoller was getting aggravated. "All right, kid. It's like this. That cop that's laying on the floor is bleeding to death. He shot at me and couldn't stop me. And he's had police training. I'm betting he knows how to shoot that thing a whole lot better than you do. So let's find out. On the count of three, I'm coming through this door shooting. I'll be aiming for you and you alone. Let's see who gets who first. Ready? One . . . two . . ."

A loud thud hit the wall next to the door, and the kid said, "Shit, I'm sorry."

"What was that?" Stoller asked.

"It was the gun," said the other kid quickly. "He tried to toss it out the door, but he missed."

Stoller leaned his head in enough to get a look at the gun lying on the floor. He leaned a little further, saw that the boy who had been holding the gun now had his hands up. Stoller stepped around, wincing as his weight shifted onto the wounded leg.

"Smart move," he said.

The officer's eyes were fixed on the ceiling, and his breathing was rapid and shallow. He didn't have long.

"Which one of you is Corey?"

They didn't answer. Stoller pointed his gun at the officer's head.

"Me," said the one who was trying to stanch the bleeding. "I'm Corey."

"Trade places."

They looked at each other.

"Now," Stoller yelled.

Corey backed away, and the other boy put his hands gingerly on the towel.

Stoller pointed the gun at Corey and said, "Stand up."

Corey complied. Stoller waved the gun, and together they moved to the door. Over his shoulder, Stoller said, "Put more pressure on that wound or he's going to die."

Out in the living area, Stoller moved them away from the doorway so they couldn't be seen from the bedroom. He pointed the gun at Corey's head and said, "I'm sorry, kid."

"Colin."

It was a voice over a loudspeaker, coming from outside.

"Colin, my name is Julie Morrison. I'm with the Siler City Police Department. We want to talk."

There's nothing left to say, he thought.

"I have a message from Pam. She's on her way here now. She says she needs to see you one last time."

She's trying to stop me.

A tenuous calm had settled in. Stoller could feel everyone

outside, holding a collective breath. Like a single organism with one thought—get the kids and the officer out safely.

The idea almost made him laugh. It was such a futile sentiment. None of them understood how meaningless a human life really was.

Afghanistan had taught him that. He had seen the worst of what people could do to one another. Men beheaded, women raped and stoned to death . . . reprisals and honor killings . . .

His unit had once discovered the body of a twelve-year-old girl with no face. The villagers said the Taliban had skinned her alive, but they didn't know why. In a village to the east, one of the elders had a different story. According to him, the girl's own father had cut her up after discovering she had kissed a boy her own age. There was no telling which story was true.

The barbarism and brutality of life in a country where people didn't live in the protective bubble of modern civilization. For most of his fellow soldiers, it was a by-product of race or culture or religion. They were savages. Different from the Americans trying to help them.

But Stoller knew better.

Life at home was an illusion. A scam that everyone agreed on so they wouldn't have to face their fear of the inevitable. It didn't matter if you were eight or eighty, when death came, it stripped away the facade of everything you had built up around you. Everything you had worked toward and fought for. It showed you how insignificant your existence had been. But life would go on for everyone else as they scurried about, hoping for the fulfillment of false promises.

Only one person seemed to understand it as well as Stoller did. And she had never let it bother her. She had embraced it, deciding to get what she could out of life before her time was done. She didn't search for meaning. She played her part in the scam because it suited her.

She would try to stop him now, only because she wanted him to stay around for her. She had collected him like all the other experiences in her life. Stoller admired the purity of that. And he had enjoyed giving in to her. Doing whatever he could to please her. In those intimate moments when they shared their inner demons, he had thought he'd found a life partner. Someone who could make his fantasy a reality. They could escape together into the wilderness, away from everyone who believed in the scam.

It was never going to happen, though. So this was the next best thing. He could go out doing his part to ensure her happiness. And the memories of their time together would be fresh in his mind up to the moment he died. Unspoiled by the passage of time.

He took his phone out and turned it on. He had brought it in case there was the opportunity to leave her a final message before the end. It powered up, and he touched her name. A moment later, she was there.

"Colin?"

"Pam."

"Will you wait for me?"

"I will."

FORTY-TWO

Patrol cars had formed a crescent on the street in front of the house, cover for uniformed officers as they kept their eyes on the doors and windows, looking for a target—though they weren't allowed to shoot unless they themselves were fired upon, lest they risk the safety of the hostages. The Chatham County Sheriff's Tactical and Response Team had gathered in the neighbor's yard in case the need came for them to storm the house. An SBI Special Response Team was en route to lend a hand.

Hughes marched Rachel, LeMay, and Braddock up to the front and introduced them to Morrison and Chief Arnold. Then he explained everything he knew about the situation. Arnold listened with his head down, nodding and rubbing his jaw with shaky fingers. When he'd heard it all, he looked up and asked, "So what do you propose we do now?"

Hughes looked at Rachel.

"We let Dr. LeMay try to talk him down," she said. "She's the only one he'll listen to."

Arnold said, "Will he answer if you call?"

"He'll answer," LeMay said. She took her phone out and called him. "It's me, Colin. I'm here. I'm right outside."

She listened for a moment. Rachel could hear his muffled voice. It sounded even and calm.

"He wants to see me," LeMay said.

"Tell him to come to a window," Hughes said.

"He heard you." She was listening and passing along each sentence he spoke. "He says no . . . you'll take a shot at him . . . he wants me to go inside."

"Absolutely not," Arnold said, but regretted it as soon as he saw Rachel grimace.

"Wait," LeMay said. "Don't . . . please don't do that. Just wait, Colin. Give me a little time. I can convince them. I just need a few minutes. Let me go, and I'll call you back." She hung up. "I'm no expert in hostage negotiation, Chief Arnold, but I have heard that you don't ever tell a hostage taker no."

Arnold looked mortified.

Rachel said, "If we have any chance of resolving this, you need to let her go in there and talk to him."

He cleared his throat and tried to regain his composure, though his face was deep red. "If she goes in there, I want a cop going in with her."

"He'll never agree to that."

LeMay said, "She's right. You can't send an officer in there with me. It'll only make the situation worse."

Arnold shook his head. "I'm not putting another civilian in that house without some kind of protection."

"I'll go with her," Rachel said. To LeMay, she asked, "Can you ask him if he'd be okay with that? If I go unarmed?"

Braddock said, "Wait, what?"

"Maybe," LeMay said. She called Stoller back and made the offer.

"Rachel, what the hell are you doing?" Braddock pulled her aside. "This psycho's already tried to kill you. More than once."

"He agreed to let you come in with me," LeMay said, putting her phone away.

"I didn't agree to it," Arnold said, weakly.

Rachel turned to Hughes. "We need a vest for her."

"Got it," he said, and took off running toward his car.

Morrison started to remove hers. "You need one too."

"No," Rachel said. "He might think I'm trying to hide something in it. Besides, if he tries to shoot me, it'll be in the head."

Arnold pointed at LeMay. "Then what good is a vest going to do her?"

"He won't shoot her. But giving her a vest will help relieve at least some of your liability if something bad happens."

He looked like he was trying to figure out whether or not Rachel was joking. Hughes came back and slid his vest over LeMay's head and secured the Velcro straps around her waist.

Arnold said, "Good God, I'm not about to let *two* civilians go in there."

"Actually," Hughes said, "she works for the Union County sheriff, so technically . . ."

Rachel took the .380 off her hip and handed it back to Braddock. As she started to pull away, he grabbed her wrist.

"No, Rachel," he said. "This is insane. I'm not letting you go in there."

"Danny, let me go."

"Rachel—"

"Danny," she said slowly, "let me go."

He looked hurt. His grip relaxed just a little, and she pulled free of it. She put her hand on LeMay's back and guided her forward quickly before anyone else could object. Hughes was right behind them. He said, "I hope you know what the hell you're doing."

"So do I," she said.

When they got to the patrol cars, Hughes fell back. Rachel led LeMay forward into the no-man's-land between the perimeter of cops and the house. They slowed their pace, and Rachel whispered, "I'm going to leave the front door open, if I can. If things go south and I tell you to run, you run. You understand me?"

"I do. But I'm surprised you would care about what happens to me."

"The last thing I need is your death on my conscience, but let's be real clear about something, Doc. I'm going in there to do whatever I can to save those kids and that cop. Beyond that, I need to see this through to the end. For myself. Protecting you comes in at a very distant third."

Rachel stepped up to the front door and opened it wide. She put her hands up and said, "Colin, it's Rachel. I'm unarmed. I'm here with Pam."

A few seconds passed, and he said, "Come in."

"Okay," she said. "I'm coming in first. Pam will be right behind me."

He didn't respond. She started into the entry hall, taking short, slow steps as she let her eyes adjust. It was dark with all the blinds drawn, and cold compared to the humid summer day outside. Rachel saw blood trails on the carpet. Thin red lines punctuated by blotches from a shoe print.

She emerged into a living area, an open-concept space with a pair of couches and a coffee table. A teenage boy stood by a leather recliner. He was facing her, watching her as she took stock of her surroundings. She was surprised by his expression. It showed no emotion, either because he was being brave or because he was in shock.

To the right, leaning against the wall, Stoller was pointing his pistol at the boy's head. He looked tired. And older, as if the day had aged him twenty years. His face still wore the dried blood from when Rachel had tried to shoot him. His shirt and his jeans were also soaked.

She looked back at the boy. "Corey?"

He swallowed hard and said, "Yes, ma'am."

She smiled. "Everything's going to be okay."

Stoller was eyeing her with a look of curiosity. "You're a very brave woman, Miss Carver."

"Oh, Colin."

Rachel turned to see LeMay looking him up and down. Horrified, she cast her eyes to the floor and looked for a moment like she might run away.

"It's okay," he said. "It isn't as bad as it looks."

"Colin," Rachel said, "I need to ask you a question. Where are Ryan and the officer?"

He nodded toward a door. "Back in that bedroom."

LeMay said, "I should go check on them," and started to move.

Rachel motioned for her to wait. "Is that okay, Colin?"

He nodded. "Yeah. Go ahead."

LeMay disappeared into the room. Rachel studied Stoller for a moment, then averted her eyes. He was staring at her intently, probably trying to figure out what her plan was.

When LeMay came back into the living area, she was dragging Ryan Calloway by the hand. She looked like she had regained her composure. Her eyes met Rachel's, and she shook her head.

The officer was dead.

"Colin," LeMay said. "I'm going to take this boy to the door. Then I'm going to let him walk out of here. This has nothing to do with him."

Stoller gave a slight smile of admiration. He apparently liked watching her take charge. Or perhaps he appreciated her desire to be protective.

Rachel heard LeMay urge Ryan out. "Go. Go." Then there were voices outside, loud and commanding. "Hands up! Put your hands up! Keep walking! Slowly! This way! Keep moving! Hands up!"

Ryan was safe.

LeMay came back into the living area. "Colin, it's time to end this."

"Are you sure about that?" he asked, tightening his grip on the gun.

"Wait," she said. "You know that's not what I meant. There's no reason for you to do this. You don't have to protect me anymore. I've told the police everything."

"I don't believe you." They stared at each other for a moment, and Stoller saw something in her expression that reassured him. "I knew you wouldn't."

She exhaled sharply, and Rachel knew he had seen right through her.

Stoller said, "I'm sorry, Pam. I have to do this."

"No, Colin, please. You don't . . ."

"You know he'll sell you out if this kid testifies."

"I don't care. Just . . . please, don't do this."

"It was good to see you again, Pam. You should leave now."

Rachel said, "Pam?"

LeMay looked at her with defeat in her eyes.

The plan had failed. LeMay had no power over Stoller. No way to make him give up his weapon, which was a trigger-pull away from claiming another victim.

Rachel had to act. She stepped forward and said, "You're pathetic, Colin."

He looked amused. "Is that so?"

"Yeah. You came here to kill this kid for what? To protect *her*? Because you love her?"

LeMay asked, "What are you doing?"

"You think she actually feels anything for you? She's been working you, Colin."

The muscles in his jaw tightened. Corey's eyes went wide with fear. LeMay said, "Stop it. Are you . . . ?"

"What? Crazy?" She looked back at Stoller with pity. "No, Doctor. But I know you think *he* is. That's what your files say."

"Liar!"

Stoller had a look of disbelief as he glanced at LeMay.

"Am I?" Rachel took another step toward Stoller but turned at a slight angle, as if trying to physically shift the tension toward her. "You don't think he's suicidal? That he's suffering from posttraumatic stress disorder?"

"That doesn't make him crazy."

There was a pained expression on Stoller's face. He must have felt betrayed by the fact that she would classify him like some random patient.

Rachel eased closer to him. "Can't you see it, Colin? She's been manipulating you. Using you to protect her and her son."

"Stop it," she said. "Colin, she's trying to turn you against me."

"She'd do anything for her son, Colin. Even if it meant sleeping with someone like *you*."

He swung the gun toward Rachel, which was exactly what she had expected. She reached out and caught his arm, turning to stay clear of the muzzle. With both of her hands clasping his wrist, she hugged his forearm tight to her torso, sinking her weight and forcing him to point the gun harmlessly toward the floor.

"Run!" she yelled.

LeMay jumped forward, seized Corey by the shirt, and pulled him toward the door. Rachel caught a glimpse of them fleeing as she tried to pry the pistol from Stoller's grip. But even wounded, he was too strong. He roared and spun and threw her into the wall. Her shoulder burst through the sheet rock, holding her for a moment before her weight pulled her free.

Rachel sank to the floor.

Stoller pointed the gun at her face. She closed her eyes and braced herself, certain that she was about to die. She tried to think of a prayer, but no words came to her. Only images. Her life, the people in it . . . people she had known and cared about. Her mother was there. So was the father she hardly knew. And she saw Ross Penter.

Then there was Braddock. There was so much she would never get to tell him.

Though it was only a matter of seconds, it felt like several minutes had passed, and nothing had happened. Rachel opened her eyes and saw Stoller sitting on the armrest of the sofa, glaring at her.

"Were you planning that when you walked in here? Or did it just come to you?"

Her voice was shaky as she said, "I can be impulsive at times."

He didn't look amused. "I don't know why I haven't killed you yet."

The gun was still pointed at her. Pretending to ignore it, she sat up and said, "Because there's no use in it, Colin. That's why. And that's why you didn't want to hurt Corey's friend either. It didn't serve any purpose. You're not crazy. You're a protector. You thought you were supposed to protect Pam and her son. But you were wrong."

He leaned forward and pressed the muzzle of the gun into her neck. "What would you know about it? Huh? Don't pretend you know me."

The pressure on her trachea made her wheeze. She lifted herself a few inches, trying to relieve it. "I didn't abandon you, Colin. I didn't use you."

He sat back. "No, I guess you didn't. You did lie to me, though."

She coughed and rubbed her neck.

He looked at the gun in his hand, but slowly his focus shifted until he seemed to gaze right through it. "You made me believe you'd seen my files. But you haven't. You didn't have a chance to break in and look at them. I don't know why I fell for that."

"Don't you?"

He looked over at her, but the anger was gone. Rachel saw something else there. Something resembling heartbreak.

She said, "You believed it because deep down, you know I'm right. I didn't have to read it in a file. She manipulated you. You trusted her, and she took advantage of that. She took the best part of you and used it for her own benefit. And she didn't care that she destroyed you along the way."

He shook his head, and the anger threatened to return. "You don't know what you're talking about."

"Yes, I do, Colin. I know because I've been through it. I know because someone did the exact same thing to me."

He gave her a skeptical smirk, but there was a hint of interest in his eyes. "Bullshit. Who's ever done anything like this to you?"

"The person I used to call my mentor," she said.

"What did he do that was so bad?"

"He took the thing that I valued most and made me betray it. More than anything, I wanted to be a good cop. A good agent. But out of loyalty to him, I lied under oath. And because I did that, there's a mother out there who thinks her daughter is a murderer. A little boy who might never know that his mom was innocent. I could never go back to being a cop again, but I always hoped I could bring the truth to that family. It's been my . . . mission."

Stoller's eyes were back on the gun. "Is that why you take Xanax? To help with the anxiety you have about what you've done? What you still need to do?" He glanced at her. "I found the bottle in your medicine cabinet."

She had almost forgotten that he had been in her apartment. She felt embarrassed and immediately realized how ridiculous that sensation was at a moment like this.

"It is," she said.

"I was on it for a while. Don't quit, if you still need it. It helps." The gun was pointed away from her now. He sat quietly for a minute. Then he said, "Do you think, if you're ever able to complete this mission of yours, it'll bring you any peace?"

She thought the right answer was yes, but she feared that he would see through a lie. "I don't know. I hope so."

"I think, if I'd been able to die knowing that Pam was going to be safe, that would have brought me peace. Now I'm not sure she ever deserved that from me."

Stoller reached into his pocket and took out his phone. He typed a password and touched the screen a couple of times. Then he started talking.

"In Afghanistan, we were always pissed about the attacks. About the fact that we were losing guys and couldn't get any revenge for it. Riley was always talking about killing villagers. He said they were all helping the terrorists, so they deserved it. Then, one day in a village in Guldara, I found an AK and a couple of old grenades hidden under a blanket next to a hut.

"There was this kid, a teenager, playing out in the field." He looked toward the door. "About the same age as Corey, but a lot smaller. Dirty. He was out there kicking a soccer ball. Riley pointed his rifle at him and said he was going to shoot him. He said the AK and the grenades were his, and that he was planning on using them on us as soon as we turned our backs on him. We all knew Riley was just talking, so Seth started giving him hell, taunting him. He knew Riley had a temper. I think he really wanted him to do it.

"So Riley, pissed off and looking like he couldn't take any more, clicked off his safety and fired. The boy took the hit and dropped to one knee. Then he stood back up, stumbling and looking all confused. Riley, Seth, Adam . . . they were all just standing there frozen. I knew what had to be done, so I opened up on the kid. Riley and Seth joined in, but Adam just watched. When we stopped, I walked over and told Adam he had to fire his weapon. I made him send three downrange. I know he didn't hit the kid, but it didn't matter. I just wanted to make sure Seth and Riley wouldn't mess with him for not joining in."

He touched a button on his phone, then locked it and tossed it to Rachel. "The password is all sevens."

He stood and rubbed his leg. Rachel gaped at the phone in her hand.

"Good-bye, Miss Carver."

He started moving toward the door.

"Wait." She jumped up. "What about Adam and Sergeant Larson? I have questions about them."

"You're going to have to figure them out without me."

He took a step, then stopped and turned to face her. "You almost died today. I was a hair's width away from killing you. That kind of thing changes a person. When you walk out of here, you won't ever be the same again. You'll either become weaker because of it, or stronger. I'm betting it'll make you stronger. If the day ever comes that you have to rely on that strength . . . do me a favor and remember who gave it to you."

He spun and limped for the door. By the time Rachel could muster a yell for him to stop, he was already outside. Officers were commanding him to drop his weapon and get on the ground. Then there were gunshots. A crescendo of weapons firing, officers taking revenge for their fallen comrades. Glass shattered and Rachel realized some of the bullets were missing the target, finding their way into the house. There was a zip and a crack as one struck the TV mounted on the far wall.

Rachel dove in front of the sofa and covered her head with her arms. More bullets came in, and someone outside yelled, "Hold it! Stop firing! Cease fire!"

And then it was over.

FORTY-THREE

Rachel heard Braddock calling for her. His voice was distant, but it rose above the flurry of activity outside. It grew louder. Suddenly, he was at the door. She stood and slid Stoller's phone into her pocket and started walking toward him. When he saw her, he nearly collapsed. He bent forward and put his hands on his knees to take a breath, then rushed to her and smothered her with a tight hug.

He pulled away and looked her over. "Are you okay? Are you hurt?"

She shook her head and tried to smile. The concern in his expression told her that she must have looked like she was in shock.

"Do you want to stay in here for a minute?" he asked.

She shook her head again. He put his arm around her and guided her outside.

The light made her squint. When she could see clearly again, Stoller's body appeared. Facedown, a mound of riddled flesh. Officers were standing around him. They looked proud to have downed the beast. The monster that had been in her life for nearly a year.

Some part of her wanted to be sad, but she knew that couldn't be right. It was a good thing that he was dead. She was supposed to have wanted him captured, taken alive so he could be jailed and put on trial for his crimes. But in her heart, she had wanted to see this. His lifeless body. The certainty that he could never harm another soul. Now that it had happened, she didn't know what to feel.

The officers all looked at her with approval. If she had looked back at them the right way, they might have cheered, but they could see it in her eyes—she was traumatized.

Braddock guided her past Stoller and out to the street. Hughes walked over, put a hand on her shoulder, and gave her a nod. Morrison was right behind him. She said, "Good job, hon. I'm glad you made it out of there okay."

LeMay was a few cars down, talking to an officer. She looked over and saw Rachel, held her gaze as a moment of understanding passed between them. Then she turned back to the officer. Nearby, Morrison approached Corey and Ryan and led them away, most likely to reunite them with their parents, who were being kept safe somewhere away from the house.

Down the street, a pair of patrol cars blocked the entrance at the intersection. News vans were parked on the other side. Arnold was there making a statement for a group of reporters. To their right, behind the last van, a black sedan sat in the grass on the side of the road. Ross Penter stood by it, watching. Rachel thought she could make out a smile on his face as he opened the door and climbed in. Then the sedan backed away, and he was gone.

★　★　★

A few hours passed, and things calmed down at the scene. The medical examiner arrived and took Stoller and the fallen officer away. LeMay had gotten a ride back to Monroe with one of the detectives from Union County, who had shown up long enough to get an official update on the fate of Gulani's attacker. After that, Chief Arnold left, taking half of his officers back to the station with him to start on the paperwork.

Rachel sat on the curb of a storm drain across the street from the house, holding Stoller's phone to her ear and staring at the spot where he had made his last stand. She listened to his confession twice, then copied the audio file, attached it to an email, and sent it to herself.

Hughes and Braddock were talking in the middle of the street, giving Rachel a little time to herself. They approached a few minutes later, and Hughes said, "We're thinking about putting together some sort of meeting with representatives from each agency and the DA. Have a sit-down so we can work through all this mess. We'll obviously need you there."

Rachel nodded. "Of course."

"It'll probably be in a week or so. There's a lot to do between now and then. In the meantime, you all should get some rest."

"Roger that," Braddock said.

"We'll have someone take you back to Monroe whenever you're ready to leave. I'd better get back to work."

"You'll need this," Rachel said, and handed him the phone.

He looked at it, wearing a look of confusion.

"It's Stoller's," she said. "He left a confession in the voice-recording app."

"Seriously?"

She shrugged. "He wanted me to have it. The password is all sevens."

Braddock shook his head in disbelief.

Hughes said, "I better get this into an evidence bag." He started to leave, then paused and turned back. "Oh, and don't forget, Miss Carver, you still owe me a murder weapon."

He winked at her and left.

Braddock said, "He told me an interesting bit of info about the car Stoller borrowed."

"Yeah?"

"Yeah, turns out he stole it from some old couple. Broke into their house and tied them up in the bedroom. Didn't hurt 'em, though, which seems like a miracle."

"There was no use in it," she said.

They stood around and watched the activity around the scene for a while, then Rachel turned to Braddock and asked, "Can I stay with you? Just for a little while?"

"As long as you want," he said.

"Thanks. We might as well get going."

They loaded up with a uniformed officer and rode back to Braddock's Explorer, still parked at the hospital in Monroe. Before leaving, they went inside and asked about Gulani. He had survived the surgery but still faced a difficult road ahead. He would be in the ICU until he improved.

It was late afternoon when they finally got on the road heading toward the mountains. They arrived in Dillard City just after dark. As they were getting close, Braddock had ordered takeout from Lexington Barbecue. They picked it up on the way home. When they got to Braddock's house, Rachel took a shower while he made a spread on the kitchen table.

Rachel managed to eat half a pulled-pork sandwich and a few fries. Then they went to bed. He offered to sleep on the couch, but she wanted him to stay with her. She asked him if he could hold her until she drifted off, and he wrapped her up in his arms and let her use his shoulder as a pillow.

The next morning, Braddock called in and said he was taking the day off. They lounged around his house and watched TV until noon, when Rachel decided she was ready to venture out. Braddock took her to Everett's Diner on Main Street for lunch. She had the meatloaf with mashed potatoes and a Mountain Dew. Then they walked the town, lingering on the bridge to watch the Tuckasegee flow beneath them.

Carly called Braddock to let him know she had just left the State Crime Lab in Asheville and was on her way to Raleigh to drop off the hair and the DNA evidence she had collected from the Camry and Rachel's gun. Their boss, Sheriff Ted Pritchard, had signed a rush request, and the lab had told Carly that, given the nature of the case, they were pushing her to the front of the line.

Then she asked about Rachel.

Braddock glanced over and smiled. "She's good. We're just taking a stroll around town." He hung up and said, "Carly said she wanted to call you herself, but she figured you probably just wanted to be left alone for a while. She wants you to know that she's thinking about you."

"That's really sweet of her," Rachel said. "We'll see what she's thinking about me when she finds out what I did to her truck."

They laughed at that and continued walking for a little while longer. It was a clear day, and the sun was burning away the cool air that had settled in the valley during the night. Rachel felt a drop of sweat running down her side as they climbed into the Explorer. They were headed for the Walmart in Franklin so Rachel could buy some more clothes. She wasn't ready to go back to her apartment yet. Not only did she not want to be alone, but the manager had said her door wouldn't be repaired until Thursday at the earliest.

On the way to Franklin, Braddock got another call. He listened and said "All right" several times before finishing with, "Sounds good, we'll see you there." Then he dropped the phone in the cup holder. "That was Hughes. The meeting's set for next Monday at the district attorney's office in Hillsborough."

And suddenly, Rachel found herself thinking about the case again. There were three things that still needed resolution: Martin had to be located; Rachel had to figure out exactly what role LeMay had played in this conspiracy; and someone needed to find a way to prove that Gordon had killed Adam Hubbard.

The last one could be the biggest challenge. Union County had already charged Kyle Strickland for that murder. They wouldn't jump at the chance to prove that they had made a mistake.

Rachel stared out the window at the lush mountains and thought about Lauren Bailey's son.

FORTY-FOUR

The meeting was scheduled for 10 AM, so Rachel, Brad-dock, and Carly drove to Hillsborough together on Sunday evening and stayed the night at a hotel. The next morning, they went early, expecting to be the first ones there. As they turned into the parking lot of the DA's office, Braddock said, "I'll be damned. Look who it is."

Rachel looked over. Standing by the front door was a man she had met while investigating the Lowry County murders. An SBI special agent with a taste for expensive suits and large amounts of coffee. He was either prematurely gray or had great skin for his age. He smiled broadly when he saw them stepping out of the Explorer. His name was Mike Jensen.

"Hey there, you three. It's great to see ya again."

"Mike," Rachel said, shaking his hand. "Let me guess. You transferred to Raleigh?"

Jensen was a political opportunist, Rachel had learned. It had put them at odds during their last encounter. Despite that, it was hard not to like the man.

"Yeah, AD Penter's promotion left a nice little vacancy to be filled."

"So they made you the new special agent in charge?"

"They did, yep. They sure did."

"Congratulations. That's great."

"Thank you, Rachel. I'll tell ya, it feels like they've thrown me right into the deep end with this one. I'm glad to have you here to help me through it."

"Don't worry, Mike. We'll get you out of here in one piece."

He laughed, as if the comment hadn't bothered him. He was good at faking it like that.

Others began to arrive and gather by the entrance, separating themselves into little groups. The Union County sheriff was there with one of his detectives. Hughes was huddled with Morrison and Arnold, talking quietly. Rachel, Braddock, and Carly stood off to one side. Jensen made his way around, introducing himself to everyone.

The district attorney showed up right on time and led everyone to a small conference room. The space started to feel cramped as everyone filed in. It only got worse with three late arrivals. The first was a detective from the Raleigh Police Department whom Rachel recognized. Second was the Wake County Sheriff's Office detective she had worked with during the Larson murder investigation. The last man in was a grim-faced assistant district attorney from Union County.

Once everyone was seated, they went around the table introducing themselves. Then the DA said, "Well, isn't this one heck of a party. I guess we'd better get started or we'll never get out of here. Who wants to go first?"

All eyes fell on Rachel.

She started from the beginning, sparing no details as she

told the story, tying together all the bits and pieces that each individual agency had into a single narrative that seemed to span almost the entire state. There were some skeptical looks and grunts along the way, but in the end, the pieces fit. No one could refute her, despite the fact that the ADA from Union County looked like he wanted to try.

"Well, ain't this a helluva thing," the sheriff said. He swiveled in his chair to look at his detective. "Looks like we've gotta take a hard look at our investigation into the Hubbard boy's murder."

The detective nodded.

"We'd like to help ya with that," Jensen said. "If it's all right with you, Sheriff?"

"Why not?" he said. "After all, we'd never get by if we didn't have a little help from the state every now and again."

Jensen smiled.

The sheriff looked at Rachel. "On another note, Manish Gulani's awake and talking. We met with him the other day, and he confirms that he did indeed call Dr. LeMay to tell her you were planning to break into his office. I guess we'll have to question her about what happened next."

The sheriff's detective said, "We searched Gordon's barn. Someone must've gone through there and cleaned it up. There was no sign of any drugs or guns. Or the prepaid mobile you said they took from you."

The ADA said, "That will, of course, make it next to impossible to charge Gordon with kidnapping and attempted murder."

"Has anyone been in touch with the Army about Stoller's phone confession?" the sheriff asked.

"We'll take care of that," Jensen said.

"Back on the subject of guns," the DA said to Rachel, "I understand you promised us a murder weapon?"

Rachel nodded. "The gun used to kill Officer Ramirez and Bryce Parker was mine."

That raised eyebrows around the room.

She said, "Colin Stoller broke into my apartment and stole it."

The detective from Raleigh spoke up. "We investigated the burglary at Miss Carver's apartment."

"So where's the gun now?" the DA asked.

"I surrendered it to the Lowry County Sheriff's Office for forensic examination."

Carly said, "It's presently at our office, along with Miss Carver's vehicle."

The DA said, "Forgive me for wanting to be thorough, but what exactly did your forensic examination reveal?"

"I swabbed the gun for touch DNA testing and took the swabs and comparison samples to the State Crime Lab in Raleigh. They were able to establish two matches. Rachel and Colin Stoller."

The detective from Union County said, "That's odd. I mean, we found gloves in his truck. I'm surprised he wouldn't use them if he was trying to frame you."

"Following Rachel's suggestion," Carly said, "I swabbed the edge of the slide near the muzzle. That swab returned the positive result on Mr. Stoller."

The detective looked confused.

Rachel said, "He was probably wearing gloves, like you would expect. But when he had to pick me up and carry me to my car, he had to do something with the gun. I figured the obvious thing would be for him to stick it into the waistband of his pants. And I was betting that, as he tucked it in, the edge of the slide likely scraped off some skin cells from the small of his back."

Hughes spoke for the first time, looking impressed. "I'll have to remember that one."

Braddock asked him, "Has the Staples boy shed any light on what he saw?"

"Afraid not," Hughes said.

"There's a sad irony there," Morrison said. "Stoller's attempt to silence Corey may have worked. As of now, his mother won't let us anywhere near him."

The DA sighed. "Well, I guess that's all there is to say for now. Thank you all for coming."

Arnold raised his hand.

"Yes, Chief?"

"I'm sorry I didn't think of this before we got started, but, in addition to the victims, I've lost two officers to this ordeal." He nodded at Rachel. "And Miss Carver has lost a friend. If everyone wouldn't mind, I'd like to observe a moment of silence for them, and maybe a silent prayer, for any who have faith."

He put his head down, and everyone in the room followed suit. With her eyes closed, Rachel saw Parker's face, eager and smiling.

★ ★ ★

When the meeting broke up, Rachel approached the sheriff. "If you're still willing to have me on as a consultant, I'd like to help finish this."

He looked a little uncomfortable as he glanced at the ADA, still at the table, packing his briefcase. "I'm sorry,

Miss Carver, but it seems the DA's office has gotten wind of the fact that you've been working for Kyle Strickland's lawyer. They're insisting that we keep you out of the investigation from this point forward."

"I see."

"It's a shame, though," he said. "You're one hell of an investigator."

"Thank you, Sheriff."

FORTY-FIVE

The sheriff agreed to release Carly's Tacoma, so Braddock drove them to Monroe to retrieve it. Standing there, staring at its rear end, Carly looked like she wanted to cry.

"I'm really sorry," Rachel said. "I'll pay for everything."

"It's no big deal," she said, sniffing. "I'm just glad you got away safe."

"I'll stay right behind you," Braddock said. "Make sure you don't get pulled over."

They made the trip to Carly's cabin. Despite her attempt to protest, Rachel arranged for a body shop in Asheville to pick up the Tacoma, giving them her credit card number to cover the repairs. Carly hugged her and kissed her on the cheek. Rachel thanked her and said good-bye.

Braddock drove Rachel to the garage to pick up her Camry. Then they went back to his house so she could pack up. When she had stuffed her new wardrobe and toiletries from Walmart into a plastic bag, she walked over and hugged him tightly.

"You know I can never say thank you enough."

He smiled. "You don't have to. You know that."

She looked into his eyes, reached up for the back of his neck, and said, "Come here."

He leaned down, and she kissed him. Their lips held together, as if testing, trying to decide how much further they wanted to go. Braddock pulled free, kissed her on the forehead, and backed away.

"You have no idea how much I want that."

She felt a rush of sadness, knowing what was coming.

For a moment, he looked like he might give in. Reach out and take her into his arms and carry her into his room. But then the look vanished.

"When I watched you go into that house . . ." He stopped himself, knowing he didn't have to explain how hard it had been for him. "I would never ask you to change who you are. And let's face it, you're always going to be that person who rushes into danger without thinking. Without caring about who else you'd be hurting if something bad happened to you. But I want you to know, if you need me, I'll always be there to back you up. As your friend."

She felt her breath taken from her. There was pain in her chest, an empty feeling in her stomach. She wanted him to change his mind. She wanted to make promises she could never keep. Then she looked in his eyes and saw a glimmer of hope.

He said, "On the other hand, should you decide that you've had enough of being a hero . . . I can't say I'll wait around forever, but you know where to find me, if you don't take too long."

She smiled, and they hugged again. Then she gathered her plastic bags and carried them out to her car while he stood on the driveway and admired her. They allowed for one more embrace and a quick kiss before she drove away. She spent the entire ride thinking about him and what he had said.

★ ★ ★

Back home in her apartment, Rachel felt lost. There was still work to be done on the most important case of her life, but she wasn't involved in any part of it. The only thing she could do was go back to work for Dunn. At the moment, though, he was insisting that they wait for approval from the Office of Indigent Services, lest he be obligated to pay her out of his own pocket. She told him she would work for free until OIS returned an answer, but he said she'd done enough of that already.

She found herself wishing she could simply put the case behind her, but that was an impossibility. Even if she could have changed her obsessive nature, the reporters wouldn't let her move on. In the days that followed, she received numerous calls from them, all hoping to be the first to break through, to get an exclusive with the woman at the heart of this sweeping investigation.

The only person she was willing to talk to from the media was Parker's editor, Cara Marsh. Rachel insisted that their conversation be off the record. And Marsh agreed, anxious to understand exactly what had happened to her colleague and why. When they finished their call, Rachel was more frustrated than ever.

She thought about Braddock and what he had said. What it had meant to have him shine a light on her biggest flaw—her need to understand. She had to do whatever it took to get to the truth. Answers were even more important than her personal safety. She had demonstrated that on numerous occasions. There would never be a time when she could let go of that. If given the opportunity, she would march right back into that house to face Stoller all over again, if only it meant being able to tell Parker's family and friends and coworkers exactly what he had died for.

There was a knock on Rachel's door.

It almost didn't register as she sat there at her kitchen table, her phone in her hand, buried in her thoughts. Another series of knocks came, this time a little louder. She stood and went to look through the peephole. She didn't recognize the man on the other side.

She cracked open the door. "Can I help you?"

The man was stocky with sun-spotted skin. He had blond hair that was cropped to his scalp on the sides with a thick mass on the top neatly combed in one direction. He wore khakis and a collared shirt. Carried himself with a stiff air.

"Hello, Miss Carver. I'm Warrant Officer Tim Vance. I'm with the Tenth Military Police Battalion of the Army's Criminal Investigation Command. I was wondering if I might have a word with you?"

She invited him in and led him to the kitchen, opened the fridge, and retrieved a can of Mountain Dew. "Can I offer you a soda or something?"

"I'm fine, ma'am. Thank you, though."

"So what can I do for you, Warrant Officer Vance?"

"To be honest," he said. "I've come to get you off the bench."

He gave her a thin smile, letting his words work on her for a moment.

"Motherfucker!"

She slammed the door to the fridge, and his smile disappeared.

"Let me explain—"

"You're Grant's mystery client," she said, tightening her grip on the can. "You started this shit."

He put his hands up and took a step back, eyeing the soda like he expected her to throw it at him. "It's not that simple."

"Oh really?"

"Well . . . okay, yeah it is, but there's a good reason why I did what I did."

Grant's text resurfaced in her memory, the feeling she'd had when she'd read it. "You'd better. Especially the part where you could've clued me in on what this case was all about from the beginning. You are, after all, the CID investigator looking into the Guldara shooting, aren't you?"

"I am now. Thanks to you and the media coverage you've been getting, the Army has decided to reopen the case."

"What do you mean, reopen it?"

"Miss Carver, you have to understand, Sergeant Larson's accusations would have been very embarrassing for the Army. Once he was killed, I tried to push it, but they took the case away from me. They said the shooting involved a Taliban weapons cache, so they were classifying it as a terrorism investigation. That meant that it had to be handed over to Counterintelligence, and I wasn't permitted to discuss it with anyone."

"You mean, they tried to cover it up," she said.

"Yes, ma'am. That's exactly what I mean."

Rachel walked to her kitchen table and sat down, willing her anger to subside. "Keep talking."

"I admired Sergeant Larson for trying to bring those men to justice. When I read Mr. Parker's article about you, I knew what had happened. At first, I wanted to go straight to the police, but a friend convinced me that would be too reckless. So I hired Mr. Grant to act as a messenger."

"So you could be protected by attorney–client privilege."

He nodded. "Also to defend me in case I got caught sharing classified information. And then I had him contact Mr. Parker on deep background to give him some context for his story."

"That's how he knew to go after Adam Hubbard."

"That's correct. And when I heard Mr. Parker had been abducted, I knew it was time to reach out to you."

Rachel didn't know whether to thank him or curse him. Suddenly, she realized he was there to do more than just confess. "What did you mean by 'get me off the bench'?"

"I thought you'd want to know that the Union County Sheriff's Office and the DA are ready to clear Riley Gordon as a suspect in Private Hubbard's murder."

"What?" Rachel nearly jumped out of her chair. "Why the hell would they do that?"

"It's a difficult thing for a prosecutor to admit that they've made a mistake."

"But after everything that's happened, they're not even going to try?"

"Sometimes it only takes one piece of evidence to convince you that you were right all along. Sorry to be the bearer of bad news."

He turned and started for the door.

Rachel went after him and asked, "Wait, how do you know this?"

He stopped and turned. "We all have our sources."

She thought for a second and said, "Jensen told you, didn't he? When he gave you Stoller's confession?"

His thin smile returned. "You have a good day, Miss Carver."

FORTY-SIX

As soon as Vance left, Rachel was on the phone.

"Hey there, Rachel," Jensen said. "What can I do for ya?"

"You can tell me what's happening with the case against Gordon."

"Uh, well . . . we're working with the sheriff's office, getting up to speed on their investigation into the Hubbard murder."

"And how's that going?"

"It's going." He was trying to sound positive. "You know, it takes a little time to work these things out—"

"They're not cooperating, are they?"

"Oh, I wouldn't say it quite like that."

"How would you say it, then?"

"Well, you know how it is, Rachel . . . you gotta give these guys time to come around, you know? I mean, they thought they solved this case already, and now here we come trying to blow that right out of the water. I'll tell ya, I think they're actually being pretty good about it, all things considered."

"I doubt that's any comfort to Kyle Strickland." Rachel recalled what Vance had said: *Sometimes it only takes one piece of evidence to convince you that you were right all along.* She asked, "What aren't you telling me, Mike?"

"Beg your pardon? I don't know what you mean."

"Yes, you do. What do they have that makes them think Gordon didn't do it?"

Jensen didn't answer.

"Fine," she said. "Maybe Ross will tell me what I need to know."

★ ★ ★

SBI Headquarters was situated in a red-brick building that fronted a large campus, a spartan structure with rows of vertical windows and a low-sloped roof topped with a tiny octagonal cupola.

Rachel parked in front and ran up the steps and inside. She checked in with the man at the front desk and waited while he called Penter's office. She hadn't bothered to call him herself. If he was here, he would see her. She had no doubt about that.

"Just wait right here, ma'am," the man said as he dropped the handset in the cradle. "Someone's coming over to take you up."

A minute later, Jensen came through the front entrance wiping his brow with a kerchief. The Capital District Office where he worked was just a short hike away, but walking over in a suit on an August afternoon was bound to make him sweat. He spotted Rachel and tipped his head toward the stairway at the end of the hall.

"Follow me," he said.

They went upstairs and halfway through the hall. Jensen waved at Penter's assistant as they passed her outside his office. Once inside, Jensen went straight for a chair. Rachel approached slowly. Penter was leaning back in his seat, watching her walk toward him. Beneath his reserved veneer, there was a hint of pride—a repudiated father figure who nevertheless indulged in admiring his favorite child. It wasn't all that different from the look Stoller had given her when he had decided to let her live.

"Hello, Rachel," he said. "It's good to see you."

"Ross." She sat down next to Jensen.

"I understand Mike wasn't very forthcoming with you on the phone earlier. You'll have to forgive him for that. He's just doing his job, of course."

"I don't blame *him*."

That made Penter chuckle. "Mike, I think Rachel would like to know why the detectives in Union County think our suspect is innocent of the Hubbard murder."

"Well," Jensen said, "turns out they checked his phone records during the time frame. The GPS data puts him on the other side of town."

"You're sure?"

"Yep. They emailed me a copy. I went through it myself."

"Maybe he just left it somewhere."

"I don't think so, Rachel. He was making calls on it and sending messages all throughout the day. Based on the timing of a couple of those calls, it would be physically impossible for him to get to and from the crime scene to where his phone was. I hate to say it, but it looks like he's not our guy."

"What if he had Stoller or Martin making the calls for him? To give him an electronic alibi?"

Penter asked, "Wouldn't that ruin your narrative? That it was a fight that turned into a murder after Gordon lost his temper?"

Rachel wanted to respond, but she couldn't deny that it blew a hole in her theory.

"The DA down there thinks they got it right the first time," he said. "That Hubbard's death was unrelated to the incident in Afghanistan."

"But that's not what we're thinking, Rachel." Jensen seemed determined to reassure her. "We're thinking it was Stoller or Martin who killed him. So we're putting all of our energy into finding Martin. We figure that's our best bet. We're also working on getting a dump from the nearest cell tower to see if either of their numbers turns up in the area during that time."

Rachel's mind was working, trying to make sense of what she was hearing.

Penter said, "Mike, why don't you give us a minute?"

"Sure thing, boss," he said. "Was good to see ya again, Rachel."

He got up and left them. As soon as he closed the door, Penter said, "How are you holding up?"

She looked at him and suddenly felt drained. "I'm tired of not being done with all this."

"That's understandable. This isn't just some random case for you. It's personal. Hell, it's almost killed you twice within the past couple of weeks."

"You think I'm not seeing straight?"

He shrugged. "I think you're afraid to admit that this might actually be over already. That you got the bad guy, but you didn't get the resolution you were hoping for. Stoller's a good fit for Hubbard's murder, if you take the time to think about it."

A surge of resentment welled up within her. "That's what you said about Lauren Bailey."

"Yes, it is. I guess I owe you an apology for that." His eyes looked down for a moment, and when they came back to her, there was repentance in them, something she had never seen there before. "I'm sorry, Rachel. I should have listened to you."

She didn't know how to react. She had spent so much of her energy being angry with him. Forcing herself to hate the man she had once considered her mentor. There were times when she had imagined what she would say to him if she were given the opportunity to unload. Now, she couldn't. He had taken away her justification with a few simple words. All that energy suddenly felt wasted.

"Thank you, Ross," was all she could say.

They were silent for a while, and then he said, "I take it you spoke with our mutual friend from the Army?"

"Was it you who told him to come see me?"

"I may have done a little more than that."

"Don't tell me you were the so-called friend who sent him to Grant."

"I didn't want the guy to end up in Leavenworth," he said. "Or wherever they send people who leak classified information these days."

"Did you know he would contact me?"

"I probably suggested it at some point."

She sat back, looking a little impressed. "I don't know what to say. I think maybe I've been a bad influence on you."

He laughed, then looked at her thoughtfully and said,

"I'm glad nothing bad happened to you. As much as I wanted you to solve this thing, I don't know what I would've done if you had gotten hurt."

A thought struck Rachel. Something about the word *influence*. About how people could be impacted by those they were closest to. By their friends and their family members. How they could adopt certain mannerisms or behaviors. Or pick up certain traits. Especially from their parents.

"Ross," she said, "it's time to finish this."

"I'm open to any suggestions," he said. "What are you thinking?"

"Right now, I'm thinking about a bottle of pills."

FORTY-SEVEN

LeMay parked her Mercedes CLS 550 in front of Sharkie's Food Market and looked around, hoping it would be safe there. It was a quarter till seven, which meant she had to sit and wait. She hated this part of town, even more so because of the people in it.

There were kids smoking cigarettes by the store's entrance. Teenagers looking to peddle marijuana or MDMA or meth, doing their best to contribute to the decline of their community. Maggots feeding off this decaying portion of Monroe. The City Council, despite its best efforts, could do nothing to revitalize it.

She checked her watch every half minute. The wait was excruciating. When it showed five till, she'd had enough and stepped out of her car.

Another rain had swept through town, cleansing the air. It was cool now, and wet. Everything seemed saturated. The soil was like a soaked sponge. Her first step off the pavement forced black water up around her trainers. They rarely saw use outside of her trips to the gym. When she heard the squishing of her steps and felt her feet turn cold, she decided she would need a new pair.

She walked around to the back of the store and found the hole in the chain-link fence. She ducked and squeezed her way through. On the other side, she stood straight and looked around but saw no one. Slowly, she proceeded into the mill yard.

The crumbled corner of the building loomed above her. She looked up into the cavity and saw a black void where there once had been a second floor. The timbers that had supported it looked like the ribs of a carcass, left bare where the red skin had fallen away. Those pieces of brick were strewn across the ground, half-buried by the soggy grass.

She stepped on one of them, felt its hard edge through the sole of her shoe, and closed her eyes in painful memory. When she opened them again, she saw a mass of objects ahead. A patchwork of small rectangles laid out across the ground. Each was the size of a sheet of paper.

She approached and saw them for what they were—photographs.

She picked one up and examined it, recognizing the scene instantly. She was there now, standing right where that photo had been taken. The only thing missing from her real-life view was the body lying in the center of the picture. The body of Adam Hubbard.

★ ★ ★

Rachel stepped lightly behind LeMay. She was almost within arm's reach when she said, "Hello, Doctor."

LeMay spun, startled. She put a hand on her chest and closed her eyes to compose herself.

Rachel said, "I've heard that people who become therapists

choose that line of work because they hope to fix something inside themselves. You think that's true?"

LeMay exhaled a sharp breath. "It can be." She looked around at the rest of the photos, all taken from the crime scene and the autopsy, all showing Hubbard beaten to death. She dropped the one in her hand. "Is this some kind of twisted game you're playing, Miss Carver?"

Rachel pointed at her collage. "This? Oh, no, not at all. I know it can seem a bit over-the-top, but it helps me visualize. Helps me relive the scene, so I can better understand what happened."

"That's an interesting process. Mind telling me why I'm here for it? You didn't say anything about this when you called."

Rachel had lured LeMay here with the promise of evidence that would exonerate her son. Proof that he was innocent of Hubbard's murder. If all went well, she would make good on her word.

"Do you remember when I first came to your office and I asked you if you thought the person who did this had exhibited uncontrollable rage?"

"I recall that, yes."

"I know it's not your specialty, Doctor, but I wonder if you think someone in that mental state could use some sort of diminished-capacity defense at a murder trial?"

"This is a waste of my time." LeMay turned to leave.

"You think that kid of yours is just a complete psycho, Pam?"

That made her stop and turn back. "What did you say?"

"Just a bad seed, maybe? He gunned down that poor teenage boy in Afghanistan." She picked up a photo of

Hubbard's body and held it a few inches from LeMay's face. "Then he comes here and does this to his friend." Rachel turned the photo around and looked at it. "You must be so proud."

"How dare you?"

"And then he goes up to Wendell with your boy-friend . . . you really know how to pick 'em, by the way . . . and together they kill Tyler Larson. Framing his girlfriend in the process. I'm still not entirely sure how they got ahold of Larson's gun, but after the way your boyfriend broke in and stole mine, it's no stretch to imagine that they could figure it out. Working together with their buddy, Seth."

"None of what you're saying is true." Her face was turning red.

"Come on, Pam. You can let it out. It's gotta be such a burden taking care of that little waste of humanity. Having to seduce and manipulate a murderer like Colin Stoller just so he could protect your worthless kid."

"Stop it," she growled with gritted teeth. "I'm warning you."

"For all the good it did. I wonder where they got the heroin they tried to kill Bryce Parker with?"

LeMay turned around and closed her eyes. Her hands were balled into fists.

"I'm sure your son will tell us when the time comes. He's in such deep shit, he'll be begging and pleading to keep the needle out of his arm."

"Shut up."

"You think he'll go quietly? Sacrifice himself the way Stoller did for you? That whining little shit who can't manage a hurt knee without Mommy's help?"

"Shut up!"

"You must be so disappointed to have given that little bastard nine months in the womb—"

LeMay reached down and grabbed a brick, turned, and swung it, aiming for Rachel's head.

Rachel stepped back, feeling the air swish by her face as the brick came within an inch of striking her. But LeMay wasn't finished. She swung again and again. Each time, Rachel moved away from her.

LeMay's eyes were wild. She bared her teeth with each attempt. Rachel's foot stepped down on another brick, and she nearly lost her balance. LeMay, seeing the opportunity, gave another scream and put all of her might into the most powerful swing she could manage. Rachel ducked it and wrapped her arms around LeMay's waist. She hooked her leg around LeMay's and drove forward, sending them both to the ground.

LeMay was on her back with Rachel on top of her. She tried once again to land a blow, but Rachel wrapped her arm and wrenched it straight, threatening to hyperextend it. This time, LeMay's scream was one of pain.

Rachel said, "Drop it," and LeMay complied. Then Rachel stood and kicked the brick away, looked around to make sure there were no more within reach.

LeMay sat up, holding her arm, and started to cry.

Standing above her, watching her come to the realization that her world was falling apart, Rachel almost felt sorry for her. She softened her tone as she said, "We've been through a lot, you and I. This has taken its toll on all of us. It's time for the truth to see the light, Doctor. Riley didn't kill Adam Hubbard, did he?"

She shook her head.

Rachel said, "It was you."

LeMay's chest heaved, but she looked like she might be searching for the strength to deny it.

"When the detectives zeroed in on Kyle Strickland, they never bothered to figure out where Adam got the Percocet from. Addicts can always find dealers. But, despite what you might see in movies, most deals are done in people's houses, not on street corners or outside convenience stores. That is, unless Adam's supplier didn't want to be seen at his house. And you sure didn't want him coming to your house. Right, Doctor?"

She shook her head.

Rachel knelt down next to her. "There's no need to deny it anymore. I had the lab run prints on the bottle. They found yours on there with Adam's. Your mobile number also pinged on a nearby cell tower during the time he was killed."

LeMay put her face in her hands and wept.

"You don't bring your cell phone when you're planning to commit a murder. And you don't handle something that you're going to give to the victim with your bare hands. That tells me this wasn't premeditated. But you have to fill in the missing pieces, Doctor. It's not enough for me to guess. If you didn't plan to kill him, tell me what happened."

She sniffed hard and patted her eyes with the back of her hand. Then she took a breath, hugged her knees, and said, "Riley found out Adam was talking to the reporter about what they had done in Afghanistan. He had left the treatment program, so I called him and asked him to come in. I told him he needed to fill out some insurance paperwork or he was going to have to pay for part of his treatment. He had no idea how it worked, so he agreed. When I saw him, I could tell he was using again. He wouldn't talk to me about the shooting. He tried to leave, so I offered to get him some pills in exchange for his time. I told him I just wanted to talk."

"And you two agreed to meet here, so you could give him the pills?"

She looked toward the back of the store. Tears streamed, and she said, "Yes. I suggested it. He had Kyle drive him because he was already high. He had taken a bunch before coming here. I think he was trying to fight the anxiety. He took too much, though. I almost didn't give him the ones I had brought for him."

"But you did?"

She nodded.

Rachel said, "Okay, you gave him the pills; then what happened?"

"I tried to reason with him. I tried to convince him to leave it alone. It was war. Bad things happen in wartime."

"How did he take that?"

"He started yelling at me. He said I didn't know what I was talking about. That I had never been over there. I had never seen what it was really like. He said it was worse than I could ever imagine, but that was still no excuse for what Riley had done. He said he couldn't sleep at night. He couldn't get by without the pills. He was racked with guilt, and it was all Riley's fault."

"Did that make you angry?"

"It did. A little." She looked up at Rachel, childlike denial in her eyes. "But I didn't hurt him then. Not for that."

"So what happened next?"

"I offered to give him money. I tried to buy his silence."

"But he didn't like that, did he?"

She sniffed and shook her head. "He hit me."

"What did you do?"

She looked at the ground, then at her hands. "I picked up a brick, and I hit him back. And I kept hitting him. Over and over again. I couldn't control it, I just . . ."

She put her hands back to her face and lay down on her side, shaking and sobbing.

Rachel raised her right arm in the air, extended her index finger, and moved her hand in a wide circle. The signal called the detective and the pair of deputies from their hiding places. The two SBI agents from the Technical Services Unit, who were observing and recording from behind a broken window in the mill, began packing up their camera and parabolic mic equipment.

Rachel bent down and whispered to LeMay, "I know there's a lot more to what you did, Doctor. I could see it when I watched the sense of purpose go out of Colin Stoller's eyes, right before he walked out in front of that firing squad. Riley told you that Larson was trying to kick-start the investigation against your son and his friends, so you went to work on Colin right then. You turned him into your own personal weapon of mass destruction, didn't you? You sent him after Larson and Bryce Parker and Ashley Ramirez."

LeMay was no longer sobbing. She lay perfectly still, her hands a pillow to shield her from the mud.

"And me," Rachel said. "I can't prove it, but you and I both know. All of this is because of you."

The detective and the deputies arrived to handcuff LeMay and escort her to a patrol car. As they lifted her to her feet, she didn't utter a word in protest or defiance. She walked quietly with her head down, her eyes staring blankly at the ground in front of her. And Rachel followed her, every step of the way.

★ ★ ★

After LeMay was loaded up, Rachel went into Sharkie's and picked out a Monster Energy for the road. The kid with the pencil-thin facial hair was there behind the register. He had seen the patrol cars arrive, and the deputies get out and walk around to the back.

"You seen them cops?" he asked. "I wonder what they're doin' back there."

Rachel smiled, paid him, and left.

Her Camry was parked on the road, two blocks down in front of a large warehouse. Jensen was standing by it. As she approached, he clapped and said, "Bravo, Rachel. I'm quite impressed."

She cracked the can, drew a mouthful, and leaned against the car. "I'm tired."

"Hey, I don't blame ya. That was quite a show. And quite a bluff, too, if you don't mind me saying so."

"Not at all."

"You think we'll actually get her number from the cell tower dump?"

"I guess that depends."

"And the fingerprint?"

She shrugged. "Hard to say. He had the bottle in his pocket, so it might've been wiped clean."

"Right, yeah . . ." He thought for a few seconds. "Of course, now this means we can't charge Gordon with anything. I hope the Army doesn't drag its feet too long."

"I wouldn't worry about that," she said.

★ ★ ★

Across town, Vance got the building manager to quietly unlock the door to Gordon's apartment. Then he asked the man to step aside as he and two civilian CID special agents rushed inside. They found Gordon in his bed, a half-eaten bag of M&M's in his hand.

"What the fuck is this?" he yelled.

Legally, the civilians had to perform the apprehension, the CID's term for an arrest. They introduced themselves as they pushed Gordon onto his side and pulled his arms behind his back, handcuffing his wrists.

Vance watched with a grin of satisfaction.

When they spun Gordon around to sit on the edge of the bed, he said, "Dammit, this is bullshit. Can't you see I'm injured?" He looked over at Vance, who was dressed in uniform. "You just going to let them drag me out of here like this?"

"Don't worry, Riley. We got a wheelchair for you right outside."

"Yeah, but you don't mind them getting all rough with me. I guess it's too much to ask for a little respect for a fellow soldier, huh?"

Vance walked over and grabbed a fistful of Gordon's shirt and pushed him back onto the bed. "You listen to me, you sorry son of a bitch. You are no soldier. And you never were. PFC Adam Hubbard was a soldier. Sergeant First Class Tyler

Larson was a soldier." He let go of him and stepped away in disgust, like he'd been holding a bag full of excrement. "You're a coward and a murderer. And when we're through with you, you'll be a prisoner for the rest of your life."

★ ★ ★

"I know you've heard this before," Jensen said, "but there's always a spot open for ya. We'd love to have ya back."

"I appreciate that, Mike," she said, "but I kinda like working for myself."

"Fair enough, I suppose. What'll you do now?"

She finished her can, opened the car door, and tossed it in. "I've got a few people I need to see. Then . . . who knows? Maybe I'll spend some time in the mountains. Decide if I'm still cut out for this line of work."

"You're kidding, right?"

She climbed in and started the engine. "Was good to see you again, Mike. You take care of yourself."

She shut the door.

As the Camry pulled away, Jensen said, "I don't think this job's done with you quite yet, Rachel Carver."

FORTY-EIGHT

Dunn called Rachel to tell her that the DA was dropping the charges against Strickland and the judge had ordered his release.

"Thanks to you," he said, "he'll be home soon."

"Team effort," she said.

"Yeah, well, anytime you feel like donating your services, you feel free to give me a call. And next time you stop into Monroe, lunch is on me. Hell, let's make it a dinner."

After they hung up, Rachel spent the rest of the evening going through all the alcohol in her apartment. In various stages of intoxication, she called her mother, Carly, and Braddock. They were all good conversations. Each of them congratulated her and told her how grateful they were that she was done with this ordeal.

When she was halfway through her Maker's Mark, she called Braddock for a second time and told him she just wanted to hear his voice. They talked for a while longer, about other cases and local politics and what was on TV. Rachel couldn't be certain, but it felt like they were on the phone for a couple of hours. When he started yawning after every other word, she let him go to bed.

At midnight, she poured her last drink and thought about what she would do when she woke the next morning. Or rather, how she would do it. One thing remained before she could say that she was finished with the Larson case for good. She was prepared to do it alone, but she hoped she wouldn't have to.

She picked up her phone and called Penter. After the voicemail greeting and the beep, she said, "Hey . . . it's Rachel. Sorry to call you so late. I just wanted you to know that I'm going to see Lillian Bailey tomorrow morning. I'll probably be there at eight . . . maybe nine. I don't know why I'm telling you, but . . . if you wanted to meet me there . . . anyway, have a good night."

She finished her drink, set her alarm, and went to bed. In the morning, she took a shower and made coffee. She sat at her kitchen table, staring into space while she drank it. There was no word from Penter. She thought about calling him again, but decided against it. Maybe this was just something she needed to do on her own.

She poured a fresh cup into a travel mug and loaded up in the Camry. Fifteen minutes later, she turned into the Blackstone Estates mobile-home park and eased into a spot in the guest lot between the sales and leasing office and the community mailboxes. She turned the engine off and wiped her hands on her jeans. She felt shaky from the adrenaline and caffeine and realized the extra cup of coffee had been a bad idea.

She stepped out, and Penter was there, standing on the sidewalk and looking at her with a warning in his eyes. As she walked over, he said, "You're sure you want to do this?"

His voice carried a note of concern, something that

went beyond his fear of the legal ramifications of what she was about to do.

"I'm sure," she said.

"All right, then. Let's go."

Until that instant, she had only expected him to try to talk her out of it.

"You're going with me?"

"Yeah, but we'd better hurry before I change my mind."

She reached out and touched his arm. It felt good to be this close to him again.

They started walking. Penter said, "By the way, I heard from our mutual Army friend today. He says Gordon's talking. He's trying to lay everything on Stoller, but they're picking him apart. Mixed in with the BS, though, was one thing we think is probably true. He said Stoller shot and killed Seth Martin instead of taking him to the hospital for his gunshot wound. Gordon doesn't know where the body is, but he's sure it happened on his property."

"Damn," she said, thinking of her last moments with Stoller. "I guess that makes sense. Can't say I'm all that sorry to hear it."

"I wouldn't be either, if I were you."

Lillian Bailey's single-wide was set back from the sidewalk by a narrow strip of grass. The home itself was white with brown streaks descending the walls where rain had chased the dust and pollen off the roof. There was a concrete patio off to one side. It held a handful of toys and a stroller covered with a black trash bag. Rachel climbed the wood steps and knocked on the door. A moment later, Bailey's voice called out, "Come on in."

Rachel had never seen the inside. She opened the door timidly and said, "Mrs. Bailey?"

"Come on in, I said. I ain't gettin' up. My feet hurt."

Rachel glanced back at Penter and then stepped inside. He came up behind her and closed the door.

Bailey was near the far wall, seated in a blue rocker with one foot on a vinyl ottoman. In front of her, Brandon Bailey played with a set of Tonka trucks on the floor. Rachel saw the boy and had to close her eyes for a moment, had to force out the memory of carrying him outside, away from his dying mother.

"Well, what do you all want?" Bailey asked.

Rachel couldn't speak. Couldn't find the right words to get her started. Penter stepped forward.

"Mrs. Bailey, my name is Ross Penter. I'm an assistant director with the State Bureau of Investigation. We've come to talk to you about your daughter's case."

"Hmph. As far as I know, I ain't supposed to be talkin' to nobody from the SBI. That come straight from my lawyer."

"I understand, ma'am . . ." He looked back at Rachel. "Uh . . . we just wanted to tell you that, officially, your daughter is no longer suspected of the crime for which she was . . . that we were attempting to arrest her for."

"I coulda told you she shouldn't have been no suspect in the first place. If y'all woulda just listened the first time around." Bailey paused for a moment to cough and adjust her glasses. "Is that all you came here to tell me?"

"We would also like to let you know that we've identi-fied the men responsible for—"

"You can save all that for Tyler's family. It don't have

nothin' to do with me." Her voice cracked and her lips quivered. "I lost my girl. I can't go back into my house no more. And I sure as hell can't sell it. What am I supposed to do?" She pointed at Brandon, who looked like he knew that something was wrong but continued to push his trucks around because he didn't know what else to do. "That little boy is leavin' me at the end of this month. I wish I could take care of him, but I can't. I'm too old now. I gotta give him up for adoption."

Rachel's eyes were welling. She stepped closer and said, "I'm sorry."

Bailey looked at her in disbelief. "You're what?"

Penter said, "Mrs. Bailey, we recognize that this was a tragedy. But our investigation was done in accordance with—"

"I'm sorry," Rachel said louder. "I'm sorry that I didn't know earlier that your daughter was innocent. I'm sorry that I wasn't able to talk her down before she pointed her gun at a deputy. And I'm sorry that you and Brandon have to live the rest of your lives without her."

"Hmph. Well, you didn't apologize for shootin' her."

"I can't be sorry for that." Rachel wiped her eyes. "That's a hard thing for me to say. And I'm sure it's even harder to hear, but that's how it is. Lauren put a man in danger, and it was my duty to protect him."

Bailey took a minute to absorb that. She said, "So that's it, then?"

"Yes, ma'am," Rachel said. "That's it."

"Well, I guess you all have told me what you came here to say."

"Yes, ma'am."

Rachel turned and went to the door, opened it but hesitated for a second. She glanced across the room and saw that Bailey's eyes were still on her. There was sadness, but no anger. Perhaps a hint of appreciation for her apology. And that was the best Rachel could hope for.

Outside, Penter closed the door, jogged down the steps, and fell in beside her. They walked quietly until they got to Rachel's car. Then Penter gave her a weak smile and said, "I guess they can't all be happy endings."

Rachel looked back at Bailey's trailer. "It's good enough for me."

Acknowledgments

To the following, my sincere gratitude:

The entire team at Crooked Lane Books. Especially Matt Martz, for his guidance and encouragement; Jenny Chen, for her insights and attention to detail; and Sarah Poppe, for her expertise in marketing and publicity.

My agent, Rachel Ekstrom Courage of Folio Literary Management. There are never enough good things to say about the person who keeps me sane, hopeful, and focused in a business I still struggle to understand.

Eric Weaver, for his counsel. Sean Wiggins, for his expertise in all things prosecutorial. And Officer Katie Anderson, for teaching me about law enforcement in North Carolina.